# THE LOCH EFFECT

## GENNY CARRICK

Cover image and design by Melody Jeffries

Edited by Cindy Ray Hale

ISBN: 978-1-957745-08-4 (e-book)

ISBN: 978-1-957745-09-1 (paperback)

❀ Created with Vellum

# what to expect

Please be advised this book includes some mild language, intense kisses, vivid descriptions of panic, an overbearing boss, heated flirtation, mispronounced Gaelic, and quite a bit of whisky drinking.

*For my silver fox*
*You can woo me any time you like*

# one

. . .

NOT TO BE DRAMATIC, but I was about to die.

Every time the plane shook, my life back home in Seattle flashed before my eyes. My dog Shatner wiggling his butt when he wanted walkies. Brunch with my best friend Jill that was really just an excuse to drink mimosas at ten in the morning. Sitting at my desk designing corporate websites while my boss sent *hurry up, Molly* texts every few hours.

That last scene kind of hogged up the memories.

My fingers shook as I notched my seatbelt a touch tighter just in case. It dug into my stomach, but that was a small price to pay for the extra security. If security even existed up here. Pretty sure we were seconds away from a free-fall.

As a point of interest, nobody around me seemed to feel the same. The young woman in the window seat next to me had pulled her hoodie closed around her face and slept slumped to the side since takeoff. The man on the aisle had watched three Marvel movies in a row, unfazed by the plane rocketing around like The Hulk had it in his big green fist.

Meanwhile, I'd spent the flight surfing a panic wave, unsuccessfully trying to distract myself with TV show reruns and wishing I was home in bed instead of thirty thousand feet in the air.

The intercom chimed, and the pilot's voice sounded over the PA. "Folks, we've begun our descent into Edinburgh. There's a bit of rough air ahead, but it doesn't look too bad. We should be on the ground in twenty minutes."

Rough air. Code for *It's about to get wild up here.* I touched the edge of the air sickness bag still neatly folded up in the seat pocket in front of me. My stomach squirmed from all this bouncing around, but I prayed it wouldn't act up. I'd made it through the flight to Boston without getting sick. No reason to start now.

*Hear that, stomach? Don't start now.*

The plane jolted sideways. *Sideways.* No way that was normal. I hugged myself tighter, sitting ramrod straight in my middle seat. Wait—were you supposed to go limp in a crash? Didn't matter, my opportunity for going limp in all this racket ended when my Valium wore off two hours ago. Even before then, I hadn't been all that relaxed.

Did I mention I hate flying?

We kicked to the side again and my brain played all sorts of harrowing images in my personal movie theater of horrors. Death from above. Plummeting doom. Crashes and nosedives and bursting into flames.

My mouth went dry and a chill sweat broke out on my forehead. Was escaping the city and my ex-boyfriend's wedding really worth this? Getting my passport stamped for the first time had seemed like a great *best revenge is living well* idea a few months ago, but now I deeply regretted every single choice that had led me here.

I'd been on exactly one flight before last night. Sixteen years ago, I'd celebrated college graduation with a trip to California with Jill. But after a horrible panic attack capped off by fainting in-flight, I'd steered clear of plane travel ever since. My vacations had stayed within easy driving distance, never requiring a boarding pass, let alone a passport. I chose from a selection of hotels on the Washington coast where I could walk my dog on the beach during the day and indulge in room service in bed at night.

But then I'd heard about my ex-boyfriend's engagement six months after our breakup, and getting out of Dodge had seemed like a great idea. I'd spent four years with him waiting for something more to happen, thinking surely this time that sense of *I like being with you* would transform into *I don't want to be without you.* But discussions about marriage had mostly consisted of vague verbal filler. *"Well...ah...maybe...uh..."* The last time I'd brought up the future, his lackluster *"I guess we could get married, if you want"* had convinced me to end the relationship. I didn't want a proposal that had all the enthusiasm of a man deciding on frozen pizza for dinner.

How had he gone from that to what I had to assume had been a genuine proposal six months later? Wasn't there some unspoken rule that the person who does the breaking up was supposed to be the first to start dating again? I hadn't ended things with Sean thinking I would immediately find someone new, but I hadn't expected to hear he'd magically overcome his fear of commitment, either. I wasn't jealous of his fiancée, I was just a tiny bit angry with him for moving on from me so spectacularly well.

The woman next to me came to and lifted the shade over the window to peer out. I'd come all this way for the sights, but not even the blur of green outside could tempt me to look. I stared at that reassuring little sliver of waxy paper in the seat pocket a few inches from my face, hoping my stomach wouldn't lose control, all while an icepick slowly drove into each ear from the change in cabin pressure.

Seriously, who thought air travel was so great? What was the draw?

I slipped the note Jill had left for me out of my e-reader cover. I'd been over it about a hundred times already, but I could stand another read-through.

> *Molly,*
>
> *DON'T PANIC. Air travel is the safest form of trans-*
> *portation in the world. Turbulence doesn't bring down*
> *planes. You're going to have an amazing time in Scot-*
> *land, I promise. Think of the lochs. The mountains.*
> *The kilted hotties. You've got this.*
>
> *Jill*

The plane bumped around like it had a bad case of the jitters, the engines whining and whimpering. No, wait—those sounds were coming from me.

Yeah, her note hadn't helped.

I shut my eyes and sank into the image that had brought me across the Atlantic in the first place. A lush green hillside with a well-worn walking path leading to a craggy pinnacle of rock. A lake shimmering behind it with low rolling hills in the distance. The scene crowned by a deep blue sky crowded with thick white clouds. Absolute heaven.

*Isle of Skye, here I come.*

Soon, I'd be hiking those paths and breathing in fresh mountain air. Biking around lochs and listening to all the bagpipe music I could handle. Taking pictures of every blessed thing like an intrepid nature photographer instead of the nerdy website designer I was. Ten days exploring Scotland without a single worry.

Fingers crossed, anyway.

The woman at the window shifted back into her seat, revealing nothing but gray outside. Tarmac. *Oh.* I stiffened up again, preparing for landing.

The slightest bump, and we'd touched down.

Now that we'd reached the ground, the terror left my body like it'd been exorcized. My rational brain took the reins again, and I laughed softly as if the anxiety had just been a little inside joke. *Oh, Molly, terrified over flying. What a silly goose.*

Definitely wasn't the time to think about how this silly goose would tolerate the return flights in almost two weeks.

The Edinburgh Airport didn't look much different than SeaTac in the United States. Rows of sad plastic seats, a carpet of indeterminate color and pattern, gates with minimally friendly airline employees—I might have been anywhere. A bit of a letdown, really. I'd expected to be greeted by men in tartan kilts tossing cabers and playing the bagpipes, but maybe that was only for special occasions. Possibly a food cart lurked somewhere in the airport waiting to dole out haggis, steak and kidney pie, and all the other organ-based dishes I'd heard about, but at first glance it struck me as ordinary.

After going through customs, I ducked into a bathroom to change out of my rumpled clothes and then perked up with a quick breakfast of coffee and eggs with toast. I turned my phone on and found a text from Jill: a picture of her newborn baby Olivia sleeping next to my old pug Shatner, basking in a slant of golden sunlight. The two cuddled in a bliss that had obviously been staged but still managed to coax a heartfelt *Aww* out of me.

Honestly, I still hadn't gotten used to the idea my best friend had become a mother. At thirty-eight, I'd seen plenty of friends marry and have children, but nobody I'd been so close with. Nobody who'd shared every last horrifying detail of her delivery and its aftermath. But also nobody who let me hold her daughter to my heart's content so I could breathe in her clean baby scent like some weird aromatherapy treatment.

The photo came with a message.

**Jill**: Have fun on your first day adventuring! Kick some mountain butt!

I chuckled over that. At first, I'd thought a tour group sounded too much like something my parents would do with their retired friends. *See the world from the comfort of your Rascal!* Just because I was nearing forty didn't mean I was ready to slide into old-womanhood like a baseball player stealing third.

But Hold Onto Your Kilts' itineraries covered everything from mountain climbs to island bicycling to castle views to whisky tastings. They included all in-country transportation, and although the accommodations weren't luxury, we wouldn't be in hostels, either. Kayaking, hiking, and biking my way across Scotland didn't sound too old womanish. I could do this. I would.

Next, I listened to the message from my mother. She either sent a one-line text or she would fill my voicemail with her musings, she had no in-between.

*"I'm sure you got in just fine. You know there's nothing to worry about. Flying is perfectly safe, I've tried to tell you. You deserve this trip, honey, after everything with Sean. Oh, that man! He wasted four years of your life just dragging his feet. Remember—one man's 'I'm not ready' is another man's 'Hell, yes.' You'll find somebody for you, a good man who knows what he wants and won't be afraid to go after it..."*

I clicked it off. I could listen to the rest of her dreams for my love life when I wasn't already exhausted. She'd been coaxing me toward dating apps since I'd broken up with Sean, and never failed to voice her disappointment I hadn't acted on the advice. She'd threatened to create a profile for me, but as far as I knew, hadn't done it yet. I could just imagine how that would read.

*Molly, 38, loves dogs, seeks man ready to make beautiful grandchildren. Don't delay!*

I had half an hour before I needed to meet up with my group in the airport car park, and I'd probably take all that time just to find them. Wandering through the terminal, a small shop caught my eye, and I skidded to a stop, my rolling luggage clattering against the backs of my knees. I didn't need the pile of tartan-clad bears, but I could do with an *I Heart Scotland* keychain. And T-shirt. And vinyl sticker. Give me all the hearty Scotland merch.

And a generous helping of chocolate bars for my troubles.

While I fidgeted in line, I caught the man next to me raise an eyebrow at my haul. Taller than me and ridiculously broad, his head was shaved bald, but he more than made up for it with his full gray beard. I could have cast him as one of the older motor-cycle riding heroes in the romance novels I read if he swapped his black fleece jacket for a leather version. His blue eyes shone as he gave me a once-over that sent unwelcome tingles over my skin.

"Tell me you're a tourist without telling me you're a tourist." His rolling accent called him out as a local, but his smirk called him out as a first-rate Scottish jerk.

All the swoony tingling going on inside me cooled. I cut him a hard look. "It's good for the economy."

A terrible comeback, but the best I could do after hours of fitful Valium-induced sleep followed up with a Shaky-Shack landing.

He chuckled. "You're single-handedly keeping the country afloat."

I shoved my goodies toward the cashier and frowned at the judgey man. "I'm probably due a medal."

"I'll keep an eye out for the ceremony."

His smile still held traces of that smirk, but it brought the skin tingles out again, anyway. *Ugh, no. You are not attracted to the brawny, snarky man, no matter how delightful his Scottish accent sounds.* Didn't matter anyway, I could tell already this man was not my type.

I'd never been into beardy, tough-looking men who chatted up women in airports. My type usually centered on the glasses-wearing IT guy who took months to build up the courage to ask a coworker out to dinner at a chain restaurant. This man…was defi-nitely not that.

I scanned my credit card and stuffed the souvenirs into my crossbody bag. As I tucked my things away, the man stepped forward to put his extra-large water bottle on the counter.

"Enjoy your visit to Scotland."

His accent twisted something in my belly, a weird, visceral response that completely ignored his smirking lips. Which I should also ignore. Definitely needed to stop looking at his mouth.

"Oh, I will." I started to walk away but looked back over my shoulder. "I heart it."

His low, rumbling laughter carried me through the airport. I would just have to pretend that getting teased by a local would bring good fortune on this trip.

# two

. . .

THE LARGE SANDWICH board emblazoned with an eye-searing tartan print let me know I'd found the loading zone for Hold Onto Your Kilts. The tour group's goofy name had been part of the draw—it said they didn't take themselves too seriously. I wanted to have a good time in Scotland, but nobody needed to get fussy about it.

An older woman stood next to the sign, apparently the first of the group to arrive. This was it. I took a deep breath and prepared myself to meet my traveling companions, Jill's reminder playing in my mind. *Don't panic.*

I moved closer, and the woman waved me over. "Are you going on the Highland tour as well, then?"

She looked to be about my parents' age, sporting a short bob streaked with gray and a vaguely British accent. I nodded, and she glanced me over, sniffing as if she expected to find something more. I'd worn loose yoga pants and a flowy top for the flights, with my brown hair in a loose braid, but I didn't look nearly as put together as she did in her neat lilac twinset.

"I'm Bea." Her accent rolled it into "bee-uh."

We shook hands, a quick, limp little exchange. "I'm Molly."

"Oh, this must be your husband." She nodded past me, smiling wide.

I turned to find this phantom husband and spotted Mr. Snarky Bearded Man just behind me. His eyebrows ticked up, like I wasn't the only one surprised by our sudden reunion. Although, the way his eyes crinkled at the edges…maybe he was more than just surprised. Pleased? No. I didn't care. I turned back to Bea before I wound up staring.

Ignoring the ridiculous thrill that had exploded to life in my chest like an uninvited Jack-in-the-Box, I addressed her assumption. "We're not together."

The man stepped forward and extended a hand to her. "We did bond over the importance of souvenirs, though. I'm Duncan."

She shook his hand and introduced herself.

He turned to me, that secret smile back on his face. Or maybe it just felt like a secret because his thick whiskers hid it so well.

"Molly." I slipped my hand into his. His firm, confident grip went right along with the alpha male thing he had going on. It also started those irritating tingles across my skin again. The handshake went on a beat too long, and I pulled my hand away. "You're taking the Scotland trip? Seems like something a tourist would do."

One side of his mouth kicked higher. "I hear it's good for the economy."

I snorted a laugh.

"You're an American, I take it?" Bea said to me. "First time in Scotland?"

I nodded, but she didn't wait for more information.

"You'll love it, darling, just the time of your life. I've been many times, of course, but this is our first time on a guided tour. I'm quite looking forward to it. My husband and I are celebrating our fortieth anniversary."

She preened a little over that, clearly waiting for praise.

"Congratulations."

"But if you're not together—" She waggled her finger between Duncan and me. "Where is your husband?"

"Lost in the mail, I guess."

Duncan chuckled, but Bea's mostly warm expression morphed into a prim smile. I probably shouldn't dole out my own snark to someone I would be stuck with on the tour, but *"Where is your husband?"* Come on. I hadn't flown all the way to Scotland for commentary on my marital status—I could listen to my mother's voicemails when I wanted that.

Another woman joined us, giving me a rest from Bea's curiosity. She introduced herself as Harlow in a thick Australian accent. Her blond, shampoo commercial hair fell in smooth, soft waves like she hadn't been on a plane for hours, and she wore a velour tracksuit that showed off her every curve like she hadn't been tempted by the airport concessions.

I'd snapped up several bars of Cadbury Dairy Milk and enough shortbread to last me the whole trip, but whatever.

"Did you come all the way from Down Under?" Bea asked.

"Oh, yes. I'm on my way to a six-month job as a yoga instructor in Dublin, but I wanted to see the Highlands first. I've already explored Edinburgh and Glasgow." Harlow had the breathless air of someone perpetually on her way to someplace fascinating. Her passport was probably covered in stamps.

"Yoga instructor?" Bea gave her the same dissatisfied once-over she'd given me. "You have the right shape for it."

Harlow lit up. "Thank you!"

You sweet summer child. Kind of felt a little jealous over this twenty-something's inability to recognize an older woman's condescension.

Soon, three more men joined our party. Spencer looked to be about my age, with dark curly hair, a slightly unkempt beard, and no trace of a smile. He introduced himself and moved to the perimeter of the group, facing away as though he didn't belong with us. A bit of a Darcy move, to be honest, even though he had a distinctly American accent.

Carlos also turned out to be American, although of a flirtier variety than Spencer. He grinned from me to Harlow, but his attention snagged on her pretty readily. Made sense, since easy money neither of them had reached thirty.

The last man was older than the rest, with artificially darkened hair and heavy-lidded eyes that made him look like Mr. Bean about to go on holiday. He handed Bea a paper coffee cup and two sugar packets.

"Thank you, dear." She puckered her lips and they leaned closer, grazing each other's mouths in mime of a kiss.

Mr. Bean shook hands all around and introduced himself as Rupert. "A fine day for this."

"The whole tour won't be done today." Bea poured both sugar packets into her coffee and took a sip.

"No, no, of course not. A fine day to get started, I mean." Still smiling, Mr. Bean didn't seem at all put-upon by his wife's tone. "Is this all of us then?"

"The maximum was eight." Bea did a quick head count. "We're short one."

Duncan looked past me at the oncoming line of cars and his mouth pulled into a grimace. I spun to see what had soured him, and watched as a mini-bus decked out in a full tartan overlay drew up to the curb. The blue, yellow, and red tartan looked striking enough from a distance, but up close, the colors burned my retinas. The Hold Onto Your Kilts logo covered the side, with a three-foot tall image of a set of bagpipes leaning lazily against the H.

"Subtle." Duncan stared at our garish transport.

"Tell me you're Scottish without telling me you're Scottish," I returned.

His low laughter gave me a little zing of satisfaction, but I shushed that away. I hadn't come here for commentary on my marital status, but I sure hadn't come here for *that*, either.

Two men hopped off the bus. The older looked like every white, mild-mannered British man I'd ever seen on PBS. The younger had warm brown skin, wavy black hair that fell strategically around his face, and a grin that showed all his teeth.

"Good morning," the older of the two said. "If you're here for the Highland tour, you're in the right place. I'm Lewis, and I'll be your guide for the next ten days, along with Arnav, here. We'll just check you all in, load your bags on the coach, and get started, shall we?"

One by one, our little group gave Lewis our names and identifications while Arnav loaded our luggage into the back of the bus. On board the sixteen-seater, only Bea and Rupert sat together. I had to hope everyone had snagged a window seat because the scenery was just too good to miss, and not because I was about to embark on a ten-day tour with six anti-social people.

Lewis climbed aboard and stood in the aisle. "Welcome to Scotland, for those of you new to our fair country. We have a great ten days planned for you. Our first stop will be the Cairngorms, where we'll spend three days in the village of Aviemore, take in the sights of the National Park, and hopefully bag a Munro or two."

*Munro* was the term for any hill over three thousand feet, and Scotland had almost three hundred of them. When you successfully climbed one, you called it "bagging a Munro." I'd learned that much in my months of reading up before my trip, but I hadn't learned a whole lot more. To be fair, most of my research had come from Instagram, one travel guide by an American who seemed to dislike other countries, and hours of listening to bagpipe music on YouTube.

Now that I'd arrived, I realized how little any of that had helped.

"We have a daily schedule," Lewis continued, "but nothing is mandatory. If you're ever tired from a climb or just not interested in what we have on the agenda, it won't hurt our feelings if you decide to wander on your own. Just let us know your intentions. All of our lodges make excellent base camps for hill walks.

"This isn't a competition. We're here to enjoy ourselves and experience a little of what the Highlands has to offer. You know yourself better than Arnav or I do—don't work yourself too hard."

His eyes darted to Bea and Rupert, the oldest of the group, but he glanced my way, too. I sat up a little straighter. I was inexperienced yes, but I wasn't out of shape. If anything, he should aim those significant looks Duncan's way, since he was clearly the next oldest of us.

Although, as I side-eyed how his fleece jacket strained around his biceps, he didn't look out of shape. At. All.

"For now, sit back, relax, and we'll be off to Aviemore." Lewis sat in the driver's seat and the engine rumbled to life. Arnav folded up the sandwich board from the curb, tossed it into the back, and we set off.

Let the adventure begin.

# three

. . .

I NEEDED a minute to get used to speeding onto the "wrong" side of the road. Probably more than one. My heart lurched, and everything inside me wanted to swerve the bus into the right-hand lanes where we belonged. So glad I hadn't opted to tour the country by myself and rent a car. I could see the headlines now.

*American woman, 38, dies alone in easily avoidable mix-up.*

I looked back at the city but got nothing of the majestic view I'd hoped for from the highway. Motorway? Whatever they called it, we were already too far away to see any of the stately Old Town buildings that crowded my new Scotland Pinterest board and filled my Instagram feed. I'd hoped to see the castle perched on its hilltop but only spotted a smattering of grayish-brown buildings in the distance.

We crossed a bridge that transported us into the countryside, erasing the city and its suburbs from view. Green hills sped lazily away on either side of the motorway—might have just been grassy pastures, but they were grassy pastures in a whole new country.

My silly little heart soared.

Carlos turned in his seat to face me. "What brought you out to bonnie old Scotland, Molly?"

Why Scotland for my first international trip ever—not that he knew that last part? It was more than just the prospect of rugged views and a long-awaited break from work, but I didn't know how to explain the rest. My ex's surprise wedding. My parents living it up in their retirement. My best friend moving into a new stage of adulthood. And me...just chugging along in the status quo.

How do you tell a stranger you haven't *carpe'd* your *diems*?

"I just needed a vacation."

He looked me over but shifted his focus behind me. "Harlow, you've been to Scotland before, haven't you?"

"Twice," she said.

A look of triumph crossed his face, a silent *Told ya*. Yeah, well, Harlow's nose probably wasn't pressed against the window glass the way mine was.

"So you've been here before?" I asked.

"Oh, yeah, I travel for work all the time."

"Is this a work trip then?"

He grinned, his teeth seeming especially white. "This is all play."

Uh-huh. I didn't want to travel with a group of anti-social people, but I hadn't planned for the frat boy package, either. I went back to gazing out the window, and he did the same. Now and then, we passed through small villages full of stone houses on our journey north. Barreling through such quaint little towns seemed a crime. I had to stop myself from leaping up the aisle and forcing Lewis to stop the bus so I could get out and take photographs. I wanted to wander the towns, hear my shoes *click-clack* on cobblestone streets, and catch the sound of bagpipes wailing mournfully in the distance.

I'd tucked my fancy DSLR into my backpack and couldn't wait to use it. I didn't use it much lately, but it'd collected photos from my camping trips and staycations, and now finally had the chance to take some truly gorgeous pictures. I would absolutely abuse my tourist privileges and cram that thing full of photos.

I stared open-mouthed out the windows over Duncan's shoulder. The highway ran parallel to a river, and on the far side, right on the water, delightful stone buildings nestled close together in a most Dickensian way. A tower with a dramatic spire stood in the center of the row as though looking down on everything around it.

"There goes Perth," Arnav chirped.

"Wow." Leaning across the aisle, I craned my neck, following what I could of the town until trees next to the roadway swallowed it up.

Duncan's mouth twitched. Probably because I was basically perched on my hands and knees on the seat, desperate for a good view. I slipped back into a more normal seated position, heat crawling up my neck. I might not have told them this was my first international trip, but it wouldn't take anyone long to figure it out if I kept drooling over everything we passed.

"Is it living up to the hype?" he asked in a low voice.

The truth was, I'd fallen in love with the country in a couple of hours, but I would never tell him that. Not when he'd already made it clear he found my touristy enthusiasm annoying.

I shrugged as though I had no opinion one way or another. "It's not bad."

He chuckled again. That sound did *not* get my stomach swooping. No. It was from the thrill of being in Scotland only.

We passed through low farmlands divided up into neat blocks that gradually turned into a sea of green and purple heather. Taking photos through the window of a moving vehicle would only end in a blurry mess, but I nearly tugged my camera from my bag anyway. I couldn't get enough of the views, and we weren't even looking at anything much yet.

Finally, a sign announced the town of Aviemore. Lewis slowed the bus up a narrow lane to our lodge. I laughed like a little kid when I saw the stone Victorian guest house with dormer windows and tall chimneys. Modern houses sat beyond the grounds, but if I looked at the guest house from just the right angle, I could pretend I'd stepped back in time. Or at least onto a Masterpiece Theatre set.

Our group filed off the bus, moving slowly to stretch our legs after the long drive. Lush green hills surrounded us, and although the lodge sat on a main thoroughfare, it was neither noisy nor busy. It was peaceful and wonderful and even the air smelled fresher.

A man and woman came out of the lodge to shake hands with Lewis.

"These are our hosts, Ian and Brenda," he said. "They'll look after us during our stay here."

"If there's anything you need, just ask," Brenda said.

"We have you doubled up in the rooms," Lewis went on, "except for Spencer, who'll have his own."

"I wouldn't mind trading you for that." Carlos bumped Spencer with his shoulder, but the other man just looked uncomfortable.

Brenda fidgeted her hands like she might sweep us all inside if we didn't hurry. "Let's get you into your rooms so you can settle in after your drive."

We followed her into the lodge, my greedy eyes scanning everything around me for potential photo ops.

She trundled up an ornate wooden staircase in the main entryway. "To the right is our dining room where we serve full breakfast and supper. To the left is the sitting room where you can relax after your adventures of the day."

Her lilting Scottish accent and kind, smiling face had me totally smitten already. She gave us a quick tour of the house, but it seemed pretty self-explanatory. At the top of the stairs, she handed out keys to the rooms while Lewis ticked off notes on his clipboard.

"We have a nice tea waiting for you in the dining room as soon as you're ready," she said.

"Take a rest, have a bite to eat, and then we'll set out on an easy hill walk to get you warmed up," Lewis called down the hallway.

As the two single women, Harlow and I had been paired up by default. Our room held two twin beds, and she dumped her bags next to the closest one. I dragged my things to the second bed but stopped to stare out the window overlooking the valley. I could see part of the town and river, and nothing but green hills beyond that.

My cheeks already ached from all this smiling.

Harlow collapsed onto her bed, burrowing her face into the pillow. I eyed mine, too, but if I laid down now, I probably wouldn't wake up again before supper, and missing any activity was out of the question.

I wandered downstairs to the sitting room and found a large fireplace set in one wall with a stag head mounted over the mantel. Three plush sofas surrounded the fireplace, each decked out in worn tartan, and a small set of shelves held well-loved books. It defeated the purpose of an adventure tour, but I could have stayed in this cozy room all afternoon.

Rupert, Duncan, and Carlos were already in the dining room when I walked in. Brenda and Ian bustled in with serving trays covered in scones, sandwiches, and fruit. Even though she'd said they only served breakfast and supper, they were sure going all-out for this welcome.

I poured a cup of coffee and heaped butter and jam on a scone before settling onto a chair at one of the tables. The men had been standing around picking at food, but as soon as I sat down, Rupert pulled out the chair across from me, and the rest followed suit.

"You don't mind if we join you, do you?" he asked.

"Not at all."

"The other young woman, ah, Harlow? Is she coming down?" Rupert spread a big dollop of cream over his scone.

"I think she's asleep."

"You're not affected by the jet lag, eh?" Carlos's wide smiles and unbroken eye contact said he didn't lack for confidence with strangers.

"I'm only awake out of sheer excitement. I'll probably pass out later." My body wilted with a vague sense of exhaustion more than actual sleepiness. I would fight it off for a few more hours before I allowed myself to fade into unconsciousness.

"Your first trip across the pond?" Rupert asked.

"My very first."

My phone buzzed in my jacket pocket. I slipped it out and glanced at the screen.

Could you sigh with your whole body? Good grief, I'd only just arrived. I already regretted signing up for my cell phone company's international plan.

"Excuse me." I left the table and walked into the empty sitting room before answering my boss's call.

"Molly, are you there already?" Lincoln's casual tone contradicted what amounted to a six a.m. phone call for him. The CEO and founder of website design firm JBQ, he had a lazy air about him completely at odds with his industrial strength case of workaholism.

Not that I had a lot of room to throw stones.

"I'm here," I intoned, knowing zero chances existed my boss had called just to check if my flights had gone well. Calling me first thing in the morning always meant he was about to ruin my afternoon.

"Great. Look, I've got some questions about one of the storyboards you left behind. I'm going to forward those on to you, I'll need you to get to it as soon as you can."

I glanced up at the ceiling as though I could see my carry-on bag perched on my bed. I'd brought my laptop "just in case." In theory, we would have Wi-Fi at every lodge, but that didn't mean I wanted to test it immediately. "I just got here."

The sound of him clacking away on his computer rattled

through the phone. I suspected he'd bought the most obnoxious keyboard he could find so everyone in the office would know when he was working. And he was *always* working.

"I'm regretting that I agreed to your vacation request so easily."

I could have laughed. He thought that had been easy? I'd practically had to beg for the time off. Whatever employment law stated, two weeks off wasn't the norm at JBQ. I'd followed along with company culture, and only asked for personal time in bite-sized chunks. A string of insignificant two and three-day breaks flashed through my mind. My last week-long vacation had been before I'd gotten together with Sean, and even that had been a camping trip in central Oregon.

"It's been five years since I had a week off."

"I get it, Moll, it's a tough industry." His placating tone didn't soothe. "But it would have been easier if you'd stayed so we could work out the details of this promotion first."

Right. Head of Design. The reminder tugged me in three directions at once. I'd been gunning for the position since I joined JBQ, and he'd finally offered it to me two days ago—along with a pointed hint I should cancel my trip to Scotland. I'd had a second there where I'd almost caved, but I needed this vacation.

I also happened to need the promotion. The extra money would be great, yes, but I also wanted the proof that these last several years had led to something.

Looking out the sitting room window at a pretty cottage garden, I released a long exhale. "I'll check out your email tonight."

"Thanks, Moll."

I would just have to hope for better internet than the lodge looked like it could possibly have. If any building still had dial-up, this one would.

Back in the dining room, I found the men still eating.

"Boyfriend?" Carlos wanted to know when I sat down again.

"Boss."

"Must be pretty important to be needed already."

"He just has questions about a client." I'd been pretty thorough in my notes, but Lincoln always found the gaps.

"Client? What sort?"

"I'm a website designer for a small firm in Seattle."

"Yeah? What's that like?"

I broke out my practiced dinner party bio. "I come up with the layouts, fonts, styles, everything that makes a website fun to look at and easy to use."

Not that I'd made anything remotely fun since I'd started with JBQ nearly ten years ago, but the principle remained. I designed websites. The fact that they weren't what I'd once envisioned myself doing wasn't really pertinent.

"What do you do, Rupert?" I asked.

"I'm in banking, myself." He didn't elaborate. Maybe there wasn't anything more to say about a job in banking.

The silence grew, so I turned to Duncan. "What about you?"

"Construction," was the whole of his response.

Now that he wasn't smirking over my airport purchases, the man had Resting Murder Face, and I couldn't look at him too long before my stomach got all twitchy. I couldn't tell yet if it was good twitchy or bad twitchy.

I turned back to Rupert. "Bea said it's your anniversary."

"That's right, forty years."

"How do you do it?" Carlos goggled at him. "That's an age to be with one woman."

He sounded like a guy who tallied up his relationships in months instead of years.

"Oh, it isn't all easy," Rupert said. "It takes a lot of hard work, you know. Compromise and whatnot. But in the end, it's worth it. I couldn't ask for more."

"Rupert! What on earth are you doing, eating all that fat?" As though summoned by his glowing review of marriage, Bea descended on him out of nowhere.

He dropped the scone onto his plate, reminding me of Shatner when I caught him with something he'd stolen off the table.

"We've talked about this, dear," she said in a firm voice. "No cream."

"Quite right, Bea, quite right." He licked his lips to get the last crumbs and dusted off his fingers. "Are you all set for the hill walk, my love?"

"I'll just have a bit of tea first." She kept her eyes on him as she inched nearer the tea cart, apparently expecting him to cram the last of the scone in his mouth the moment she turned away. "Molly, dear, would you check on Harlow? I tried to knock her up but got no answer."

Bea turned away to serve herself tea, leaving me baffled by her request.

"You tried to…?"

Duncan's mouth ticked up. "She tried to wake her."

See, these were the kinds of things my travel books should have mentioned. Slang and common phrases would have been way more helpful than lessons on which hand should hold your knife and fork.

"Right. Got it."

Upstairs in our room, Harlow slept on. I debated leaving her to sleep, but I wouldn't like to be left out of anything if it were me. I gently shook her shoulder until she stirred. Her eyes fluttered open, but she looked at me with a blank expression.

"Did you want to do the hill walk, or would you rather sleep?"

"Sleep." She snuggled deeper into the pillow and winked out again a second later.

Lewis and Arnav waited at the bottom of the stairs.

"Is she coming?" Lewis asked.

I shook my head. "She's choosing sleep."

"How are you holding up? It's understandable if you'd rather rest, too. It's just going to be a light walk to break us in."

"Oh, I'm up for the hill walk." I had my hiking boots on and my camera in my backpack, ready and waiting to take photos of quintessential Scottish scenery.

Arnav rounded up the others while Lewis and I waited by the bus outside. I pulled out my phone and snapped a few quick shots of the lodge to send to Jill.

> **Molly**: What's this? Oh, nothing, just the country house where I'm staying for a few days. NBD.

# four

· · ·

NOW THAT THE *adventure* part of the tour had started, my confidence faltered just a touch. I walked Green Lake every day, but I didn't always walk the whole three miles around my neighborhood lake. This excursion wasn't classed as one of Hold Onto Your Kilts' most strenuous outings, so I hadn't thought I'd needed to do anything but show up.

Man, I hoped that's all it would take.

We walked through pinewoods until we reached a lake surrounded by low hills. The crystal-clear water reflected a mirror image of the cloudy sky above. Our path hugged the lake's edge next to green reeds and knotty, multi-trunked trees growing out of the shallows.

"Everyone, Loch an Eilein." Lewis swept his arm out toward the lake.

I repeated it under my breath as I walked, stamping it on my brain. *Loch an Eilein, Loch an Eilein.* I practiced making the Gaelic "ch" sound that stopped in the back of the throat and drew out the vowel sounds, trying to mimic Lewis.

Still muttering to myself, I realized Duncan had fallen in step with me, his eyebrows hitching higher the longer he watched me.

"I'm just practicing." As though there could be another reason I would endlessly repeat the name of the lake.

"You're doing well."

"You're being generous." On the credibility scale, my Scottish accent fell right beneath Groundskeeper Willie's on *The Simpsons*. "I'm not used to making the Gaelic sounds."

"Most Americans aren't."

We kept on, his pace matching mine. "Where do you live, Duncan?"

"London."

"Really? I thought your accent was Scottish." Pretty sure his deep, rolling cadence didn't match any London accent I'd ever heard, but I probably wasn't the best authority there.

"You're not wrong. I was born and raised outside of Edinburgh. I've only lived in London the last ten years."

"What took you there? Work?"

He nodded, his gait steady on the dirt path. "I had an opportunity I couldn't pass up. But I've been wanting to get back to my roots lately, and so—the Highland tour."

"Couldn't you just drive up here and do all this yourself?"

"I could, but I've never been a tourist in my own country before."

"Aha." I pointed an accusatory finger at him. "You want that medal for helping the economy, too."

He exhaled laughter. "I think it's all yours. What brought you out here?"

"Oh. I just needed a vacation." I hadn't thought I'd needed a cover story for my trip, but I wasn't eager to share the factors that had combined to bring me here, either.

"Yes, I heard that much."

He waited, his clear blue eyes watching me like he had no doubt I'd spill my guts. Less alpha motorcycle man and more mafia don right now.

No—I needed to stop casting this guy in my romance novels.

I wasn't ready to open up about my tale of woe, so I opted for the most direct answer. "I wanted a place to get away from it all, but nothing too exotic. Trekking through the Scottish Highlands seemed more my speed than a trip to Tahiti or something like that."

"You wouldn't like Tahiti?"

"Not alone."

"Fair enough."

"Alone in Tahiti is sad and pathetic, but alone in Scotland is rugged and endearing." Or so I'd been telling myself these last few months. "A triumph of the human…something or other."

"Humans triumphing over something or other is our nation's motto."

I laughed, pleased to see the humor that lay beneath his stern appearance. Maybe he wasn't as annoyed by me as I'd initially thought. "I don't remember that in the pamphlet."

"You have to be told by a Scotsman. More dramatic that way."

Carlos and Spencer walked ahead of us, Carlos chattering away while Spencer carried himself like every step hurt. The two men couldn't have been more different. Carlos looked at everything with satisfaction as though he had partial ownership of it, while Spencer seemed physically pained by the views.

Personally, I thought the views were the most incredible thing I'd ever seen.

We came to a clearing in the woods where another group of walkers stood gazing across the lake. Following their lead, I turned my head, and a jolt of excitement stopped my feet.

A ruined castle stood in the middle of the water. An actual, factual castle. Water came right up the sides of the stone walls, the roof was gone, and the surrounding shrubs looked about five minutes from tearing it down completely—but it was a *castle*.

"That is amazing," I whispered. "How old is it?"

"It was built sometime in the twelve-hundreds." Lewis's normal speaking voice felt too loud for the reverential awe the castle deserved.

"Wow." It would have been forbidding to see in its prime, but now, ruined and flooded, it was mysterious and enchanting. The afternoon light cast a golden glow over the stones, making the castle stand out unnaturally against the still lake.

"A shame they let it get into such a state."

I couldn't tell whose neglect Bea meant to criticize, but clearly she blamed someone for the castle's downfall.

I took dozens of pictures as we moved on, stopping every few feet to get a slightly different view of the castle, zooming in for close-ups of birds in the trees that grew through the broken walls.

Duncan paused next to me as I snapped away with my fancy camera. "Are you usually such a keen photographer?"

"No, but I'm not usually in Scotland."

"Looks like you've remedied both with enthusiasm." One side of his mouth quirked up as he skirted by me on the path.

Maybe taking a lot of photos was a touristy thing to do, but I *was* a tourist. Goggling open-mouthed at Scotland was my right—nay, my duty—for the entire ten days I would be in the country.

Leaving the flooded castle behind seemed an insult to its beauty, but Lewis shepherded us up a hillside. I kept peering over my shoulder for last glimpses until I completely lost sight of the ruins. The detour led us up a grassy slope where trees turned into low heather. Atop the hill, we gazed at the Cairngorm mountains in the distance—a swath of green stretching for miles in all directions punctuated only by white clouds hovering low in the sky.

*This.* This was why I had come here. I needed this distance from everything familiar and routine and hectic back home. I needed this soaring, glowing excitement that filled my heart.

Looking out over the gorgeous scenery, I swore the countryside whispered, *Welcome to Scotland.*

By the time we finished our walk along the lake's edge and returned to the lodge, exhaustion had me teetering on the edge of a crash, possibly literally. My body felt leaden, from my bones to my eyelids, and every move I made took extra effort, as though my limbs would really rather just stay put, thanks. Sleepiness had taken hold, but my stomach ached from having had nothing for lunch but coffee and a scone. If I didn't tough it out through dinner, I'd risk collapsing from hunger.

After changing into a fresh T-shirt and checking on Harlow lightly snoring in her bed, I joined the others in the lodge's homey dining room just as Brenda brought out a giant tureen of stew and platters of boiled potatoes. The rest of my body might have been half asleep, but the warm smells coming from the crockery had my mouth watering and my stomach growling its eagerness.

Jet lag must have messed with my senses, because the simple meal of meat and potatoes with thick, fresh bread tasted better than any high-priced restaurant dinner in Seattle. I'd been so focused on gobbling down the delicious food, it took me a second to realize Bea had spoken to me.

I patted a napkin across my mouth, mildly mortified to see several of the others watching me. Did this have something to do with breaking British table manners? I casually switched my fork and knife. "Sorry, I didn't catch that."

Bea's mouth pulled into a patronizing smile, and I already regretted asking.

"I was just saying it's a real delight to see single women in their forties traveling alone like you are. It shows how far we've come."

I stared, my hunger forgotten. "I'm thirty-eight."

"When I was thirty-eight my children were teenagers."

Rupert nodded confirmation over his stew, and she went right on staring at me like she expected a gold star.

"It's a different time for women these days," she persisted. "You don't need a man to provide for you. You're free to flit from one relationship to the next without the burden of a husband or children."

Backhanded compliments over dinner. So fun. I was suddenly wide awake. "I'm sorry, was there a question in there?"

The men's eyes flickered from me to Bea while they chewed in silence.

Bea considered me with a mix of sorrow and scorn. "I'm just

saying that you're lucky. A single woman your age isn't seen as the persona non grata she once was."

Hoo boy. Persona non grata. At least she hadn't gone straight for pariah. "No, and we're never made to feel uncomfortable in conversation with strangers, either."

She nodded as if she hadn't heard me. "Though, of course, the biological clock keeps ticking. That hasn't changed."

I couldn't even come up with a smart remark. My brain had absolutely shut down over the words *biological clock* being thrown at me. Not even my mother would have stooped so low. I was trying to come up with the most polite way to say Bea needed to keep her nose in her own business when Duncan spoke up.

"How many children do you have, Bea?" he asked.

She launched into a description of her three children and their various successes, detailing their careers, spouses, and accomplishments from birth to present. My unseemly singleness became all but forgotten in the flow of praise for her family.

Duncan's gaze flickered to me, his mouth turned up at the corners.

I smiled back in silent thanks. He might look like the tough alpha, but I was starting to suspect he had some cinnamon roll in him, too.

# five

· · ·

WHEN I CRAWLED INTO BED, I felt like my muscles had been replaced with cement. Not just from the jet lag, or the hike, or even the extra time I'd spent after dinner answering Lincoln's questions until my eyes had turned into dried husks.

Bea's pointed comments at dinner had found their mark and hooked in.

It wasn't like I'd planned to be single at thirty-eight. I'd gone into each of my three major relationships thinking they'd surely turn out to be The One, but then they just…hadn't. No tragedies there—I'd always consoled myself I'd rather be single than make a permanent mistake like marry the wrong man. But Bea's conclusion my singleness stemmed from some kind of failure on my part left me lying in bed staring into darkness, cataloging inadequacies.

I didn't get nearly enough sleep before my phone alarm woke me in the morning. Hazy light shone through the window as I scrabbled to shut off the low buzzing. Rubbing at my bleary eyes, I thumbed off the alarm and found a text from Jill. It included a picture of Shatner, his eyes shut and tongue lolling, tucked in bed next to her husband Ed, along with a note.

**Jill**: Who's the Silver Fox?

I stared at the screen trying to decode her message. Shatner did have gray hair, but silver fox seemed a stretch—although I would have to start calling him that when I got home. Ed's blond head wasn't remotely gray. Maybe I'd missed a text?

I scrolled up to the braggy photo I'd sent of the lodge. Duncan stood on the doorstep with his arms folded, glowering straight into the camera. I'd been so taken by the glorious old building, I hadn't even realized he'd loomed in the doorway when I took the shot.

I enlarged the picture until his face filled the screen: stern brow, the barest shine of stubble on his head, impressive full beard. Staring longer than I would have dared in person, I did find him handsome, in a *Don't mess with me* sort of way.

Silver Fox was on point.

Not that Jill needed to know I agreed with her. If she caught so much as a whiff of interest, she would hound me about this guy the rest of the trip. Happily paired off friends always wanted everyone else to have the same happiness.

**Molly**: Duncan—he lives in London

Harlow's bed sat empty. She'd probably woken early and already gone down for breakfast. I sorted through my luggage for appropriate clothes, but my phone buzzed. Jill must have been up with Olivia, because she'd texted right back.

**Jill**: Vacation hottie's not bad

I laughed at how quickly my prediction had come true. If she knew his last name, she would probably stalk him online for me and write up a report with every last detail of the man's private life.

**Molly**: I'm just here for the scenery
**Jill**: Loser. Keep me updated on the sexy Brit
**Molly**: Scot
**Jill**: Even better!

My mom had sent one of her rare texts.

**Mom**: Keep an eye out for available men!

Lovely. Now I had three women ready to harass me about my love life.

The pathetic water pressure took a little of the shine off the thrill of staying in fabulous old lodges. I had a quick shower under a dribbling stream, but I might as well have rubbed myself down with a wet wipe. At least the water stayed hot. I wrapped myself in a fluffy white towel and stepped out of the ensuite to find the room door wide open. Carlos leaned against the jamb mid-conversation with Harlow, who rummaged through her suitcase.

"Good morning."

His wide, cheeky grin somehow made me feel even more naked. Would it be more or less dignified to run right back into the bathroom? Since I wasn't sure how much of my backside the towel covered, I stayed put.

"Do you mind…?" I flicked my fingers toward the door.

He caught the hint, but he wasn't quick about it.

"I'll catch up with you outside, Harlow." He smirked at me as he backed out, finally pulling the door shut.

Harlow hadn't looked up from her luggage. "Carlos wanted to know about my yoga practice so I'm going to take him through a session out on the lawn. I just needed a strap. Do you want to join us for a few asanas?"

Strap in hand, Harlow finally stood and realized I still dripped in the bathroom doorway.

"After you get dressed."

As though if she hadn't clarified, I might have joined them in the nude. Wait, was naked yoga a real thing? I didn't want to know.

"No, thanks."

"No worries." She waved and slipped out the door.

Great start to my morning.

Dried, dressed, and ready, I walked down to the lodge's lower level. One wall of the staircase was covered in portraits and photographs, mostly of men in various levels of kilted regalia, but a few tartan-clad women popped up here and there. Maybe these were relatives of the lodge owners, photos prominently displayed as a source of family pride.

Or maybe vintage photos could be purchased at any Scottish flea market for a few pence each. I chose to think of them as the ancestral owners and nodded at them as I passed.

Harlow and Carlos were probably doing sun salutations on the front lawn, but the rest of the group had assembled in the dining room. An appalling assortment of food had been laid out on a side table—everything from sausages to boiled potatoes to hard-boiled eggs. I peered at a tray of small, fried black coins of unknown substance, trying to sort out just where they fell on the breakfast spectrum.

"Blood pudding," said a deep voice over my shoulder.

I looked up to see Duncan at my side. Jill's *Silver Fox* assessment pinballed through my mind, lighting all the bumpers. This close, his piercing blue eyes and furrowed brow worked a tingly little shiver up my back.

*Not* how I normally reacted to strangers, but...yeah.

"Good morning," he said with a nod.

"Good morning." I dragged my attention away from the silvery Scot and back to the questionable subject at hand. "What's it like? Blood pudding?"

"It's just sausage, but the flavor can be a little coppery. This lot has a texture that melts in your mouth in a way that could be disconcerting if you're prone to overthinking such things."

"I'm definitely an over thinker." With a name like blood pudding, my imagination didn't have to stretch far. I leaned a little closer to him and dropped my voice. "Is it rude if I don't take any?"

His mouth tilted beneath his beard. "I don't think they'll kick you out."

Relieved I wouldn't be obligated to start my day with a hearty helping of blood, I grabbed a plate.

"You'll want to avoid this, then, too." He gestured at a pile of what could have been heavily spiced ground beef. "Haggis."

"Right." I inspected the would-be beef. "What's in that again?"

"If you have to ask, you don't want to know." He paused a beat and matched my secret whispering. "Organs stuffed inside other organs, mainly."

I shuddered. "I do not heart that."

"That's one of the main ingredients."

I rolled my eyes at his teasing and filled my plate, steering clear of the blood pudding and haggis, and found an empty spot at one of the tables. Next to me, Rupert had taken extra servings of the blood pudding. He savored it, rolling each bite in his mouth as he chewed. My stomach turned at the unfortunate sound.

*Don't overthink it.*

"Not trying the haggis or black pudding, then?" Rupert nodded at my plate of eggs and fruit.

"Not today." I tried to sound optimistic, as though maybe I would be willing to try organ meat some other day.

"You have to try haggis, at least. What have you come to Scotland for, if not for the adventure?"

I dropped my gaze to the pile of haggis on his plate. I wouldn't call it unappetizing, exactly, but the ingredient list didn't make my mouth water. "I wasn't really thinking of gastrointestinal adventures."

"You know what's in it, don't you?" He looked all too eager to tell me.

I glanced at Duncan. "I heard the basics, yes."

"Sheep's lungs and heart ground up and stuffed in the intestine." Rupert laughed at the way my mouth curled back with his every word. "It's not so bad as it sounds." He ate a bite to prove it. "Though some call it *offal.*"

He snickered, and I had to laugh, too. Even Duncan's mouth twitched in amusement. Dad jokes, Scotland style.

Harlow and Carlos walked into the dining room, cheeks flushed pink from their exercise. As they passed the table, Carlos leaned over Duncan's shoulder to speak to me.

"Good to see you with your clothes on, Molly."

Immune to my glares, he followed Harlow to the buffet.

Duncan raised his eyebrows in silent question, but I slashed my hand through the air like an over-eager Jedi mind trick to erase whatever he had in his head.

"I wasn't totally naked."

His eyebrows hitched higher.

"I was wearing a towel!"

He rested his chin on his clasped fists as though ready to hear the rest of the story.

"Actually, never mind, that's the best I can make it sound."

"You see, Rupert," Bea said only semi-confidentially. "There's another difference between our generations. Women in our day had a sense of shame."

After breakfast, we loaded onto the tartan mini-bus for a twenty-minute ride to where we would start the day's hike. The road climbed into the foothills of the Cairngorms, and as the slopes grew steeper, I began to have serious doubts about what exactly constituted a *walk* on this trip. Yesterday's trek had been mostly flat, since it circled a lake. Loch. Whatever. But this hike would involve actual ascent. The last thing I wanted to do was lag behind Bea and Rupert and hear more about the failings of modern women.

From the car park we hiked up a steep and rocky climb, but eventually it leveled out and led to a small green lake surrounded by pine trees. I had my camera out of my bag in a heartbeat, snapping as many pictures as I could, and experimenting with angles and zoom.

"Do you want one of yourself?" Duncan asked.

"Thanks." I handed over the camera and walked a few steps off the path, close enough for my hiking boots to sink a couple of inches into the silty lakeshore.

"Say 'lohan ohanye.'"

"Lohan ohanye?" The words didn't roll off my tongue the way they did his, they just sort of fell out of my mouth and flopped onto the ground. I envied the ease with which he pronounced the Gaelic, although of course he would be used to it.

He snapped a single photo and offered my camera back. Pictures were clearly not a priority for him. We took our places back on the trail, our boots crunching along in unison.

"What does lohan ohanye mean?" I asked, trying to emulate the cadence of his pronunciation. "Is it like saying 'cheese' in Gaelic?"

His brows tugged together, and he stared at me as if I were the one not making sense. After a beat, he laughed and jerked his thumb toward the lake.

"It's the name of the lochan. The little lake there."

Idiot. *Lochan Uaine.* I'd read the sign for it at the car park but neither knew what it meant nor how to say the words. Apparently, the pronunciation of Gaelic had little to do with the spelling.

"It could just as easily have been cheese," I grumbled.

He looked like he struggled not to laugh any harder. Clearly, I had the whole oblivious tourist thing down.

The trail turned sharply uphill, and my lungs burned as I panted along the rough path. Next to me, Duncan didn't even seem winded. Meanwhile, dampness spread under my arms and the smell of sweat came off me with every step. But if I must reek, at least I reeked in Scotland.

Finally, we reached a plateau and stopped for a breather. Below us lay a gorgeous glen with the misty peaks of the Cairngorms in the background and dark green swaths of forest all through the valley.

I exhaled a breathy laugh. I almost reached out to Duncan to get him to share in my raptures. "It's incredible, isn't it?"

He seemed more entertained by my reaction than awed by the sights. Maybe my grin gave me an air of a madwoman, but what did I care? It. Was. Glorious.

Staring my fill of the otherworldly view would be impossible, so I took more photos as we climbed the last of the way to the cairn that marked the summit.

"Welcome to Meall a' Bhuachaille." Arnav swept his arms out wide to take in the hillside.

I tried to repeat the name with about as much success as I'd had with Lochan Uaine. Which was to say, none. "Meow and Vuhchuluh?"

I couldn't take offense at his good-natured laughter. The Gaelic sounded so awful coming from me, it probably insulted his Scottish pride.

"Close."

We tried a few more times, with him patiently pronouncing the name of the hill we stood atop, and me butchering it in echo.

"You're trying anyway, which is more than most Americans do."

"Are we the worst?" I asked. "I always hear that we are, so it won't hurt my feelings if you say it's true."

I'd read several articles detailing what American tourists shouldn't do overseas. Most of it boiled down to not being a jerk.

Arnav laughed again. "Americans aren't bad, really, they just tend not to want out of their comfort zone, they call it. They speak a certain way, eat certain food, have certain entertainment, and they want to speak, eat, and do the same things everywhere they go. Anything else is strange to them."

"Is it weird to do the same things all the time?" *Asking for a friend.*

He grinned. "Never hurts to try something new."

"I'll try not to be a rude American, at least." No guarantees on the *something new* part. Especially when it came to things like haggis and blood pudding.

"The worst offense Americans make," Duncan said with a dramatic pause, "is to accuse a Scot of being English."

Bea and Rupert looked away, suddenly very interested in the views.

Arnav shook his head over the insult. "Or the Irish of being English."

"Or the Welsh."

"Pretty bad, is it?" I asked. I wouldn't be able to tell one nationality from another based on accents alone.

"Safest to assume anyone you meet in this country is Scottish." Duncan winked, but I was pretty sure he meant every word. "We're old enemies, you know."

"But I thought you were a *United* Kingdom." I brought my hands together and laced my fingers to demonstrate.

His deep laughter raised the temperature on the mountainside by a couple of degrees. In my immediate vicinity, at least.

"Bit of a myth."

"So I shouldn't say this is the loveliest mountain in England?"

He pulled his mouth into a dour frown. "No."

"Or that you have quite a nice accent for an Englishman?"

"Don't." The crinkling around his eyes betrayed his amusement, ruining the glower.

I shrugged in playful innocence. "It's all British to me."

"You're not wrong there," Rupert called out. "We are the *British* Commonwealth."

The other men looked unmoved by his helpful emphasis.

The descending trail from Meall a' Bhuachaille wasn't nearly as rough as the climb up. A long stretch down faced a lake Lewis identified as Loch Morlich. The lake proved extremely photogenic and had the added benefit of being easier to pronounce than Meall a' Bhuachaille.

I'd never seen views so stunning in all my life and continued to snap away at every turn. Maybe views were like accents, and I had only grown used to the beauty of Seattle because I saw it every day. If I brought Duncan to Seattle, he would probably stare in amazement at Mount Rainier and the shining Puget Sound, sights I took for granted. Would coming home to them after being away change how I saw them? Or would I go back to not really seeing them at all?

I couldn't imagine ever getting used to the views here.

Each bend in the trail or drop in elevation gave a new vantage I wanted to preserve with a picture, and I stopped every thirty feet or so. I didn't want one piece of this trip to slip through my fingers. I would be back in my office soon enough—I needed to cherish every minute.

"I hope you brought an extra memory card," Duncan said dryly.

"I did. If I take more than four thousand photos, I'll need another one."

He laughed, but something about the low sound didn't warm me up this time. "If you take four thousand pictures on your vacation, you're not doing it right."

I wilted under his teasing assessment. I had never been on a big vacation before, and now I wasn't doing it right? He didn't know the effort it had taken me just to get here. I wouldn't admit just how far inside my comfort zone I'd been, or for how long.

"There's nothing wrong with wanting to remember all of this."

"No there isn't, but will you remember what you did, or your photos?"

I splayed my hands. "Remembering what I did is the whole point of taking the photos."

Photo books, prints, wrapped canvases—I already envisioned all the mementos I would create when I got back home. I had a whole shrine to Scotland in the works in my mind.

He lifted one gargantuan shoulder. "At some point, chronicling it is no longer experiencing it."

I scowled at his casual judgment call. "Okay, Scottish Zen Master."

"Collum MacZen, thank you."

I trudged the rest of the trail walk, my spirits defeated as I tried to sort out the difference between chronicling and experiencing. I reminded myself that I didn't know this guy, and his opinion on my photography habits didn't matter. He probably lumped photos in with souvenirs, and I knew already he didn't have a high opinion of those.

Still, I hated to admit it, but he kind of had a point. The whole purpose of this vacation was to get away so I could unplug and reboot, not spend every minute looking through a lens. I tucked the camera into my backpack and zipped the pocket shut with a stout nod. I could experiment with simply enjoying the moment.

My goal disintegrated five minutes later when a new view of Loch Morlich proved too good to pass up. I took eight pictures of it.

# six

. . .

HIGHLAND COWS ARE MASSIVE, in case anyone wondered.

Lewis had driven us to the McFarland Estate, an old manor with grounds that sprawled for miles. Kilometers. Whatever. He'd parked near the entrance gate so we could walk up the lane, and as soon as we left the tree line by the fence, I realized why.

Great, shaggy Highland cows roamed the pasture along the road, and a few lay in the shade beneath an old oak. They were so big and fluffy, I might have squealed a little.

Duncan side-eyed me, his mouth tipping up at my ridiculous response.

I pointed at my face. "Tourist, remember?"

He exhaled laughter, gesturing me toward the cows. "Tour away."

I did, taking endless photos of the hairy red animals, and managing to almost totally ignore the amused looks he kept shining my way.

Two baby cows trotted out from the cluster beneath the trees, and our group's collective *oohs* rose up like a soft sigh. Even Spencer seemed enamored with them, but by the time his face fully turned my way, whatever spark of joy he'd held had already been snuffed out.

Lewis and Arnav herded us toward our ultimate destination, which fortunately wouldn't be anywhere near the sweet brutes in the pastures. I wouldn't want to risk hurting them—or them hurting *us*.

Walking up the lane toward the great house was like being transported onto the grounds of Pemberley. Fingers crossed we would find Darcy stepping out of a lake. Despite the cows roaming out front, the lawns close to the house had been meticulously manicured, with hedges trimmed at neat ninety-degree angles and rose bushes carefully pruned to get the largest blooms. But as the road curved around the side of the manor, the golf-course-perfect lawn relaxed back into meadows, free-growing shrubs, and rambling roses.

I laughed to myself and turned to Spencer, who was nearest. "Can you imagine living here?"

He looked at the manor as though I'd pointed out a grave. "The last owners probably died from consumption."

"Wow. That's grim." Although, given the age of the house, he might have been right.

"How do you think they'd feel about their family home being turned into a tourist trap?"

Pretty comfortable with it, given the income it must have brought in.

"You're one of the tourists it's trapped, you know."

"Like a bug under a glass."

"You didn't want to come here?" I ventured. He hadn't enjoyed much of anything yet. Seemed like an awfully long way to come just to hate your way through a country.

He regarded the flowers and grasses as though they'd stabbed him in the back. As for me, I wanted to breathe in the beautiful sights until they filled my lungs, just live off the views like oxygen, but to each their own.

"There was a last-minute change of plans." He took a deep,

shaky breath, and his smile looked one hundred percent fake. "I'm going to go check out the...plants."

He quickened his pace to get ahead of me, and I let him go. I supposed he could regret his travel decisions by himself. I certainly had no regrets.

James, our burly archery instructor, led us to a field outfitted with bows, arrows, and a line of targets. Lewis and Arnav didn't participate. They must have done this sort of thing enough they didn't need to anymore. They watched from beneath a shady tree, probably ready to laugh over our attempts.

He showed each of us to a hay bale laid out with gear. Along with the bow and arrows, I found protective goggles, arm pads, and weird-looking gloves that only covered the middle three fingers. James went through a lengthy spiel about safety, not aiming at anyone, being super careful, and ended with a reminder that, oh yes, one could kill a person with these bows.

Just the sort of pep talk I liked to hear.

"Have any of you ever used a bow and arrow before?" he asked.

Only Duncan raised his hand, which didn't seem all that surprising. His shoulders said he'd played his fair share of sports and then some.

Since the rest of us had no idea about the finer points of archery, James gave a basic rundown on holding, aiming, and shooting the bow. He made it all sound so easy, but I'd never been a quick study. Once he got well out of target range, he encouraged us to give it a go.

I slipped on the protective gear and picked up the bow. Surprisingly light, this sucker still meant business, as evidenced by the *it could kill you* part of the lesson. I nocked an arrow, pulled the string back, and aimed at the target, channeling Legolas hunting orcs.

The arrow flew through the air and skidded into the grass ten feet away from the target. I groaned over my pathetic display. Next to me, Duncan hit his center ring and selected his next arrow like nothing could be unusual about an afternoon of shooting at targets on an ancient, luxurious estate.

James must have been able to sniff out amateurs, and strode over to give me a few pointers. He helped me hold the bow properly and showed me the correct way to draw back the string. I released an arrow again, and this time it sailed to the right of the target.

Duncan's arrow hit center.

"Show off," I said over my shoulder. His smirk proved him unharmed by my teasing.

James walked me through it again, and again my arrow hit the grass well short of its mark. I'd never shot any sort of weapon in my life, but I'd thought it would be easier than this. I wasn't expecting to run out and take down wild game, but I might have at least hit the target, for goodness' sake.

"Just keep trying, and you'll get it," James said. "I have a rule that no one can leave until they hit the target at least once."

"In that case, I live here now."

Farther down the line, Harlow, Spencer, and Carlos were doing pretty well—they'd all hit their targets once, anyway, a feat currently beyond my skill. Bea and Rupert had fallen into an argument about the proper positioning of the bow. Bea pressed her case, shifting her body until she nearly had a clear shot at Rupert. James ran downfield to give them a little more attention before Rupert wound up impaled.

Left to myself, I shot another arrow that resolutely missed its mark. My skills were too ridiculous even to be embarrassed over —I was straight-up terrible at this. Superhero movies had lied to me when they made archery look easy.

"Do you want some help?"

Duncan set down his bow and stepped closer to me. Two arrows stuck out of his center ring, with three others surrounding them. Not a shock, honestly.

"James has given me up as a lost cause." Behind us, he struggled to get Bea into proper position while Rupert peppered him with helpful advice.

"You can't expect too much from your first try," Duncan said.

"Is hitting the target too much?"

"For some people."

I found his dry humor charming, even if it was at my expense. He gave me a new arrow and moved behind me, placing one hand under my elbow to help keep my arm level. Then he reached around me, demonstrating how to draw the bow back more fully. He gave instructions while he moved me into place, but I struggled to process everything he said.

He had me practically nestled in his arms—I couldn't help it if the words *Silver Fox* overtook my brain. His warmth seeped through my clothes and I just caught the spicy scent of his after-shave. Wait. Would he use aftershave on his *head*? No. Maybe I smelled beard oil.

I'd never given a second thought to that particular product but suddenly couldn't think of anything else.

I tried to look like I possessed a scrap of concentration for my aim, nodding now and then at whatever he was saying, but I struggled to shake off the effect he had on me. I needed to focus on the target, not the heat of his hands on my bare skin.

I definitely needed to stop thinking about how good he smelled. Aftershave, beard oil, I didn't care. Earthy, like a forest, but with something bright and crisp in there, too. Maybe Old Spice had a new scent—SilverFoxalicious.

*Way to focus, Molly.*

I released my arrow, but it zoomed toward Duncan's target. Apparently, everything was drawn to him.

"That would have counted."

"You're letting the bow drag over your fingers when you let go," he said. "Try for a quicker, smoother release."

He moved in front of me, clenching his fingers back and forth to demonstrate, and I mimicked the motions. He cupped my hand in his, showing me the move with his fingers over mine. Did I think his hands were warm before? His palm practically seared as it swallowed up my smaller hand. Kind of wished we weren't wearing these freaky gloves.

"This is certainly a detailed archery lesson." I'd shot for casual sarcasm, but like everything else I'd aimed at today, I missed. Awkward and breathy weren't all that convincing as casual.

His eyes sparkled with mischief. "It's good to be thorough."

Yeah, I would just forget all the thoughts *that* sentence fired up. In a minute or two.

He nodded toward my target. "Give it another go."

Ignoring the excited flurries in my stomach, I took a deep breath, raised myself to full height, and positioned the bow and arrow. Duncan put his hands at my arm and shoulder again, either not knowing or, more likely, not minding that his attempt to keep me steady had the opposite effect.

Trying to think of the bullseye and not his hands, I released the string. The arrow hit the target with a satisfying *thunk*. It lodged just outside the ring in the upper corner, but it'd hit.

I raised the bow in triumph. "Yes! Take that, you lousy English!"

Bea gave me a sharp look.

"Not you." I waved at her like we were chatting over a back-yard fence. "You're fine."

I turned a guilty look on Duncan, who shook his head at me.

"The old enemy," I whispered.

"Possibly a new enemy," he whispered back.

Pretty sure Bea had fired the first shots, but I would try to tone down my jabs.

"When did you learn to do this? You obviously have some skill with a bow." I delivered my best Aragorn impression, but it seemed lost on him.

"I first learned when I was a boy, but I took it up again a few years ago."

"Why?"

"I have this annoying neighbor…"

I faked a gasp. "You wouldn't."

He ticked his head toward the targets. "It's a sport is why I took it up. I enjoy it."

"Well, I'm crap at it."

"You've shot four arrows. Twenty-five percent of them hit the target."

"Hey, when you put it that way, I sound pretty good." I nocked another arrow. Focusing on my fingers, I released it, and watched as it sailed over the top of my target. "Pretty damn good."

# seven

. . .

AFTER DINNER, our host, Ian, reminded us that no trip to Scotland could be complete without a few sips of the "water of life," and encouraged us to visit the lodge's extensive whisky bar.

Harlow, whose body was a temple, went upstairs to bed, and Bea, who turned her nose up at the offer, made a nest for herself in the sitting room. Spencer had begged off and slunk away to his private room, leaving me to have whisky with the other men.

I'd given up on Scotch as a drinkable alcohol long ago, but I agreed with Ian—no better way to participate in Scottish traditions than by sampling it now. When in Scotland, and all that.

The bar held narrow wooden shelves packed with dozens of bottles of various shades of golden whisky. A few older vintages had peeling labels but most looked new. Acting the proper barman, Ian stood behind the counter and nodded for me to come forward.

"Ladies first. What'll it be?"

"I have no idea." I scanned the array of whisky bottles. I had no clue what constituted a good one, or even how to order one properly. *Give me the orange-labeled one* didn't sound especially sophisticated. "What do you suggest for someone who doesn't normally drink whisky?"

"Drink more whisky, of course." He gave me a good-natured look of reproach but found a bottle and poured some into a small glass. "If you're new to whisky, I have just the thing. Slightly sweet, excellent for beginners."

I didn't love being called out as a beginner, but admitting all the Scotch I'd tried before had tasted equally terrible probably wouldn't impress the very Scottish barman.

He passed a glass to me. "There's a wee dram for you."

I took the little glass and swirled the golden liquid around as though I could fake my way to classiness. Duncan leaned an elbow against the bar, watching me take the tiniest of tiny sips.

Ian scoffed. "Aw, doing it that way, it's a wonder you can even taste it."

I took a slightly less tiny sip. I caught a thick, almost caramel flavor when it hit my tongue, but it burned just as much as I remembered on the way down.

"It's surprisingly not awful." I jiggled the glass again and took another sip. I'd call it drinkable, but only in small doses.

Ian laughed. "That'll have to do as a compliment. Gents?"

The men had a better idea what they were after, and once we each had a drink, we took over one of the stout wooden tables. I sank onto a plush chair, sipping at my *wee dram* of whisky. The flavor could grow on me, but the bite would take longer to get used to.

Like, a whole lifetime.

"What do you think of it?" Rupert asked.

I wanted to be honest, but…not as honest as I could be. "It's better than Jack Daniels."

Duncan shook his head. "That compliment's as good as an insult."

"You're bad-mouthing perfectly good ten-dollar liquor?"

"It costs ten dollars now?"

I laughed, feeling lighter already. My thoughts skipped around the way they did before sleep, and I stopped sipping so frequently at my glass. What was the alcohol content of whisky versus wine?

I wasn't the best at liquor-related math, but judging by how out of sorts my brain had gone after a few sips, the whisky must have been something like two hundred proof.

I rubbed my foot against the table leg to try to ground myself, hoping the repetitive motion would keep me from drifting away on the alcohol. Trying whisky was one thing, but I didn't need to get trashed with these men.

"Maybe you just don't have a taste for American whiskies," I said, scrambling for a little more conversation. If I had something to focus on, maybe my thoughts would stop folding in on themselves.

Duncan indulged my belated retort. "Given that most of their whiskies have definite notes of jock strap and old horse leather, I think I'll stick with Scotch."

"Old horse leather?" I repeated with a grin.

His eyebrows quirked up, but he didn't explain. Should I know the difference between new and old horse leather? What was horse leather? Was this a Scottish thing or a Duncan thing?

Oh no, I'd gotten drunk on two tablespoons of whisky.

"There's a great whisky bar I go to in L.A." Carlos looked around at the lounge's dark wood paneling, somehow both admiring and judging. "Not as authentic as this place, though. Too crowded. Sometimes the waitlist to get in isn't worth it."

Los Angeles made sense for Carlos. Something in his charm and bright smiles felt a little too curated to be totally real. Handsome for sure, but he didn't give off *effortless* vibes.

Unlike someone else at the table.

"I didn't hear where you're from," Carlos said to me.

"Green Lake." That earned blank stares all around. "Seattle. I live in the Green Lake neighborhood, which probably means nothing to you unless you live in Seattle, too. Which you don't. But I do."

Yup. Definitely drunk on two tablespoons of whisky.

Rupert's drink had gone straight to his face. He flushed bright red from the tip of his nose to the tops of his ears. "You'll be eager to head back home straight away, I'd imagine."

"I don't know." I paused to let my sluggish brain contemplate the question. "It's so beautiful here. I was thinking today about how the views we see every day become tired and common, and it takes something new and exciting to make us feel alive again."

Even my tipsy mind knew that could be an apt analogy for this whole trip. I needed a boost, a change of scenery, *something* to carry with me when I went back home.

Rupert sputtered into his drink and set it down. "That's an interesting sentiment. I think I'm off to bed."

He stood and left the table as though a banshee chased after him.

No, not that. Banshees were Irish. I frowned at the last of my whisky, trying to think of the Scottish equivalent of a howling nightmare. All I could come up with was Mel Gibson yelling, *Freedom!*

"What got into him?" Duncan looked at the empty doorway where Rupert had disappeared.

I shrugged and moved my foot against the table leg again, only, I didn't find it. I waved my foot around in the air, confused how I could have lost it. I wasn't *that* drunk. Table legs didn't just up and leave—

Realization punched me in the gut.

"Oh, no." I collapsed forward onto my elbows, sinking my forehead into my hands. "Oh, no."

"Yes?" Duncan said slowly.

I peeked out at him from between my fingers. "I was rubbing my foot against his leg."

How long had that gone on? Five whole minutes? More? *Way to be mortifying overseas, Molly.* I could have cringed myself into another dimension.

"You vixen," Carlos said with a naughty smile.

"I thought it was the table leg!"

"Must be one bony leg." Duncan kept his eyes on me as he took a drink of his whisky.

Sure, they could have a good laugh over it. I had to spend the rest of this trip with a man as old as my father who thought I had the hots for him. No wonder he'd escaped so quickly.

But wait…

"No," I moaned. "The thing I said about something new and exciting making us feel alive. He probably thought I meant *him*. Or *me*. Or *me and him*."

The whisky in my stomach churned.

"What are modern women thinking," Duncan scolded, "flirting with men twice their age?"

"It was an accident!"

He tipped his head down at me. "Try telling that to Bea."

Yeah, I was definitely going to be sick.

# eight

. . .

IN THE STARK light of day, nausea crept over me like waves against something slimy that had washed ashore. I couldn't say which made me feel sicker: the whisky or my evening with the men. I dreaded facing Rupert again, knowing how I'd shamelessly—however inadvertently—flirted with him last night. That he thought I was coming onto him would have been laughable if I didn't have to face him every day for another week.

Not that facing him would be much of a problem, apparently.

At breakfast, he flatly refused to make eye contact with me. He gave me a wide berth at the buffet and kept his wife closest to me at the table. Nerves tumbled around in my stomach as I watched Bea, but she seemed ignorant of the whole situation. If she'd known, she would probably have already made a nasty remark about brazen women going after married men. I flinched every time she opened her mouth to speak, waiting for the blow to fall, but it never did.

Rupert was wiser than he appeared at first glance.

Today's itinerary would take us up Ben Macdui, the second tallest mountain in Great Britain, according to a laminated placard in the lodge. After a hearty breakfast, we piled into the mini-bus for the drive into the Cairngorms. We went deeper into the mountains than we had yesterday, winding our way up hillsides whose imposing, rocky slopes were softened somewhat by the lush green grass that clung to them.

At the car park, Lewis reminded us to bring our jackets, no matter how little we thought we would need them. The temperature hovered in the low sixties in the valley, and I'd stowed my fleece-lined rain jacket in my pack.

"Any snow?" Duncan asked as he slipped a water bottle into his backpack holster.

"Latest report says there's no concern for ice or snow fields," Lewis said, double-checking his supplies.

"Snow fields?" I said. "But it's summer."

"You're in Scotland now." Duncan buckled his backpack's chest strap, drawing my attention to the way his hunter green shirt hugged his upper body.

This marked the first time I'd seen him without a fleece on, and I had to stop myself from doing a double-take. He had a slim stomach, defined pectorals that stood at attention beneath his shirt, and round biceps that strained mercilessly against his short sleeves.

Would it be rude to whip out my camera so I would never forget the sight?

We got going, but my enthusiasm flagged pretty quickly. The track cut over a mild slope, but a half-hour of even that gentle climb had my legs burning. Gravel rolled underfoot as I crunched along, and we had to scramble around bigger rocks that covered the path.

At least after this I would spend the next few days kayaking, where I could abuse my arms instead of my legs. Spread the misery...er, joy.

Clouds hung low in the sky, bringing with them a chill wind, and although I hadn't felt a drop of rain yet, my lifelong experience in Seattle said it was inevitable. I stopped to pull on a wool cap and my jacket. Even another layer more would have been welcome protection against the elements on the bare mountainside.

Summer, my behind.

The mountain fell sharply away, carving out a little lake at the bottom of the valley. Other hikers scrambled down to it, and judging by their tiny figures, the lake was a lot bigger than it appeared from up here.

"It's a perfect spot for wild swimming, if anyone's up for it," Arnav said.

"Followed quickly by hypothermia," Spencer put in.

"Worth it."

Spencer didn't look tempted. Honestly, I voted with Spencer here.

I took more and more pictures just to have an excuse to stop on the trail. The Cairngorms were wide and round, massed together in giant ripples all the way to the horizon. Beautiful, but oh, so hard to climb.

The track grew steeper, and I silently cursed myself for ever thinking I needed an *adventure* tour. I could have gone on one of the group vacations my parents kept trying to get me to join, full of fit and active people in their seventies. But no, I'd had to prove to myself that approaching forty hadn't put me on a downward slope. So noble—so misguided.

My legs ached, my lungs burned, and my exhaustion seemed premature compared to the rest of the group. At least I wasn't so miserable I'd had to stop to throw up, but that didn't give me a lot to cling to.

The clouds broke into a mist that hung low in the air, narrowing visibility and leaving my clothes damp. I'd seen a lot of overcast days in Seattle, but never experienced anything quite like this hanging mist. It formed a perfect cap to the hilltop, even if it meant we couldn't see the rest of the Cairngorms now.

Next to me, Arnav just noticeably breathed hard as he paused to take a drink of water. He wiped his mouth with the back of his hand. "Have you ever heard the legend of Am Fear Liath Mòr?"

"I don't even know what you just said, so no."

"It's the Big Gray Man of Ben Macdui." He put a sinister edge in his voice like we were sitting around a campfire telling ghost stories. "Some say he's a tall creature covered in fur. Others say he's the spirit of a climber that haunts the summit where he died. Whatever he is, the Big Gray Man can send icy fear into the bravest heart."

Even as he spoke, the mist curled in around us, and I took a step closer to him. He was putting me on, of course, but the gloom made anything seem possible.

"Have you ever seen anything up here?"

"Nothing for certain. But I was hiking here last year with a mate, a day just like this, with heavy cloud cover, we could barely see anything. We heard footsteps behind us, but no matter how many times we stopped, they never caught up. I can't say it was the Gray Man, but we didn't see anyone else."

With one last hitch of his eyebrows, he turned and continued up the trail, leaving me rattled by his story. Enclosed by the creeping mist, every footfall and scatter of rock echoed around me. Sometimes the sounds seemed separate from our group as though farther away, but with the thick fog, I couldn't be sure. It would have been awful to be alone out here in the mists.

Just as I moved to follow Arnav, a hand clamped down on my shoulder.

My heart went into overdrive, and I screamed before I could stop myself. Duncan stood beside me, a surprised grin twitching at his mouth.

"Why would you do that?" I brushed his hand off my shoulder and told my fight or flight response to save the panic for something serious, like an actual flight.

"I am sorry, Molly." He would have looked more penitent if he toned down that triumphant grin. "It was too good an opportunity to miss."

Farther along the trail, Lewis, Bea, and Rupert had stopped to stare in our direction.

"I'm fine," I called. "Just frightened by the big, gray man, here."

I gestured at Duncan, and my fingers brushed the solid muscle of his arm. My heart rate spiked again, ignoring all my attempts to calm it down.

"Ouch." He grimaced at my teasing epithet. "I suppose I deserve that."

"Well, you're not totally gray."

"Not really helping."

I tilted my head, examining him. "More of a salt and pepper. Heavy on the salt."

He stared me down, thoroughly unimpressed. "Mm hmm. Best quit while you're ahead."

"Silver fox?"

One eyebrow ticked up. "I could live with that." Merriment danced in his eyes. "I really wasn't expecting a scream."

"You're lucky I didn't punch you." Although, as exhausted as I already was, pretty sure a punch would have wound up embarrassing me more than the scream.

"Very lucky."

We carried on with the climb, bringing up the rear of the group.

I still hadn't pinned down Duncan's age. The solidness of his body and his general athleticism gave his age more ambiguity than his severe gaze and gray beard originally implied. Still, I couldn't think of a question indirect enough to get the information I wanted without *looking* like I was asking.

"You said you've lived in London the last ten years. How long did you live in Edinburgh before that?"

"All my life."

Swing and a miss.

"And you?" he asked. "Have you been in Seattle long?"

"Same. Born and raised." I'd gone to college in the city, too, and now lived ten miles from my childhood home. Nobody would ever call Seattle sheltered, but the reminder I hadn't explored much beyond my own backyard sat uncomfortably in my gut.

The rocks became larger and more difficult to work around the closer we got to the summit. If a path existed, Lewis had left it in favor of a more direct route to the top. It wasn't steep, but the boulders made for slow going.

I put my weight on one, and the rock rolled enough to throw me off balance. I fell onto my shins and hands, and my mind lit up with a searing stab of pain.

Duncan knelt beside me before I could right myself. He put a hand on my shoulder, assessing me with a piercing gaze. "Are you hurt?"

"Just my pride."

I shifted to sit and dusted the mud from my hands. Blood welled up in tiny droplets where the skin on my palms had been scraped off. He slipped off his backpack and used his water bottle to wash away the blood and dirt. I could tell he was trying to be gentle, but the cool stream of water still stung my open wounds.

*Killing it on the adventure tour, Molly.*

Lewis doubled back to us and pulled a green first aid kit from his pack. "Are you hurt anywhere else?"

"No." I couldn't focus on anything beyond the fire in my palms.

"Her leg." Duncan nodded at my shin.

Exposed by my cropped leggings, my right shin must have taken the worst of the fall, and a two-inch gash seeped blood. It didn't look deep, it had just…removed a lot of skin. I didn't even feel it yet. Probably a bad sign.

"Oh." My stomach fluttered, but for some reason, I thought about breakfast, and an awkward giggle bubbled out of me.

A line formed between Duncan's eyebrows. "Are you uncomfortable with blood?"

"No, I was just thinking about Rupert's blood pudding." Now he looked at me like I'd hit my head instead of my leg. I patted his arm. "I'm okay."

"I think I'm supposed to be reassuring you, here."

"Everything okay down there?" Bea called from farther along the path.

Great. Next I'd have to hear about how women in her day didn't go around falling about on mountains, either.

"Arnav, would you take the others on up to the summit while we get Molly wrapped up?" Lewis ripped open an antiseptic pouch and gently swabbed at my bleeding leg.

I hissed as the wipe did its work. The numbness went away, at least. "That stings."

He cleaned my injuries and dotted on salve before bandaging everything up. "How do you feel?"

I felt like a child who had fallen off my bike away from home —one part reassured, and two parts unsettled. Mostly, though, I just wanted to move past the "Molly embarrasses herself daily" part of this trip.

"I think I've experienced a little undue pain and suffering."

Panic spread across his face. I could almost see the word *litigation* flashing behind his eyes. Injuries on tours like this must be every guide's nightmare.

"I'm kidding. I'm fine, really." Scraped palms and road rash on my leg weren't all that bad. Also, I only had my own negligence to blame.

Worry still creased his brow. "I'm glad to hear it."

Each man got a hand under one of my elbows and helped me stand. The pain in my leg wasn't awesome now that I put weight on it, but I would power through and say nothing more of this stupid fall for the rest of the trip. Maybe someone would fall into a lake to draw the attention away from me.

"Steady there?" Duncan asked.

"Steady as a bagpiper in a hurricane." My giddy laugh didn't seem to reassure him.

"That's not a thing."

I climbed the last of the way with Duncan at my side like a bodyguard ready to throw out a hand if I looked shaky, but we finally reached Ben Macdui's summit. A cairn marker stood at the top, and a dial pointed to the other peaks in the mountain range. It hadn't been a perfect trip up, what with all the bandages plastered on me, but I'd made it to the top of a mountain.

Triumph coursed through my veins. I'd bagged a *munro*.

Some of the threatening clouds had cleared, and although the foggy cover still hemmed in most of the view, the mist that enveloped the nearby mountains made them mysterious in the quiet. I took dozens of pictures as I spun in a slow circle, entranced by what I could see of the crags, glens, and lochs below.

High-pitched bagpipe keening carried to me on the wind, tingling up my back like fingers tracing along my spine. Arnav held his phone aloft, blaring out Scotland's national anthem, its rhythmic tune familiar thanks to the countless YouTube videos I'd watched leading up to this trip.

The others mostly ignored this show of national pride—only Duncan seemed at all moved by the gesture. Looking out at the Cairngorms below, his stoicism increased tenfold. With the pipes ringing in the background and his stern brow facing into the harsh winds, I could imagine him as a Highlander decked out in his kilt and claymore two centuries ago.

I didn't hate the image. I might have even lingered on it way too long.

He caught me watching him, and a spark of something primal lit inside me. I had a sudden urge to go to his side and…I wasn't even sure what. *Anything.* Equal parts unsettling and thrilling, I hadn't had this sort of reflexive response to a man in ages. Maybe ever.

Playing it cool like my eyes hadn't fallen out of my head while I ogled him, I went back to snapping pictures of the mountain range around us. After all, I'd come out here to experience the rustic scenery, not flirt with rugged men.

I slowly made a circle around the mountaintop and came upon Spencer off on his own, looking down into the glen. His contemplation of the Cairngorms was less like Duncan's Highlander and more like a janitor surveying a cafeteria after a food fight.

I took a few steps closer. "Pretty amazing, right?"

The morose look he turned my way said he very much disagreed. "It's just hills and grass. You can see that anywhere, and for a lot less effort."

Okay, then.

Leaving him to write his bad Yelp review of the Cairngorms, I joined the rest of the group at the cairn. I lowered myself onto a stone between Harlow and Rupert, wincing every time my leg moved or I clenched my hands too much. As I dug through my pack for my lunch, Rupert stood, dusted off his pants, and sat down again, putting Bea between himself and me.

Across our little circle, Duncan caught my eye. Ever so slightly, he moved his booted foot in a sultry motion in front of him. I guess nobody had forgotten about my tipsy, inadvertent attempt to seduce our companion. His mouth curled up as he teased me, pinning me with his gaze.

I made a show of rolling my eyes, but my cheeks probably flamed bright red. In spite of my protests a minute ago, the fluttering going on in my chest said flirting with rugged men in Scotland sounded like a great idea.

# nine

· · ·

BY THE TIME we hiked down Ben Macdui and returned to the lodge for dinner, my legs were begging for mercy. Shakiness this early in the game didn't bode so well for my big adventure trip. Still, I gloried in what I'd done. Climbing a mountain ranked infinitely higher than any exercise class back home.

I changed into fresh clothes to head down to dinner when my phone buzzed. I glanced at the bright screen, and my glorying came to a crashing halt.

"Lincoln."

"Molly, how are things in Scotland?"

"Great." Details would have been as lost on him as Spencer.

"Good to hear. Look, the design team has some final mock-ups that need approval before going to storyboard. I've sent you an email with the specifics."

Laughter rumbled somewhere downstairs, reminding me I should have been with the rest of the group getting ready for dinner, not taking phone calls from my boss. At least approving the mock-ups wouldn't take much time.

"I'll look at them tonight."

"Thanks, Moll. There are also some change requests I'd like you sort through, and a few bugs in the layout engine to fix."

"Bugs?" I prayed I'd heard him wrong. Fixing bugs could turn into a massive time suck.

"That's one of the tasks you'll be tackling now as Head of Design. You've got this, right?"

I didn't like the note of concern in his voice, as though maybe I *didn't* have it. I hadn't failed him or this company in all the years I'd been with them, and I wouldn't have him start questioning my abilities now.

"I've got this."

I tossed the phone on my bed. I considered tossing it straight out the window, but that would wind up hurting me more than Lincoln.

Downstairs, I found two vacant seats at our table, but no way would I pull up a chair next to Rupert and further his belief in my unrequited affections. Instead, I took a seat at the opposite end of the group beside Harlow.

"How's your leg?" Duncan asked as I sat down across from him.

"Sore, but not bad. I still feel like an idiot." My one comfort was that since I'd pulled up the rear at the time, nobody had witnessed my actual stumble.

Nobody but the mythical Gray Man.

"I'm sure it's not the worst injury to befall a person on Ben Macdui."

"I hadn't considered that. Is it bad I'm encouraged by it?" The fall could have been a lot worse. I imagined being carried down the hillside on a stretcher while Bea *tsked* over my clumsiness in the background.

"You just need a stronger core," Harlow said.

Wow. That advice struck me as markedly unsolicited. "I lost my balance when a rock rolled beneath my foot."

"When your core is strong, it won't be so easy to lose your balance." Her matter-of-fact tone only added to the slight. "That's one of the things I help my clients with in our sessions. You just don't have any muscle tone. When you strengthen your core, it will take care of the rest."

An indignant flame burst to life as I looked down at my stomach. It wasn't quite as flat as hers, but saying I didn't have any muscle tone went too far. I ran a hand over my stomach and clenched the muscles there. They moved—I had muscle tone.

I glanced up to find Duncan had seen my little muscle test. I dropped my hand and flashed a defiant look. "Abs of steel."

He nodded solemnly. "No doubt."

Brenda and Ian brought out serving trays wafting up delicious smells that might have come straight from heaven. I focused on my best table manners even though my hunger urged me to shovel food into my mouth as fast as possible. Harlow, meanwhile, carefully selected food from each tray, singling out the roasted vegetables and avoiding the fish and bread.

"Are you a vegetarian?" I asked as I cut a piece of fried fish. I'd enjoyed everything I'd eaten here. Brenda's culinary expertise had even managed to make the organ-based dishes look palatable— not that I'd had the courage to try them.

Harlow shook her head. "Paleo. I eat meat, but this fish has been cooked in batter and I can't eat flour."

"That's too bad, the fish is delish."

She turned up her nose as I shoved a forkful of battered fish into my mouth.

"We really aren't meant to eat grains. Our ancestors didn't grow wheat."

I took a bite of bread slathered with butter, ignoring her look of dismay. I didn't mean to rub it in her face, but I wouldn't miss out on a tasty meal just because she had chosen to. I had a few friends who'd tried Paleo, but I couldn't think of a good reason to eat the way cavemen did aside from the trend factor.

"Cavemen didn't live very long." Pretty sure I'd already exceeded the average caveman's life expectancy by several years.

"That's a myth. They lived long, healthy lives without all the grains, processed foods, and chemicals that people eat today." Harlow sounded more like she was trying to get me to go to church with her than get me to cut wheat from my diet. "If people would just eat healthy, no one would get sick at all. Since I started on Paleo, my auto-immune disease has cleared up and I haven't had a single cold."

I shared a look with Duncan, whose lips moved into the slightest smirk. *Bull.*

"Paleo?" Bea said. "Who's doing Paleo?"

"I am," Harlow said.

Bea scowled out her judgment. "I tried it for a while—didn't like it."

"You just need to give your body enough time to adjust. It's the natural way for humans to eat."

"Cancer's natural, too," Spencer put in.

She didn't even acknowledge him. "Our ancestors didn't eat dairy products, and they didn't harvest grains or eat sugar. There's no reason for us to, either."

"Sounds awful to me." Carlos popped a bite of breaded fish into his mouth and waggled his dark eyebrows at Harlow.

She frowned back, apparently unimpressed by his charms.

"I didn't even think of sugar," I said. "I could never do it."

Sure, I might wind up healthier, but at what cost? Without sweet treats I'd only be living half a life.

"I've never felt better since I gave up chocolate." Harlow's angelic smile was smug as hell.

"Give up chocolate? That's a *heck, no* from me."

"You love chocolate so much you'd trade your health for it?"

"I think I'd trade just about anything for chocolate."

"Really?" Carlos leaned over the table, suddenly interested. "Would you trade men for chocolate?"

"Absolutely."

I might have answered too quickly. I didn't really see myself as *that* woman, angry at the world because I was still single in my late thirties, but come on. *Chocolate.*

Carlos looked at me the same way I watched ASPCA commercials on late-night TV. Sad and maybe a little horrified, but he couldn't bring himself to look away.

"Pretty set on that choice, are you?" Duncan asked.

Was it me, or was the lighting making his eyes sparkle? Had to be the lights.

"Well…" I pretended to at least consider the alternative. "I've had a *lot* of first rate chocolate."

One of his eyebrows lifted. "No first rate men?"

I made a face. "More like generic store brand. You think it's going to be good, but then you actually get it and realize you're stuck chewing on tasteless, sub-par candy."

Okay, maybe I *was* that woman. I didn't have a line of awful relationships behind me, they'd just been…less than expected. Underwhelming. Nothing I'd give up Godiva for without some serious thought behind it.

Laughter rumbled through him. "Sounds like we need to find you a better quality man."

"Amen to that."

# ten

· · ·

THE NEXT MORNING, Duncan sat next to me for the hour ride to Inverness, and I opened up the conversation by yawning massively behind my hand.

He side-eyed me. "Don't tell me this trip is too much for you."

"I think it's still the jet lag." I'd stayed up past midnight sorting out website bugs, but jet lag sounded better than admitting to working furtively in the middle of my vacation. "What do you do in construction? Everyone seems to dance around those kinds of questions here, but I'm curious."

Basic questions about jobs back home hadn't cycled through as typical small talk among the Brits in the group. Carlos had no problem asking people questions about themselves, but the others mostly discussed things like food and places they'd been.

Duncan laughed, but it wasn't unkind. "Americans are more straightforward. You ask personal questions right away. In the U.K., we're more reserved until we get to know people. Then you'll have a hard time enduring our forthrightness."

"Then Bea must feel she knows me very well," I whispered.

"It isn't the same across the board," he whispered back.

"I didn't think asking about someone's job was a personal question."

He tilted his head to the side. "Depends on what the someone does."

"So you're saying you're some kind of construction ninja spy?"

He laughed, but I went on watching him, waiting for an answer.

After a minute, one side of his mouth turned up. "I run a construction company that specializes in historical renovations."

Why did that sound like the coolest job around?

"How long have you been doing that?"

"Since I was a boy, really. My father was a carpenter. He did custom trim work, windows, doors, mantelpieces. I learned at his side."

I thought of the old house I rented with its original crown molding and wooden built-ins. Might be nice to see it in all its glory. "So that was your opportunity? The thing that took you to London?"

"London is a good market for my line of work, so I made the decision to leap out on my own."

"Just like that?"

He nodded. "Just like that."

I'd had that kind of confidence when I set out to make it on my own, too, but with very different results. My unfettered optimism that I only needed to want it badly enough and everything would fall into place hadn't gotten me as far as I'd hoped. Reality had proved a little harsher than that.

I'd had a few successful months creating custom websites, logos, and branding for small businesses, followed by a slow decline that burned through my savings until I'd had to move into my parents' basement.

Basically, the highest point of my adult life, followed right after by the lowest.

"That's great it's worked out so well for you. It can be hard to set off on your own."

"I knew what I wanted, so I went after it. Didn't make sense not to take the leap."

Duncan seemed like he could catch himself pretty well if he fell, but I'd sworn off swan dives after mine had ended in a belly flop. Despite my optimistic hopes, following my dreams had turned into a nightmare of destitution and humiliation. I'd taken the path of practicality and solid plans ever since. Maybe my path wasn't the most exciting, but it kept a roof over my head.

He narrowed his eyes on me like my expression had given my whole inner monologue away.

"You don't like leaping into things." Not even a question, an assessment.

I bit my lip. The brief rise and long, painful downfall of *Molly Clarke Designs* wasn't exactly happy mini-bus banter. "I just think things don't always work out the way we hope."

He watched me for too long, and I didn't like all the conclusions he must have been drawing. Most of them were probably pretty accurate.

"Do you come back to Scotland very often?" I asked. Anything to move the conversation along.

"I have lately. My mother still lives outside Edinburgh, and I visit her when I can."

"Do you drive up?"

"Sometimes, but it's only an hour flight. The best way to travel, though, is by train. A luxury seat with a dining car and a bar, riding through spectacular scenery—nothing better."

"I'd thought about doing that for this trip, but I couldn't add the extra days off." Pretty sure Lincoln would have lost his mind if I'd asked for any more time.

"Your work isn't very flexible?"

Laughter bubbled out of me. "I don't think my boss is familiar with that word."

I'd known Lincoln would ask me to work over my vacation, but I hadn't anticipated just how much he would want me to do. I'd already logged several hours, and the trip had barely begun.

But arguing with him—especially with my new promotion hanging in the balance—would only make the problem worse.

"Anyway, I've got a little time in Edinburgh before my return flight. I want to see the castle."

Duncan gave a disinterested hitch of his shoulders. As a former resident of the city, he must have long ago grown immune to the wonders of its castle.

"My guidebook says it's the crown jewel of the city." I laughed at the face he made over that flowery description. "Well, it's written by an American travel show host, and I'm not sure I always trust his opinions."

"Steering you wrong, is he?"

"His motto seems to be 'Never look at anything twice.'" His trips were obnoxiously designed to avoid even a few feet of back-tracking.

Duncan nodded. "That does seem to be at odds with your motto of 'If it's worth taking one photo, why not take thirty?'"

I lightly shoved his shoulder, and he laughed at my efforts. He was all taut muscle beneath his soft fleece. "I can't help it, I want to remember everything."

"How many photos have you taken so far?"

My camera's display currently read 376, but he didn't need to know that. "A couple hundred."

He dipped his head closer. "Per day?"

"*No.* Ooh, that reminds me." I fished my phone from my messenger bag. Jill had sent a photo of Shatner staring out her front window, his tongue dangling as he waited for someone to walk by so he could menace them.

I showed the phone to Duncan. "This is my dog, Shatner."

"Shatner, as in William?"

His fingers brushed over mine as he took the phone, and a flood of warmth rippled across my skin. I would have thought the days of getting worked up over phone hand-offs were long gone, but nope. Still in full swing.

"Yup. I'm a bit of a Trekkie." Understatement, considering I basically had the original series memorized. "Plus, it's just a great name."

"It is." He smirked at the photo and handed the phone back.

I looked at the pic of my dog's adorable mug but then died a little inside. The tail end of last night's text session with Jill peeked out above the photo.

**Jill**: What's the status with the hottie Scot?
**Molly**: Goodnight, nosy
**Jill**: Snoopers gonna snoop

I could have shriveled up into a tiny raisin of humiliation. I shut off the phone and stuffed it deep in my bag. Had I signed some sort of stipulation that said I was required to embarrass myself every day of this trip? If so, I was doing a bang-up job.

What was I supposed to do here? Say *That's not about you!* like a teenager whose crush found a note about him? No way. Best to pretend he'd never seen the text—even if the twitch of his mouth and glint in his eye said he certainly had.

"Shatner's a chubby little tub, but he's a good boy. My friend Jill is dog-sitting for me, and she's been sending pictures of him every day." Among other things. "I used to think he couldn't get along without me, but he seems to be doing fine. He'll probably pee himself when he sees me again, though."

He chuckled. "A sign of true love."

My belly did a little flip when Duncan's deep voice rumbled *true love*. He made everything sound good, but those words worked a special magic.

"What about you? Is there anyone at home ready to pee themselves when you get back?"

"If you're asking if I have any pets, no." He paused a beat. "If you're asking if I have anyone else, also no."

Was I asking that? No. Sort of? He was attractive, not that I needed reminding, with a good sense of humor, and his rich, mellow voice was all kinds of sexy, but—no. We were just on vacation together, nothing more.

Probably nothing more.

# eleven

· · ·

THE STONE GUEST house on the outskirts of Inverness made my heart skip. I had to hand it to Hold Onto Your Kilts— even though staying in such small lodges meant we had to double up in our rooms, they were ridiculously quaint. A little like going across town to visit Grandma in the heart of the Highlands.

"This will be our home base just for one night," Lewis said. "Today, we'll focus on Scotland's history with a trip to Culloden, and end with an afternoon on Loch Ness. We're just going to drop off our things before we head to the battlefield, so let's not get too comfortable inside."

The two men who ran the lodge greeted us with warm handshakes like grooms in a receiving line.

"Good morning to you all," Jack said. "Welcome to Inverness. Step right in, Kenneth will show you to your rooms."

Kenneth handed out room keys as he led us through the lodge. Harlow and I had a twin bedroom on the second level, and aside from slightly different wallpaper, it might have been the room we'd just left behind in Aviemore. Cozy, homey, and perfect for an American still stunned to find herself in Scotland.

"What did you do on your other visits here?" I asked. She

hadn't seemed impressed by much of anything we'd seen or done so far, but maybe more experience with travel did that to people.

"I came for a yoga retreat in Glasgow one time, and the other I went to Edinburgh with my ex. We mostly stayed in the city and saw live music." She laid out her bags in the cramped communal space around the beds and aired out her clothes.

"I still can't believe I'm here." I peeked out our small window onto the lane below. The houses boasted dormer windows and chimney stacks topped with half a dozen vents each that just begged for a little soft-shoe action by a scruffy chimney sweep.

"Is this your first big trip?"

"Yup." I'd been to Vancouver, British Columbia, a few times, but it didn't compare in light of international travel stories. Anyway, nothing I had done there was worthy of mention. Visits to museums and botanical gardens wouldn't impress anyone under the age of seventy.

"Watch out," she said. "You'll get addicted. I try to add a stopover to every trip I take, just for the pure need to see one more place."

"I don't travel much for work." Seemed a pathetic excuse, all things considered.

Harlow grinned. "Get a new job."

I laughed a little too loudly at her ready solution. She might as well have suggested I fly without the valium. Not going to happen.

Following Lewis's instruction not to drag our feet, I hurried back outside, but the grounds caught my attention. Ivy covered a low garden wall that protected sweet little flowers in purples, reds, and oranges. I could have spent my whole vacation in the lodge's yard, breathing in the scent of wildflowers. All I needed was a blanket and a book, and I'd be set.

When I joined the others by the bus, Duncan lifted one teasing eyebrow at me. "Really? That little garden is worth chronicling?"

I swatted his arm. "It's picturesque."

"Half of it's weeds."

"Hush."

We climbed into the most Scottish mini-bus in all of the U.K., and Lewis navigated the short drive through Inverness to Culloden.

"Have you been to the battlefield before?" I asked Duncan, who had slid into the seat next to me again.

"Yes, but not since I was a boy."

I tried to picture him as a child but couldn't do it. Not when confronted by his bushy beard and wide shoulders. "Don't you mean lad?"

"Oh, aye, I was a wee sprite of a lad the last time I was here, my kilt barely scraped the ground." He laid his accent on thick, and I laughed at the change.

The travel book I'd skimmed included a lengthy sidebar about the battle at Culloden. In the 1700s, it had been the last battle in the struggle to retake the crown from King George, and a decisive defeat for the Highlanders.

If I were being honest, I didn't look forward to this leg of the tour. Loch Ness would be fascinating for its legendary beauty, but a battlefield where hundreds of soldiers had died would hardly be the pick-me-up I'd hoped to get from the trip.

Even if Jill had asked me to take a dozen pictures for *Outlander*-related reasons.

At the battlefield, we joined a guided tour of the grounds. We strolled the paths that snaked through open fields while our young guide explained some of the political history of Scotland and England before ending with the crushing defeat at Culloden. As expected, it made for an immensely depressing story.

She led us to a giant memorial cairn, but smaller stones with clan names carved into them dotted the field. The guide explained that they marked where the men of those names had fallen in battle. All told, some twelve hundred men had died in less than an hour that day so long ago. Here in the field where they'd been cut down, unexpected sorrow washed over me, and tears pricked behind my eyes.

"After their victory, the government determined to destroy the Highland way of life." The guide's voice sounded thick with emotion as though she might cry, too, even though she must give the same speech several times a day. "They sent their armies across Scotland punishing anyone suspected of sympathizing with the uprising. The clan system was dismantled, their lands and weapons seized, and kilts and tartans were banned."

A mournful hush fell over the group. Eventually, we split up and walked through the battlefield at our own pace, my party lost among other tourists. I stared at a clan marker and feigned reverent contemplation when really, I was just willing myself not to break down into a puddle of tears.

I had no ties to Scotland that I knew of, no long-lost family members who'd been killed here, but standing in the middle of Culloden, the sad history reached through the mists of hundreds of years to take hold. I didn't know the right or wrong of it, but the thought of so many lives lost so brutally weighed on me.

Duncan came up beside me to read the marker name but stopped when I didn't move along to the next.

"Do you have family with this clan name?" he asked.

I'd been pretending to contemplate the marker for so long, it would have made sense if I had. I shook my head, brushing ridiculous tears from my cheeks.

He examined me and moved a step closer. "Are you all right?"

Ugh, that gentleness in his voice. Did I look so torn up as that?

"I'm just—" I gestured at the battlefield surrounding us, ending with the marker. *Donald.* "It's a terrible story."

"It was terrible. The battle, and how the people and their way of life suffered under forced acclimation. It's a dark time in our history."

I tried to laugh at my weepiness, but it came out a strangled sob. "I don't know why it's affecting me like this. I guess Scotland's getting to me."

He watched me with a tenderness that made my embarrassment evaporate. Wasn't that why he had come here? To commune with history? He briefly placed a hand on my arm, offering comfort.

"Does your name have a clan marker?" I asked.

"It does." He gestured forward, inviting me to find it with him.

We strolled through the grass, pausing to study each marker in turn. The worst of my crying jag passed, and I could read the names without tears clouding my vision. I barely sniffled any more at all.

Duncan gave me a sidelong glance. "This is really unfair of you, you know."

"What is?"

"A pretty American woman who comes to Culloden to cry over our dead? It's hard to resist."

That compliment swelled inside me, squeezing out the sorrow that had gripped my heart and replacing it with the warmth of being praised by this handsome Scot. He might have taken his words back if he'd guessed how quickly my mourning had turned into exultation.

"Ah, here we are." He stopped in front of a marker. "Clan Stewart."

He touched his fingertips to his forehead and gestured toward the marker, a little salute to the long-gone men who'd died here. The rough-hewn stone was like the others we'd passed, largely unremarkable except for where we were.

"It's unreal to have such a tie to history."

He exhaled a soft laugh, shifting close enough his shoulder brushed mine. "I feel I must tell you, I can't guarantee direct lineage. We claim this branch of the Stewarts, but I haven't looked into it to verify."

"I won't dig into it, then. Still, I wouldn't even know where to start looking to find any part of the Clarke family tree. My dad always jokes that we're American mutts—a little bit of everything. I think we're on the Irish side of the Clarkes, but we don't really have a connection to it. Nothing like our name carved in stone on a battlefield, or a tartan just for us."

"On behalf of Clan Stewart, I invite you to wear our tartan whenever you want."

My ribcage fizzed with the warmth of that sweet offer. If he was trying to charm me, it was working.

"I didn't know the English banned kilts and tartans." The plaid prints were such a well-known symbol of the country, the fact that they'd been forbidden for any amount of time seemed unbelievable.

"Makes me wish I'd worn one today, to be honest."

"Do you wear one?" My question probably came out a little too eager.

"I've been known to on occasion."

*Hello, Highlander.* I looked away before he could figure out just how vividly I was imagining the scene. I didn't have to work hard to conjure up a picture of him in a kilt showing off his toned calves. Throw a sword into the mix, and I just might swoon.

We wandered back to the information center, pausing to acknowledge clan markers along the way. Bea and Rupert examined a sign by the entrance but strode over to meet us.

"It's quite a sight, isn't it?" Bea sounded more gossipy than reverential. "You're not the only one with tragic history, Molly."

I had to guess she meant the American Civil War instead of my personal life, but the comment came across so vague, I had no way of knowing. My broken relationships had little in common with a field of dead, but maybe Bea saw things differently.

"Of course," she went on, "all of this could have been avoided had they just accepted King George's rule."

My eyes drifted to Duncan's. "And what do the volunteers here think of your theory?" I asked.

She gestured as though brushing the volunteers' opinions away. "They have a more nationalistic view of it."

"They would," Duncan said dryly.

Lewis rounded everyone up, guiding us toward the parking

lot. We would have just enough time to return to the lodge for lunch before setting out again for Loch Ness.

Before climbing on board the bus, Duncan turned to me and spoke low. "The banning of the tartans was unforgivable, but for this monstrosity, I'd be willing to make an exception."

"I don't know, it's growing on me." I patted the tartan-bedecked bus's frame. "Good old Tarty."

He barked a laugh. "Old Tarty? I'm not sure you've thought that through."

"The Kiltmobile?"

He frowned. "Ye Olde Eyesore is more like it."

"Pride of Scotland?"

"Get on the coach."

# twelve

. . .

HOPEFULLY, an afternoon on a lake populated by imaginary monsters would be less depressing than the battlefield had been. Loch Ness's claim to fame, apart from the legendary creature that supposedly lived in its depths, was falling just short of being either the longest or the deepest lake in Scotland. It did, however, claim the title of largest lake by volume, which even the most interested of tourists will tell you means nothing.

On shore, Arnav led the way to the docks where the rental canoes waited. He would paddle on the lake with us while Lewis drove to the retrieval site a few miles away to wait.

The day had no cloud cover for a change, and I'd opted to wear capri pants and a light T-shirt, despite Lewis's steady stream of reminders to dress in layers. Anecdotes about Scotland's unpredictable weather had been a frequent topic of dinner conversation, with everyone seeming to have been suddenly caught in one freak storm or another. I toted along my fleece jacket but counted on staying warm enough from paddling the canoe while wearing a bulky flotation device.

At the docks, Arnav pointed up the lakeshore to Urquhart castle, just visible against the blue sky. At full zoom, my camera couldn't capture more than a hint of the structure in shadows.

Even though I had wanted to steer clear of the old woman tour, I wished for just a minute we had time to visit the castle.

Well, that and everything else we'd missed so far. Seeing all the sights in Scotland would take a lifetime.

Our canoe instructor Lily gave us a two-minute rundown on the basics of canoeing. Take smooth, even strokes, don't stand in the boat, don't lean overboard—not much to tell. I'd canoed quite often on Puget Sound, and although I didn't consider myself an expert, I planned to show far better skill here than I had during the archery lesson.

Not that I hadn't appreciated Duncan's detailed coaching. Maybe I could finagle my way into one-on-one rowing lessons.

Lily looked us over as though trying to guess how much we could bench in her quest to make sure each boat had one strong rower. I wouldn't have minded being paired up with Duncan, but she stuck him with Bea. Arnav went with Harlow, and Spencer with Rupert, leaving me with Carlos.

Carlos and I sized each other up. I might have had a decade on him, but I wasn't so sure I had anything over him when it came to muscles.

Lily helped us buckle into life jackets before loading us into the boats, strong arm in the rear. I sat hard on the front bench while Carlos chuckled behind me. So I wasn't the strong arm—he didn't need to gloat.

We paddled onto the lake, and with a few parting words of encouragement from Lily, we set off. Arnav and Harlow took the lead, skimming along not far from the shoreline.

Experiencing such a quintessential Scottish activity as rowing a canoe on Loch Ness felt a little surreal. A few boats drifted on the green water, leaving hardly any wake. The sun warmed my skin, and I congratulated myself for stowing the fleece on such a perfect day.

"They say it's most often seen in this area, as it's the deepest point." Rupert's voice held a layer of awe to it. "Sometimes they get just a peek at the tail, but the lucky ones get a glimpse of her head."

"Who is 'they?'" Spencer asked.

"They, *they*, the Nessie experts. There are two exhibits in town. Bea and I visited both of them three years ago on holiday."

"Rupert considers himself quite the authority on all things Nessie." Although voices carried in the stillness, Bea shouted like she was in the bottom of a well.

"I thought someone confessed on their deathbed to faking the photos," I said. That scandal and a grainy black and white photo were the sum total of my knowledge of the Loch Ness monster. Sitting in the little canoe, the idea of mysterious creatures swimming in the depths made my stomach creep. A lot could hide in eight hundred feet of water.

"Those photos weren't the whole of it." Under his sunhat, Rupert looked smug, as though he possessed secret knowledge. "Nessie sightings took place long before cameras were invented."

Duncan turned slightly to catch my eye. "How would you have survived such times, Molly?"

"I feel faint just thinking about it." See also: the way he said my name.

His answering wink made my stomach dip.

My canoe suddenly tilted hard to the left. I shrieked and crouched low, my mind filled with giant sea creatures ready to overturn my boat. When nothing more happened, I stared over my shoulder at Carlos.

"I thought I saw Nessie." He spoiled his sham innocence with self-satisfied laughter.

"Let's be safe, everybody." Arnav sounded like a little brother trying to get family events in hand, shouting against aunts and uncles who were determined to ignore him.

Everything I might say to Carlos involved curse words, so I kept my mouth shut. He grinned away, but his dimples couldn't win him any favors here.

"It's all in good fun," he said, uninjured by the daggers I stared into him.

Facing forward, I got back into the groove of paddling. Gliding behind Duncan's boat, I watched his shoulder muscles move beneath his shirt, his deltoids flexing with every smooth, powerful stroke. The other muscles in his back and arms must have had names, too, but I was too transfixed to remember specifics.

I'd never been particularly drawn to muscular, direct men before. My type tended more toward slender desk jockeys, or *massive geeks*, as Jill described them. Tech guys who talked code and had inside information on Apple's latest rollout and took an age just to ask me to get coffee. Men who led with their brains. Predictable men. Safe men.

In a lineup of my exes, Duncan would have stood out on all counts.

But oh, it couldn't hurt to look.

In front of him, Bea shifted from side to side, lightly dipping her oar into the water but adding little forward momentum to the effort. She was in high spirits on the lake, chattering away about the Loch Ness cruises she and Rupert had taken, which had provided excellent views of Urquhart castle and zero Nessie sightings, to Rupert's utter dismay.

"We met a couple on their honeymoon, do you remember, Rupert?" Bea paused for his requisite, "Quite right, quite right," before continuing. "Honeymooning on Loch Ness, can you imagine? It's not what I would have chosen, I can tell you. We spent our honeymoon in the Lake District. It's where all the poets used to go, you know."

I really didn't need to think about Bea and Rupert on their honeymoon right now.

"Is this a Scottish tradition, Duncan?" she asked. "You wouldn't choose Loch Ness, would you?"

"Choose Loch Ness for what?"

"For your honeymoon."

He made a sound that might have been a snort. "No."

"Lifelong bachelor?" she asked over her shoulder.

"Divorced."

This silenced Bea, who seemed to fault him for the confession she had forced. The lake stayed quiet for a while except for the slap of the oars cutting into the water.

I wasn't surprised to hear Duncan was divorced—given his admitted lack of anyone waiting for him at home, there weren't many options. Single. Divorced. Liar. Widowed was an option, too, but I'd run into more liars than widowers.

Canoeing would have been a lot more enjoyable if my hands hadn't been so scraped up after my fall on Ben Macdui. I'd replaced the bandages this morning, and although it hadn't hurt then, it sure did now. Gripping the oars sent sparks of fire through the torn flesh on my palms, the dull ache creeping deeper into my hands. Maybe I should take a page out of Bea's book and just phone in the paddling.

The winds over the lake picked up, bringing a gentle tail-wind to aid our progress. Now and then, I paused my paddling to slip my camera from the small dry bag I'd tucked into my fleece so I could take a few photos of the lake, the surrounding hills that loped down to the water's edge, and our little group of canoes.

Finally, we came in sight of another set of docks where Lewis waited for us. Rowing closer to the end of the trip, Rupert lamented we hadn't spotted a single sea monster.

"If there were dangerous creatures down there, you'd think boats would be their first targets." Spencer seemed to have nothing but cheerful commentary at the ready.

"You never know," Rupert said, ignoring Spencer's doubts. "There are many more mysterious things in this world than we could ever guess."

Actually—I couldn't fault that logic. Maybe something did lurk in the deep. And I couldn't deny it added an air of mystery to the loch. How many tourism dollars had been added to the area over the last several decades by people hoping to find the definitive answer to the question of Nessie?

Really, it was great PR.

Two cormorants flew low over the lake as though in slow motion. In an instant, I had my camera out of the dry bag, ready to take a few parting photos of wildlife. Rupert and Spencer's canoe blocked my view, so I crouched low to give myself just enough height to capture the shot.

Carlos shouted, "What was that?"

I turned to look, and before I knew what was happening, the canoe pitched and I fell into the lake.

# thirteen

· · ·

MY LUNGS instantly froze as tiny needles pricked all over my skin. My life jacket bobbed me to the surface, and I gasped for air.

Everyone shouted at once, but I couldn't understand them over the deafening sound of my own wheezing. I kept gulping in air, but my lungs couldn't seem to exhale in release. I was dimly aware I should swim or tread water or move my body in some way, but my whole focus had stuck on trying to breathe.

The moment of panic might have only lasted a few seconds before my lungs remembered how to function. Warm breaths seared through my chest, shuddering in and out. My body ached in the frigid water, my limbs flailing uselessly.

Carlos paddled so close I had to kick out of the way so he wouldn't crash into my head. I didn't need a concussion on top of everything else.

"Molly, are you okay?" He looked appropriately worried, at least.

"I'm freezing, Carlos!" I sounded like my throat had been scraped raw.

"I'm sorry, I'm an idiot! I'm sorry!" Repeating the hasty apology, he reached down to take my hand. He caught hold of me, but tipped the canoe and nearly dumped himself into the lake, too. I

"

slipped back into the water, my worries shifting from my quickly numbing body to how, exactly, I would remedy this situation.

Arnav shouted instructions on how to pull me back into the canoe without capsizing. My breath hitched in my lungs as I boosted myself up while Carlos tried to pull me in. Instead of bringing me into the boat, he only managed to cop a major feel.

"That's my butt!" I sputtered, scrabbling on the side of the boat.

He let go, and I dropped back into the water. Arnav paddled closer and offered to help me into his canoe, but I couldn't bear the spectacle of this rescue attempt any longer. Lewis waited on the dock forty feet away—I would swim it.

My life preserver had lived up to its name, but it sucked when it came time to swim. I could barely move my arms, and the vest rose up so high it almost blocked my face. I kicked up a storm, though, and my improvised crawl stroke got me to the dock, where Lewis pulled me out of the water *without* touching my butt.

"Are you all right?" Worry sat in the creases around his eyes and in the deep furrow on his forehead. Poor Lewis—another potential for injury and litigation on this trip.

"I'm fine." I tugged off the life jacket and let it drop onto the dock. My wet clothes clung to my arms and legs, making me as cold out of the water as I'd been in it. Every breeze that played over the lake was like ice skidding over my skin.

A man I assumed worked for the canoe rental place frowned at me as if I might keel over dead. "I don't have any emergency supplies here."

Lewis flashed another look of apology. "I've got some towels in the coach."

He dashed up the dock, leaving me a shivering mess. I hugged my arms around my chest. Glancing down, I realized that the shirt I'd chosen for the day had been an excellent choice for breathability but no better than tissue paper when wet. It would have earned high marks for an impromptu Loch Ness wet T-shirt contest, but right now, it just added to the indignity.

I couldn't catch a win in this country.

The others docked their canoes and climbed out to fuss over me. Duncan hovered close, wearing a grim expression, but he couldn't do much unless he wanted to trade clothes with me. Harlow complimented my strong swimming, which was gratifying after the struggle it'd taken to get back to the dock. Bea shot a disappointed glare at the clear outline of my bra through my shirt, as though this ensemble had been an intentional fashion statement.

Carlos came up to me with huge, sad eyes, like a puppy who expected to get kicked. "Molly, I am so sorry. I really am. What can I say? I'm an idiot. I only mean to give you a scare. I never thought you'd actually fall in."

"If I weren't frozen stiff, I'd deck you right now." I might have sounded more threatening if I hadn't wheezed after every other word.

"I'll do it."

Duncan's threat carried much more weight. Putting his Murder Face to good use, he looked every bit ready to slug Carlos. Even if I didn't actually want him to, his offer warmed me.

Figuratively.

Carlos took Duncan at his word, and moved closer to me like I could protect him. "I'm sorry, I can't say it enough."

I could do without standing on the dock freezing cold, but I was fine. It hadn't been a near-death experience; I wasn't going into the light. I still kind of wanted to punch him in his stupid, careless face for his prank, but I was fine.

Lewis returned with a single towel and a foil emergency blanket he'd probably pulled from a first aid kit. "This is all I've got. You need to get out of your wet clothes. The lake is only about fifteen degrees Celsius. We need to warm you up as quick as possible."

I looked around, but the dock didn't even boast a port-a-potty, much less a restroom. Oh, this would be fun.

Harlow helped me drape the emergency blanket around my

shoulders so I could strip out of my shirt and bra, while the others tried to look busy. Arnav brought my fleece jacket from the bottom of my canoe, and I zipped into it. I moved my makeshift privacy screen down and shimmied out of my soaked pants, wrapping both the towel and emergency blanket around my lower half.

At least I'd worn my sneakers on the boat instead of my hiking boots—those would have taken an age to dry out. The sneakers had turned into blocks of ice on my feet, but they would be fine to wear again in a day or two.

I collected my wet clothes into a messy bundle, keeping my bra and panties at the center of the ball of shame. I patted my phone, still in the dry bag in my fleece's pocket, and finally remembered what I'd been doing when I fell into the lake.

I sucked in a breath as nausea unfurled in my stomach. Lost. I'd lost it, all for the sake of a few pictures of birds and a stupid joke.

"Idiot," I seethed. I wasn't sure if I was angrier with Carlos or myself.

"What is it?" Duncan asked. He hadn't left my side since he'd climbed up on the dock.

I didn't have the heart to say the words. I just looked at him and focused on not crumbling. My lower lip wobbled, but I held it together.

Understanding my unspoken thoughts, his expression softened. "Your camera."

My sigh hit just this side of a sob. It'd been the day for crying, apparently. I stomped up the dock, tossed my wet things in the back of the mini-bus, and climbed on board. Bundled in my jacket and the emergency blanket, I stared out the window, feeling every bit as miserable as my faint reflection looked.

Outside, Lewis lectured Carlos while Duncan silently glowered like a bouncer ready to throw out the riff-raff. I wished they would just let it go. Carlos was a charming, self-centered idiot, but the whole disaster had been an accident. He hadn't meant to dump me into the lake, or for me to lose my camera.

Oh, but my camera. Four days of chronicling my visit to Scotland, lost at the bottom of Loch Ness. Loch an Eilein, Meall a' Bhuachaille, Ben Macdui—the baby highland cows. All those captured memories, gone.

The chill in my skin sank right into my heart, but I absolutely would not cry. First, tears would probably freeze on my face if I did. And second, they were just photos. I had a few pictures on my phone. I'd still done those amazing things, even if I didn't have all the pictures to prove it.

Still. I really wanted those pictures.

Eventually, Duncan sat down beside me as we prepared to leave the lake. He watched me in silence, his quiet scrutiny worse than fawning pity would have been. Measured breathing and pretended stoicism kept my tears at bay, but I couldn't do anything about the shivering or my clacking teeth.

"Here." He pulled his jacket out of his backpack and offered it to me.

I slipped it on over my own without a second thought. Zipped up all the way, I nuzzled my chin down into the soft fleece. "Thanks."

I soaked up that delicious smell—SilverFoxalicious. Like wood with a tinge of something brighter. Whatever it was, I wanted to swim in the scent.

*Must not make it obvious I'm smelling his coat.*

I rubbed my face against the fleece, trying to bring some feeling back into my icy cheeks, and only ducked my nose into the collar every other minute.

He wrapped an arm around my shoulders and ran his hands over my arms, probably trying to draw a little warmth into them. Keeping me alive with his body heat, and all that.

*Must not make it obvious I'm thinking about his body heat.*

"Okay?"

I nodded, my answer the same whether he were asking about

my spirits or his touch. I leaned against him, telling myself it was all in the name of first aid. Not cuddling the sweetheart silver fox.

But the cuddling was pretty dang good.

Carlos sat as far away from me as he could—either out of guilt for his stupidity or fear of my threatening bodyguard. Whichever it was, I didn't really care.

My teeth chattered the whole way back to the lodge, broken up occasionally by whole-body shudders. I just wanted to sleep and leave all this behind, but as soon as I closed my eyes and let my head drop against Duncan's shoulder, Lewis called back to say I shouldn't rest until after I warmed up.

Wasn't that what they always said about hypothermia? People went to sleep and never woke up again. I couldn't possibly have hypothermia. I'd just taken a bad chill. Nice of Lewis, though, to want to stop me from drifting into death by catnap.

Rude, too, to take away my excuse for even more Duncan-snuggling.

As soon as we got back to the lodge, I ran myself a hot bath. Lewis told me to use lukewarm water so I wouldn't shock my system, but I ignored that—I cranked the water up as hot as I could tolerate. It hurt a little getting in and my skin turned bright red, but it did the trick.

I scrunched down in the tub to defrost, contemplating how else I could mortify myself on this trip. Seemed like I was running out of options, but we had plenty of days left for me to find new and unusual forms of embarrassment.

Weirdly though, I didn't regret the trip, despite all my stumbles. I held close every memory, and I couldn't wait to make the next one. Even if it meant falling into a dozen more lakes, I wouldn't turn back now.

Once I was reasonably thawed, I returned to my room. My phone sat in the clear dry bag on my bed—that bag was supposed to have been a genius move for canoeing. If only I'd actually left my camera in it.

I stared at the phone, a little coil of dread slithering in my stomach. Was it ESP, or an old habit I'd long grown used to?

Sure enough, I pulled it out and thumbed it awake to find an email from Lincoln.

He'd sent a flurry of questions about a site's revamp. I didn't even read through them before I turned it back off and tossed it on the bed. So far, I'd spent every night in Scotland sifting through website skeletons, answering his questions, and managing the design team from afar. I could handle this later. Right now, I needed to eat.

I pulled on a long-sleeve shirt, my fleece jacket, and flannel pajama pants, and went down to dinner. More informal than I'd normally choose for a communal dinner with strangers, but hey, I'd swum in Loch Ness. I was all about informal now.

Dinner had nearly wrapped up by the time I joined the others, and I noticed Carlos wasn't with them. Could he have felt so guilty that he wouldn't even come to dinner? He didn't seem like the type to let guilt eat at him for long.

I hooked Duncan's jacket on the back of his chair. "Thank you."

"Better?" He looked up at me as though examining his patient for any lasting injury. His attention warmed me up almost as well as the hot bath.

"Better," I confirmed.

Lewis had less subtlety, and questioned me the whole time I ate, tallying my responses against a checklist to see how near death I was. He seemed satisfied with the results, but tossed worried looks my way the rest of the evening.

After I ate a greedy dinner, Jack and Kenneth made me comfortable by the fire in the sitting room with a thick blanket thrown over my lap, fussing over me in showy displays of concern.

"We sometimes get the odd loch swimmer, but none have ever taken a dip by accident," Jack said.

"Can I bring you anything else?" Kenneth's look of apprehension matched Lewis's, as though I might die of hypothermia in his armchair.

"I could use a drink."

"Now that, we can do. What'll it be?"

Wasn't brandy the traditional remedy for cold? I couldn't remember ever trying it, but it didn't sound nearly as good as what I wanted. "Can you do a hot chocolate?"

"I'll be right back."

Duncan and Harlow joined me in the sitting room, flanking where I sat in my cozy armchair.

"How are you feeling?" Duncan asked.

"I'm feeling less like a popsicle now."

His eyes narrowed, and I suspected he wasn't just asking about my chill in the lake. Was I really so attached to my camera as all that?

Yes, and he knew it. I wanted those pictures, and the undeniable proof I'd really come all the way out here. I'd planned all sorts of ways I could turn those photos into mementos, tangible reminders of my journey to last long after the trip ended. I needed *something* to carry this with me long after I'd gone home.

Snuggled up under layers of quilt next to a roaring fire in the Highlands, it hit me—the Scottish Zen Master was right. Chronicling the trip wasn't the same as experiencing it. Did I need a photograph of every minute to know I wouldn't forget it? Planning all the ways to memorialize the trip, I lived it in the past tense. Mentally, I was already home, putting pictures on my wall.

I needed to *relish* this trip.

"Someone once said something about the importance of remembering one's experiences rather than simply one's photos," I said.

"Sounds like a wise man. Although not a terribly articulate one."

Behind my hand, I whispered, "Scottish."

His answering grin had my chest fluttering wildly.

Kenneth returned with a big mug of hot chocolate, and I

burrowed deeper into my covers, savoring the heat from the mug in my hands.

Duncan nodded at my drink. "Keeping with the theme, are you?"

I hugged it closer to me. "It's helping me warm up."

He twisted his mouth. "That's one way to do it."

Now *that* curled warmth through me better than the bath or the chocolate. Yeah…I could think of other ways to warm up, too.

"I'm curious," Harlow said. "Did you have to pay extra for the Nessie encounter?"

"For all we know, my camera is taking pictures of Nessie right now."

"You should have seen the look on Arnav's face," she said with a laugh. "He was so freaked out."

"*He* was freaked out? I couldn't get my lungs to work." I didn't like to think just how bad I'd looked in the water, my ponytail plastered to my head while I flailed around gasping like a fish.

"Arnav and Lewis were really worried about you."

"They might have to rethink the canoeing portion of this trip." They could carry a few more emergency supplies for surprise dunks in a lake, at least.

"They might have to reiterate the lesson on not being a total arse on the canoeing portion of the trip." Duncan didn't sound ready to let go of his blame for Carlos, but I waved him off.

"He was a total ass, but it was an accident. I'm over it." He raised one eyebrow at my easy dismissal. "He didn't really mean for me to fall in. And it wasn't completely his fault."

Now he gave me a curious look. Suddenly, I wasn't all that eager to admit my part in the day's unexpected adventure. How many different ways could I prove myself inept on one vacation? "I was kind of standing when it happened."

"You were standing," Duncan repeated, his voice flat. "In a canoe."

"Don't you start." I shook a finger at him. "Go back to feeling sorry for me."

"I need more information."

"There were cormorants. I needed a better angle for a picture." I swallowed the rest of my story. In all the rules of canoeing, there was only one truly stupid thing you could do, and I had done it.

Because I'd needed pictures.

Duncan tried to look disappointed, but laughter broke through his frown. "I guess it's for the best I didn't brawl with Carlos."

"He did try to rescue Molly," Harlow pointed out.

"Sure, by grabbing my butt," I said.

"A national hero." Duncan's eyes stayed stuck on me in the soft lighting.

Speak of the devil—Carlos walked into the sitting room. He looked as sheepish as when I'd first crawled out of the lake, but he had a little more pep in his step this evening. More telling, he had his hands behind his back, concealing something.

"I've come bearing a peace offering." He stepped closer to present a plastic shop bag. "I really am sorry about today, Molly."

My suspicions growing, I took the bag. I peeked inside to find a brand-new camera staring up at me. "You didn't have to do this."

"I'm pretty sure I did."

I looked it over and did a double take. "This is nicer than mine."

I'd splurged on that camera years ago. This had to have set him back quite a bit.

He shrugged. "I wasn't sure what you had."

"Thank you."

He smiled, and I had the feeling he expected me to leap up and throw my arms around him in gratitude. When I didn't, he sat down next to Harlow.

"Standing in a canoe," Duncan said so low that only I could hear him. I smiled a little at his look of consternation. "I'm going to have to keep my eyes on you."

I liked that plan.

# fourteen

. . .

BACK IN MY ROOM, I phoned Jill before I went to bed. I'd promised phone calls when anything exciting happened, and falling into Loch Ness qualified, even if it wasn't the kind of excitement she'd hoped for.

"It was a disaster." I described my tumble into the lake, complete with the ill-fated rescue attempt. "I made a fool of myself and lost hundreds of pictures."

"That's kind of a lot of pictures, isn't it?"

"Not the point."

"I know it sucks, but look on the bright side. Now you have a hilarious story to tell whenever there's a lull in conversation at parties."

I groaned. "I don't know if I'd call it hilarious."

"Try it at a party sometime and see."

I had to laugh at myself. Jill's brand of pep talk was just what I'd needed. I'd only lost pictures, and I was still here, ready to make new memories. "What's new with little Olivia?"

"Still acing tummy time. Sometimes Shatner comes up to sniff her like he hasn't figured out what she is yet."

"He thinks she's a puppy who hasn't figured out how to dog." I couldn't resist gentle pokes at the Mama Bear.

"Hmm." Jill didn't sound as amused by the comparison. "He isn't sure what to do with himself at night. He wants to sleep with me, but he wants more room than Ed gives him. He'll get up and down six times a night. He's as bad as Olivia."

"So you're saying taking care of my dog is exactly like caring for an infant. Good to know."

"It's really not. Even if he does have the same number of special creams as my baby."

"I bet hers smell better, though."

"Enough about us," Jill said, switching into gossip mode. "I want to hear more about your trip. What else have you seen? Have you tried haggis yet? I need to know about the sexy Scot already."

I gave her the Cliffs Notes version of my first few days in Scotland, ending with Carlos presenting me with the replacement camera for his part in my dip in the lake. I still wasn't sure if our mistakes didn't even out, but I'd accepted the camera anyway.

"Now," she coaxed. "Tell me about Duncan MacBeard."

I looked around the bedroom as though I might find him crouched in the corner just waiting for me to start talking about him. Harlow was downstairs with Carlos, so whatever I had to say to Jill was safe. Or as safe as anything I told Jill ever could be.

"He's funny and sexy and I think I could listen to him talk for about ninety days straight, but…" I dropped my voice even lower, as if Duncan could hear me down the hall. "He's not really my type."

"I like him already."

"Seriously? What's that supposed to mean?"

"How do I put this?" She paused while Shatner barked at some mystery sound in the background. "Your type sucks."

My mouth dropped open. "Hey!"

"In the nicest, blandest, most boring way possible. Nice, nice guys." She faked a yawn.

I wanted to argue, but her assessment wasn't that far off from my mental boyfriend lineup earlier in the day. Duncan wasn't like any man I'd ever dated. So far, that hadn't stopped me from thinking about him an alarming amount of the time.

"Duncan's nice." Weakest defense of a man ever.

"Sure, but you could think of other words to describe him, right?"

"So many." I sighed a little, descriptions parading through my head. *Thoughtful. Funny. Pulling me in like a charismatic magnet.*

"See? I've been saying you need to find someone less cerebral. Get yourself a man of action."

My stomach dipped over that phrase. Duncan fit it to a tee. "But it's ridiculous to think of him like this at all. He lives on the other side of the world."

"You're together now. Enjoy that."

"But nothing real can happen." Despite whatever Bea thought of my poor relationship history, I still wanted something lasting— a life-changing, world-rocking love. That didn't really seem like the kind of thing we could have over a vacation and let go when we went home again.

"Seriously, Molly, live a little. You're on your first real vacation in forever, you're with a man you clearly like. Just enjoy yourself. I want you to be happy."

"I am happy."

"I mean man happy. Anyway, you know what they say about older men—snow on the roof, fire in the pants."

I laughed over her awful idiom. "I'm not even sure he's that much older."

"So get it, girl."

Duncan didn't strike me as a man I'd easily forget. Then again, if things went wrong, I'd never have to worry about running into him again. Win-win?

"I'll think about it."

She made a sound of disgust. "I know you, Molly. 'I'll think about it' means 'I'm going to drag my feet until it's too late to do anything about it.'"

I frowned over that, but Olivia's crying and Shatner's barking brought an end to the conversation before I could come up with a believable defense. Jill made me promise to let her know if anything fiery progressed.

"Send a text, at least. S.O.S.—Snogged our Scotsman."

Thinking about that S.O.S. made it hard for me to drift off to sleep.

By morning, I'd fully recovered from my unexpected dip in Loch Ness. I had never been in much danger of dying from hypothermia, but I'd warmed away the last of the chills and slept off the worst of my regrets over my camera.

Now, we'd packed our bags and were headed north to the Black Isle. Duncan and I had become seat-mates, an arrangement that grew on me with each passing mile. He spent most of the drive reading while I stared out the window watching scenery go by, fogging the glass with my breath.

I side-eyed him, Jill's call sign on my mind. I didn't do short-term relationships or vacation flings. I wanted the Real Deal. I just hadn't found it yet. Hidden way down in my heart, I longed for a soul-deep connection, that spark that let you know *This is It*, but it had been so long since I'd felt anything resembling a spark.

Until now.

———

Despite Dingwall's small size, the lodge we stayed in was the largest we'd visited so far, and in sight of the Cromarty Firth where we would go sea kayaking later in the day. We didn't see any other guests when we checked in, leaving us tucked away in our own little world.

Unfortunately, Lincoln kept intruding on that little world. He'd sent an email asking for front-end mock-ups for a newer site. I'd started notes before I left, but now he needed visuals for the design team's meeting so they could get a feel for my vision and start the storyboards.

Wait—I read through his email again, sure I'd read it wrong.

He wanted the mock-ups for *today's* meeting? With the time difference, I had at least two hours of work to do, a narrow window to do it in, and no chance to tell Lincoln *no* before the deadline to get the work to the design team hit. I could only get the mock-ups done in time if I opted out of the kayak trip.

An afternoon of sea kayaking on the Moray Firth, surrounded by gorgeous glen scenery—how could I even consider missing it? The firth shone in the distance, a stripe of blue I was meant to be out on in less than an hour. I didn't want to back out of any part of this trip, but three little words pushed me to my decision: *Head of Design*. Providing vision layouts for the team would be my new normal when I got home. I just wasn't usually distracted by hikes and views and sizzling men back home.

Flexing my bandaged palms, I resigned myself to it. I would have another opportunity to kayak once we got to the Isle of Skye, so missing out in Dingwall wouldn't be the end of the world. A poor justification, but it was all I had.

I wandered through the lodge and found Arnav and Rupert in the dining room looking over a tray of cookies, pastries, and assorted sweets. Rupert defied Bea's "no fat" edict, nibbling on a small pastry.

"Those look amazing." I drooled over the buttery shortbreads, golden-brown hand pies, fat cookies, and jam-dotted tarts that filled the trays.

"House-made." Arnav raised a doughy cookie in toast.

I chose a caramel covered shortbread square that melted in my mouth, the perfect balance of sweet and salty. "Incredible."

Rupert wiped his fingers at the jam that had oozed onto his lips. "Be a dear and don't tell Bea about this, would you? She's worried about my fat intake, you see."

I shared a conspiratorial smile. My tumble in Loch Ness must have softened his chilly attitude. He'd been much more sympathetic since I'd climbed out of the lake. "My lips are sealed."

Arnav started to leave, but I remembered why I'd wandered into the dining room in the first place. "Oh, Arnav—" I swallowed down the shortbread bite. "I wanted to talk to you about the itinerary."

"Let me guess—you want to go back to Loch Ness?"

"Ha. Funny." Maybe Jill had been right about telling the story at parties. "No. I don't think my hands have quite healed enough for more paddling."

True enough, but nobody needed to know I would be firing up my laptop as soon as they left.

"Lewis is taking Bea and Rupert on a hill walk straight from the lodge in a couple of hours. You're welcome to join them. It's a good little town if you want to just walk around. There are some nice shops and a good pub."

I thanked him and headed back to my room. Wandering the village didn't sound like a bad idea, and the hill walk timing was perfect, even if that would involve spending part of the day in close proximity to Bea's helpful criticism.

I ran into Duncan and Lewis as they came downstairs. I couldn't help but notice Duncan had on another tight shirt. Maybe all shirts were tight when you were built like that. His defined muscles could only be the result of hours in the gym every week. I got tired just looking at him.

Not that I stopped right away.

Reminding myself not to ogle, I told Lewis I planned to join his party on the hill walk later in the afternoon.

"Understandable. We'll see you this evening."

He nodded and headed down, probably to find Arnav.

"No kayaking for you today?" Duncan said.

I held up my palms to display the fresh bandages. "Probably not a good idea."

"We'll miss you out there."

I forced a smile, silently shushing my unwarranted disappointment. I'd wanted and maybe even expected him to choose the hill walk, too. *Note to self: Duncan's vacation is not about you.*

He leaned closer, and I caught that heady, warm scent that

made my stomach do flips. Also: when had eye crinkles become so attractive?

"What do you think the odds are that Carlos rolls his kayak?"

"Don't," I said, even as I mirrored his smile at the idea.

He placed one hand over his heart as though vowing innocence. That man was a lot of things, but innocent wasn't one of them.

Upstairs, I flopped onto my bed and opened my laptop. The sitting room might have made a better workstation, but with all the picture windows overlooking the firth, I probably wouldn't accomplish much. Gravel crunched as the mini-bus pulled away, and I had to force myself not to run down the lane after it. Had I really given up kayaking for work?

I closed my eyes and took a deep, cleansing breath that would have made my yoga instructor proud. *Head of Design.*

Its power as a motivational mantra had already started to fade.

# fifteen

. . .

I HAD the mock-ups drawn and sent off to the design team in Seattle in time to set off on the walk with Lewis, Bea, and Rupert. I collected my backpack and light rain jacket and zipped the camera Carlos had given me into the jacket pocket.

Downstairs, Lewis, Bea, and Rupert waited in the sitting room.

"There you are." Bea sounded as though I'd held up the King's coronation. "Have a nice nap, did you?"

Her assumption I'd been resting irritated, considering I would have rather been doing literally anything else. "I had to do some work for a client."

"Oh. Well, that's hardly right, is it? You being on vacation and all."

The tightness inside me loosened. Her frank commentary was refreshingly supportive for a change.

Lewis led us to a walking trail that cut through Dingwall and into the countryside. As we left the lodge and approached the village, I wondered how the others were doing out on the water.

Honestly, I was only thinking of one of the others: the man with the tight shirts, sea-blue eyes, and sexy voice.

"I know what you're thinking," Bea said.

My smile froze. Just how obvious had I been these last couple of days?

"You're thinking a day in the hills will be easier than a day out on the firth, and I agree with you."

I breathed out a sigh. Maybe I wasn't mooning over Duncan so obviously that Bea had found me out.

"I don't mind canoeing," she went on. "It's easy enough and only a simpleton could run into trouble—oh, not you, dear."

She patted me on the arm. *No offense, dear, but you're an idiot.*

"But kayaking is tricky business. Rupert and I tried a few years ago, but we had a poor outing."

"I fell out just climbing into mine." Rupert didn't seem distressed by this announcement.

"Have you kayaked before?" Bea asked me.

"I have, but only on a lake. I'm not sure how firths compare."

She leaned toward me, ready to share the inside scoop. "Take the wind on Loch Ness and double it. And today's not the clearest of skies for a trip on the firth."

The morning had been pleasant, but between the winds and the rough skies rolling in, I couldn't predict how the afternoon would play out. It could be sunny and warm, or we could be caught in a downpour. Apparently, unexpected heat waves sometimes rolled in, too, but I wouldn't count on being that lucky.

"They'll do fine," Lewis said. "Arnav knows to bring them in if the waves get to choppy."

"Has he been working for your company very long?" I asked.

"Three years now. We hired him right out of university."

Arnav was only twenty-five? No wonder he had so much youthful enthusiasm—he was still a youth.

"I've been here eight years now, myself. I've led all the tours several times over. I could probably climb Macdui in my sleep." He winced as though he didn't like his words. "Not to boast, of course."

"This can't be your only source of income," Bea said.

Now I winced on his behalf. What would it be like to have

immunity from embarrassment? Was that a package deal that came with being an older woman? Between Bea doling out critical commentary and my mother freely discussing her love life with my father after sixty-five, verbal filters seemed to fade with age. Something to look forward to, I supposed.

"I also teach history part-time," he said.

That explained all of the tragic little side-bar stories he'd told on our hikes.

"I'd like to get a full-time position, but that hasn't panned out yet. Hopefully it will soon, as my wife is expecting and I'd prefer to stay closer to home."

Bea, Rupert, and I offered a chorus of congratulations which he accepted in his modest style.

"It's so nice for women these days that so many husbands want to hang about and help with the children." Bea's disapproving tone somewhat diminished her praise. "Rupert here hardly changed a nappy, did you, dear?"

"Not a one."

I told myself it'd been a different time for them, but it sounded like classic weaponized incompetence to me.

The houses and cottages grew more sparse, and views of the countryside took over, a patchwork of fields and hedgerows spreading out on either side. The country lane was just the sort of path Elizabeth Bennett might have strolled down had she been a Scottish Highland lass instead of an English lady.

Bea walked next to me, pink-cheeked and eyes shining. "It's nice for Lewis, isn't it?" She spoke as though he weren't five feet away and able to hear her every word. "About his wife and child?"

Lewis steadfastly looked straight ahead. He'd obviously had some practice at ignoring clients' conversations.

"It is nice." I knew she would accept nothing else.

"I only wonder that you don't want the same things for yourself. Some women don't, and I can respect that, but you seem like the type who would."

I doubted Bea respected the choice to opt out of marriage and family—not that I had made those choices. I debated digging into her assumptions about me, but I chose the high road.

At least, I didn't start an argument, which was as high of a road as I could manage.

"I do want the same things." I probably sounded a little testy, but she had to know she was prying. "I just haven't found the right man to have those things with."

"Unlucky in love?"

*I'm a single thirty-eight-year-old woman. You do the math.* "A bit."

"The right man will come around. You just need to broaden your horizons. You can't have such high standards that no man can ever attain them, you know."

Ah, yes. The good old *lower your standards* speech.

"I don't think expecting a man to be faithful, to make me feel alive, and to make me laugh is too much to ask." I wasn't sure why I chose to admit that to Bea, of all people. I blamed it on the fresh mountain air—too much oxygen in the brain or something.

She flashed a beady eye. "That's all you want, is it?"

Additions to my description of Mr. Right flashed through my mind. Confidence, a stable career, a life beyond me that still included me, and the ability to kiss me until I forgot my own name were first in line, but I didn't say them out loud. My hesitation gave her all the answer she needed.

"So you're saying beggars can't be choosers."

"I'm saying you should be open to the unexpected. Just look at me." She glanced over her shoulder at her husband. "Rupert and I met in university on a train back from Edinburgh to London. I expected a simple rail trip but wound up with the love of my life. We've been married forty years, and I wouldn't have it any other way."

I wasn't sure how to take Bea's advice. In my world, being open to the unexpected usually meant accepting a guy's all-consuming gaming addiction, not love at first sight. Did that even exist anymore? I wanted to believe in this fairy tale version of love, but my experiences hadn't reflected it. Real love took years to build, if it ever developed at all.

Mostly, for me, it hadn't.

Still, it was a romantic story. If I didn't think too hard about Bea and Rupert being the principal characters.

"And you know dear, you only have so long," she went on. "You're not so young you can expect the men to keep calling forever."

*There* was the critical Bea I'd come to expect.

Lewis led us up a short scramble to a hilltop that provided wide views looking down on Dingwall and the inlet beyond. I scanned the firth, hoping to see an indication of our group of kayakers, but the distance made everything too tiny.

I took a few pictures and then tucked the camera back in my bag and just stood there for a while, enjoying the view.

# sixteen

· · ·

WE RETRACED our steps to Dingwall and the others returned to the lodge, but I wanted to explore the town. I found a nice stretch of road paved in cobblestones, but was disappointed to discover my hiking boots hardly made a sound on them. Few of the village's stores were open so late in the afternoon, but I didn't mind window shopping among the locals.

Nothing much caught my eye until I came to a small café with a sign advertising homemade pastries. Despite the delicious treats waiting back in the lodge, I bought a bag of "biscuits" fresh from the oven, lacy confections with a tangy sort of orange marmalade filling.

I ate three immediately.

I passed a butcher shop, and the sweet treats in my stomach turned sour. A cold case sat in the front window showing off fat little rolls of haggis and long black links of blood pudding and other assorted meats. Just looking at them made my insides churn. Was throwing out the organs really all that wasteful?

"That dip in the loch changed you if you're tempted by this lot."

I turned to find Duncan standing behind me. His cheeks and forehead glowed pink from the sun and the lines at the corners of his eyes stood out as though he'd been squinting all afternoon, but he only looked better for having been out in the elements. Rugged suited him.

"I'm just browsing," I said with a smile. "Although isn't there some sort of law that says all visitors must try haggis while in Scotland?"

"The Haggis Act of 1974, yes."

None of the others from the kayak group were on the street—just Duncan. Had he set out to find me, or had it been chance? Fate. Whatever. "How was the firth?"

"Excellent. It's a good day for it, and the water was as calm as could be expected." He paused as though measuring his words. "I have a feeling you're going to regret not joining us, though."

"Why? Did Carlos actually fall in?"

"Nothing quite so satisfying. A few dolphins swam with our kayaks."

"What?" I took hold of his upper arm to dramatize my shock and his warm bicep was all firm goodness beneath my fingers. *Wow.* "I missed kayaking with dolphins?"

"I'm sorry to say so. How was the hill walk?"

"Hilly." I let go of him and tried not to pout. I was a grown woman after all, but how many opportunities in my life would I have to kayak with dolphins? "The countryside was really beautiful. We could see the local castle at one point, and then we climbed this little hilltop for views of the firth."

I laughed at my description. *Local castle.* I'd already become spoiled from being surrounded by scenic ancient ruins.

I tipped the bag of cookies toward him in silent offering, and he took one. We strolled down the lane and looked in shop windows, our shoulders jostling as though pressed in by the minimal crowds. Every little touch sent fluttering wings sailing around in my chest. An absurd reaction...but I didn't put any distance between us, either.

"Between the crags and the Cairngorms and your swim in Loch Ness, how are you enjoying Scotland?" he asked.

I didn't even pause to consider. "I love it. I don't think I've seen a single thing I wouldn't call beautiful. The people are amazingly kind, and the weather is perfect."

He laughed at my enthusiasm. "I can't fault the beautiful views, but amazingly kind locals and perfect weather aren't two of the more common conclusions about Scotland."

"Everyone we've met has been very kind to us."

He nodded. "As we're paying them to do."

"Still. And I do love the weather. I can't handle too much heat."

"Ah, you're a fair Scottish rose who withers in the sun."

"I thought it was an English rose."

He nudged me with his shoulder. "We have roses, too."

"Then maybe I am. Overcast, drizzly days are perfect for staying in all day, snuggling into a blanket, and reading a good book."

"Mmm. Or staying in bed all day with a good companion."

I couldn't get enough of that mischievous glint in his eyes. Whatever he might have seemed at first glance, Duncan had a playfulness about him that made it all too easy to drop my defenses.

"That, too." I thought about beds, blankets, and companions until the silence between us grew tangible. "Are you enjoying the trip?"

"It's fantastic. I've seen parts of the country I'd never visited before, and you can't beat bagging munros and kayaking the firth." He gave me another arch look. "And then there are the people in our group."

"Oh, yes? What do you think of them?"

His half smile made my stomach flip. "I'm quite taken by them."

I made a little noise as if to say "fascinating." He wasn't so bad, himself.

"So this is helping you get back to your roots?" I asked before my thoughts could stray back to the bed and blankets.

"It is. There's nothing like standing atop Ben Macdui to make one's blood run blue for Scotland. I'd made a list of things I wanted to do before I turn fifty in December, and climbing Macdui was one."

*Forty-nine. Finally.*

"You're doing very well for your advanced age." I flashed him a grin.

He scowled back. "You're this close to being tossed into the firth."

"You have to admit, at first glance you do look a bit older than forty-nine."

He scoffed. "Your flirting is atrocious."

Laughter burst out of me that he'd so directly named my teasing. It was the right word, though.

"I suppose my flirting's not much better," he said. "When I spoke to you in the airport, I saw that coming off much better than it did."

I stared at him. "Wait—that tourist jab was flirting?"

He grimaced. "Hardly counts when you have to be told, does it?"

"This puts things in a new light. I'm not sure you have room to criticize flirting skills."

"Hmm. Perhaps we should work on our skills together."

Damn, this man was good. Okay, the tourist remark not so much, but right now? He had game all over the place. "It's probably a good idea. I'm out of practice."

His eyebrows pulled together. "Why is that?"

"I spend most of my time at work. In-office flirting is heavily discouraged."

"What about off-the-clock vacation flirting?"

I probably glowed so bright they could see me all the way in the States. "Heavily encouraged."

He grinned, and my eyes traced the line of his mouth. What was it about this man that he could so easily tie me up in knots? His mix of confidence and charm proved absolutely intoxicating.

"Then I'll prepare myself to receive your flirting. Preferably without further commentary on my *advanced age*."

I scrambled for an apology, but he laughed it off. "It's the beard. It's grown monstrously gray these last few years. Maybe it's time to shave it again."

He stroked his whiskers as though in deep contemplation. Lucky. I wanted to run my fingers over his whiskers, too.

"Oh, I like the beard. It suits you."

He leaned just a touch closer to me, his eyes practically throwing sparks. "Then I'd best keep it."

I tried to pretend I hadn't lit up with warm fuzzies, but I was pretty sure he wasn't falling for my ruse anymore. Not after all this forward business about flirting. "What else is on your list of things to do before you turn fifty?"

"Let's see…I wanted to run a marathon, which I did this spring. My time was wretched, but I finished, which was all that mattered. I've visited new countries. I'm reading more."

"I noticed that. What are you reading?"

"*Into Thin Air.*"

"People dying on Mount Everest isn't exactly an inspirational vacation read."

"The one before was *Robinson Crusoe*." He pulled an exaggerated face.

"I'm sensing a theme," I said with a laugh. "You're really charging at fifty head-on. Here I am just sort of lazily meandering my way toward forty."

"Meandering is good, too. More time to enjoy the views."

He wasn't giving me a hard time about my picture-taking, but that's where my thoughts went. Capturing moments from a distance. Living life through the lens instead of soaking up every moment.

"I don't know if I've done that, either."

"You know the best time to start, don't you?"

I did. *Now.*

———

Back in my lodge room, I pulled my phone from my bag. Lincoln had sent a quick *Great work, Molly* reply first thing this morning but no further update on the design meeting. I'd have to take that as a sign that everyone was on board with my plans for the site. Any concerns would have been forwarded to me immediately.

Dinner conversation mostly centered around the dolphins the kayak group had encountered on the firth. I tried to suck it up, but I had a hard time squashing my jealousy of people who had seen dolphins in the wild.

"They were so close," Harlow said. "One kept swimming right in front of my kayak. I could have touched it."

"That was a once in a lifetime experience," Carlos said. "I wouldn't trade that for anything."

Bea refused to be outdone. "We had a lovely time on the hillside. The views were not to be missed. I'd imagine dolphins can be seen from shore, but the views can only be seen from above."

"That one experience made the whole trip worth it." Harlow flatly ignored Bea's praise.

"Just that one?" Carlos countered. His slow grin made me think they were talking about something very different from dolphins.

"I find kayaks too unpredictable," Rupert said as he buttered a roll. "I much prefer the hill walk, even if the ladies did bore us with their talk of man troubles, eh Lewis?"

Good Lord, take me now. Lewis looked as alarmed as I felt. He continued chewing rather than answer. Seemed like a wise course of action.

"Man troubles?" Duncan echoed, pinning me to my seat with his eyes.

I wasn't about to get roped into another dinner conversation about my love life. I made a face as though I had no idea what Rupert was talking about.

"I was just suggesting Molly broaden her horizons," Bea said, ever so helpfully.

Duncan raised his water glass to me. "To broadened horizons."

I was pretty sure my cards were already on the table with this man, but I raised my glass and clinked it to his. "To being open to the unexpected."

After dinner, I browsed the bookshelf in the sitting room, pretending I wasn't idling away my time until Duncan came back downstairs. Every good book collection should have a copy of *Pride and Prejudice*, and this one didn't let me down. I took it to one of the cozy couches and settled in. Skimming to where Darcy catches Elizabeth by surprise at his estate, I lost myself in Pemberley.

Bea wandered in and sat down beside me, e-reader in hand. After a while, Duncan joined us, took over one of the armchairs, and opened his book, ready to read about disaster in the mountains. I snuck glances at him, my eyes darting between Darcy and Duncan.

"I've been thinking, Molly." Bea leaned closer as though we were having a private conversation but didn't lower her voice at all. "About you finding a man."

Oh, don't do this now. Or ever. Never would be perfect. "Thank you, but it's fine, really."

She ignored my attempt to shut down the conversation. "Don't underestimate the power of clothing. You're pretty, but your outfits could do with a little touch-up. You want to dress like a lady now and then, show a little leg but not too much."

As though I should hike Ben Macdui in a dress and heels. "Well, Duncan's here, so…"

I'd thought my veiled argument against such helpfulness in present company would speak for itself, but she seemed unwilling to take the hint.

"We can get his opinion." For all her interest in other people's lives, Bea had no skill at all at reading them. "Duncan, wouldn't you agree that men like to see a little leg now and then—but not too much?"

He smiled as though he'd been waiting for someone to ask him such a ridiculous question.

"For the first, I'd say absolutely we like to see a little leg, but I have to disagree with you that there's such a thing as too much."

Bea thinned her mouth into a prim line at his saucy answer. She angled her body toward me to cut Duncan from our conversation.

"Let the man make the first move," she went on, unrelenting in her desire to be my dating coach. "Make polite conversation, show interest, but let him take the initiative. Men like to feel they're in charge."

"Is that true, Duncan?" I asked.

His smile ticked up. "Oh yes, we love the illusion that we have any control at all."

"Above all," Bea went on, "you want to be elusive. You're not a fish to be caught and thrown back into the pond, if you understand me."

She couldn't possibly have been clearer. No, strike that. I had a feeling she could make her meaning horrifyingly plain, and probably would if I gave her enough time.

"Understood." I'd had enough dating tips from the 1960s for one night. I put *Pride and Prejudice* back on the shelf. "I could use a drink."

"Great idea." Duncan snapped his book shut and leapt from his chair.

We left Bea harrumphing her disapproval behind us. I had just ignored several counts of her advice. If I'd stayed any longer, I probably would have been told not to drink alcohol with men, either. Considering what had happened when I'd had a drink with Bea's husband, this was sometimes sound advice.

When we reached the main corridor, I turned to Duncan. "Can we pretend that conversation didn't happen?"

"As long as I get to pretend I suggested it."

The lodge had a small lounge seemingly laid out as an afterthought, with mismatched chairs and random tables strewn about the room. We collected our drinks and snagged a table among the other lodge guests. I sipped my whisky, relieved and oddly proud that drinking one whisky a night hadn't affected me much.

"This one isn't bad at all." I'd trusted Duncan to choose my drink tonight. Hints of apple and vanilla came through the malt, and it had less burn than the others I'd tried, although still stronger than anything I normally drank. If I took small sips and nursed my dram as long as possible, I wound up only mildly drunk instead of *flirt with Rupert* drunk.

"How is your dog faring today?" Duncan asked.

I beamed just thinking about my little guy. "He's good. The picture this morning was of him sitting in Jill's baby stroller."

Along with a text noting that men traditionally wore nothing beneath their kilts, followed by several winking emojis. I would never show him that conversation.

"Sounds like a good dog."

"Lazy enough to ride around in a stroller, anyway. No pets for you, though?"

"No. My ex-wife was allergic to dogs. Since the divorce, I haven't given it much thought."

"How long ago was that?"

"Four years."

"Do you have children?"

"Two girls. Louisa is ten, and Sophie is seven." He pulled his phone from his back pocket and called up a photo. He flipped it around to me, revealing a picture of him crowded by two cherubic girls with bright blue eyes like his and mops of unruly brown hair that blew in front of them. They all wore huge, glowing smiles as though we were peeking in on them on the best day of their lives. My heart soared just looking at the picture.

He took one last look at the phone, his expression nothing but sweet tenderness, before tucking it back into his pocket. "I know more about princesses and tea parties than you would expect."

"I can imagine." My poor heart wanted to burst imagining this big, tough man playing with his daughters. "Do you see them often?"

"Weekends. Part of summer breaks. Alternating holidays." He ticked his head to the side. "Not often enough."

"I'm sorry."

"It's not ideal, but we're making the best of it." He shrugged as though long used to the arrangement, however disappointing. "They're off on holiday with their mum just now, so it seemed a good time for me to get away."

"It, um, ended amicably between you?"

"Eventually." He drummed his fingers against his whisky glass. "For a long time, I let my business consume me. I worked long hours, weekends, holidays. By the time I thought to take a step back, the damage had been done."

"You couldn't make it work?" A stupid question. The answer was obviously no.

"I wanted to try, for the girls. But she was just done. Didn't want to put in the effort on a sinking ship, she'd said."

His grimace made me ache. I knew how much it cut to have someone give up on you. "That's awful."

"I don't pretend I was blameless, but...it hurt that she wouldn't fight for us." He raised a shoulder. "She remarried two years ago. She's happy enough where she is, and so am I."

He looked at me so long after that, I had to take a gulp of whisky. "Have you had other lady friends since your divorce?"

"Lady friends?"

He cocked an eyebrow. I kind of loved the way his bald head put his eyebrows on display—they were wonderfully expressive.

"You know. Companion. Cohabitant. Partner. Romantic associate."

He nodded. "Yes, I see where you're going, but why the roundabout terms?"

"Oh. I've heard that people of a certain age can get a little sensitive about using terms like boyfriend and girlfriend."

"I'd say I'm more sensitive about being described as being *of a certain age.*" He kept his eyes on me as he drank his whisky. "There have been no particular romantic associates of late. You?"

"No one to give up chocolate for. My last relationship ended almost a year ago."

"How long were you together?"

"Four years."

"That's a bit. What happened?"

What could I even say? We'd had no big blow-up, no huge betrayal that had caused the split. We'd drifted into dating—Sean and I had met through Jill and her husband, and worked in similar fields—and eventually, we'd drifted out again.

In the aftermath, I felt like I'd blinked and lost those years. They hadn't been bad years, but they'd been a little like drinking lukewarm coffee—not ideal. I just hadn't fully realized it until everything ended.

"Do you ever read a book or drive your car and realize you're on autopilot? You're not really paying attention to the words or where you're going, you're just acting out of habit? Our relationship was like that."

"Autopilot's no way to experience love," he said. "Love should be wants and needs, hearts and minds coming together in fire and passion until being apart isn't even an option."

My inhale sounded too close to a gasp. His words stirred my body to life like dying embers catching fire in the wind. Look at me, worked up over a few choice sentences. The whisky wasn't helping.

"Men with Scottish accents should not be allowed to say things like that to slightly drunk women."

He threw back his head and laughed. That sound didn't help things, either. I wanted to swim in his delicious laughter.

His eyes sparkled when they hit me. "What am I allowed to say?"

"I'm thinking."

I was thinking I wanted to drink in his easy smiles and his blue eyes that seemed to see beyond surface-level. I was thinking about his hands as he held the whisky glass. His years working in construction left their mark in shimmering scars, a nick here, a scrape there. I imagined those hands in action, and my breathing sounded entirely too loud.

"You should probably restrict your comments to boring things like street names and places of note."

"Reducing me to a GPS, are you?"

"Seems safest, yes."

He leaned closer, his eyes full of mischief.

"Loch an Eilein. Meall a' Bhuachaille. Ben Macdui."

He practically purred, drawing out every syllable until my insides shook like thunder. If I had Duncan voicing my GPS, I would never get out of my car.

I threw my hands up in defense. "I take it back. You're not allowed to say anything at all. Just—" I mimed zipping my lips.

He roared with laughter, making some of the other patrons turn our way. "We won't get very far if I'm not allowed to talk to you."

"With you? I think eye contact is plenty."

He leaned forward again, eyes intent on me. My stomach dipped and my skin heated like I'd walked into a furnace. How was this *worse*? I'd met a lot of men, been on plenty of first dates and had a few long-term relationships, but I'd never had anyone flip all my switches with a look.

"Maybe we should just be pen pals."

He gave a slow shake of his head. "That would never be enough."

No, it would not.

We were in a crowded lounge and barely knew each other, and all I could think about were the span of inches between our faces, the way his fingers moved against his whisky glass, the light in his eyes that said he knew *exactly* how he was affecting me.

I had enough attraction blazing inside me to light a football stadium. Worse, that photo of him and his daughters had set off something tender and sweet that settled dangerously close to my heart. Feelings for a strange man weren't remotely what I'd come to Scotland to find.

This wasn't Real Life Molly responding to him—this was Vacation Molly. Real Life Molly got to know men over weeks and months and years, not hours and days. I took my time, made sensible and safe choices. The last thing I'd rushed into had burned down around me in a puff of pretty custom logos and branding. Rushing led to mistakes, and mistakes led to heartache.

The man smelled divine and I wanted to listen to his laughter all night, but I had to be realistic. Anything that started between us would end in a matter of days. As interested in him as Vacation Molly was, I couldn't open myself up to that.

Real Life Molly wasn't prepared for the fallout.

"It's late. I should probably get to bed." I sounded way too peppy for a woman who had just chosen to walk away from her Scottish temptation.

Duncan worked his jaw as though debating whatever it was he'd thought to say. In the end, he nodded and said good night. Probably for the best, since I wouldn't have needed much encouragement to stay.

One well-timed *"Lochan Uaine,"* and all my resolve would unravel like a cheap sweater.

# seventeen

. . .

I MIGHT HAVE LEFT Duncan in the lounge last night, but he'd followed me into my dreams.

Unfair of him, really, to catch me in such a vulnerable state. When I woke, my mind flashed with images of him from my fevered, sleeping fantasies. Most of the dream had faded away like mist in the morning light, but wisps of Duncan's mouth on mine and vague imaginings of his broad, bare chest remained.

Pretty sure a kilt had been involved at some point.

I sat up in bed and checked my phone, hoping for a picture of Shatner to remind me of my life back home when everything inside me wanted to get swept away here on vacation.

Instead, I found two texts from Jill.

**Jill**: Call me when you get up, doesn't matter the time. Important
**Jill**: Shatner's fine, it's not about him

My heart had jolted so hard after reading the first text, the second didn't do much to soothe it. Why couldn't she have led with that? *Dog is fine, please call* would have been the preferable order there.

Harlow moved around in the ensuite, but I touched the phone icon anyway, figuring whatever Jill had to say couldn't possibly make my nerves any worse.

She picked up right away. "Good timing, I hadn't even gone to bed yet."

"You scared the crap out of me, just so you know."

She groaned. "I knew it, I'm sorry. I didn't think how that sounded until after I sent it. Your dog is perfectly healthy. He's currently sleeping on my pillow. I'll have dog hair on my face all night."

"Getting hair everywhere is his love language. What's so important then?"

She made a small sound like she didn't really want to tell me after all. My nerves kicked higher, even though after news about Shatner, I couldn't think what else she might have to tell me.

"Ed got a promotion."

Oh. Her husband worked for a popular search engine company and had climbed fairly high up the ladder. We didn't run in the exact same circles, but between the two of us, we had enough tech contacts to fill a phone book. If anybody still made phone books.

"That's great news, though! He's been wanting to move into a new position for a while."

"Yeah, we're really thrilled."

She drew in a slow breath, and that pause made me realize I hadn't caught the full picture. My stomach twisted as I guessed the rest of her news.

"The position's in San Diego."

"That's…" Hard to say quite what. I was nearing forty—I couldn't tell my best friend of twenty years I didn't want her to move away.

Even if I was really, really thinking it.

"I know," she said, hearing everything I hadn't said.

"When do you move?"

"In a month."

Harlow left the ensuite, flashed a little wave my way, and ducked out of the room, but I barely registered it. A month. And I would be here in Scotland for another week of that precious time. After that, it'd be nothing but packing and scrambling to get everything ready. And with a newborn? I couldn't imagine all the work in front of her.

"I'm sorry, I know it sucks," she said.

That woke me up. I would *not* rain on their parade. I loved them and only wanted the best for them. I could still do that from a distance, even if I would be a little sad about the change.

"No, it doesn't." I would not be someone whose friends felt the need to apologize for the good things in their lives. "I'm happy for you guys. This is what you've been hoping for."

"Yeah, we just hoped it would be here. We've only been in our house two years."

"Hey, think about how much it's appreciated since then." Seattle housing prices had climbed to slasher-movie levels scary. My very generous landlady had kept the rent on my little house modest for the neighborhood, but the dollar figure still made me wince every month.

"San Diego isn't much better. I've already started looking at house listings and—oof. I'm emailing you some of the houses so I can get your color commentary."

"I guess you can be grateful his position isn't in Mountain View."

"I'd have to sell a kidney for a house in Mountain View." She laughed, but it died out. "It's going to be hard to leave, but this is a really good opportunity for us."

"I know. He's going to kill it down there, and you're going to become a perfect granola mom."

"I doubt it, I've already switched from cotton to disposable diapers. Granola moms would eat me alive."

Her high hopes of doing everything *naturally* diminished with every natural thing she did, starting with childbirth.

"When I get back, we're doing brunch and girls nights whenever you need a break, and I'll help you pack whatever you want."

"You'd better. And hey, you overcame your fear of flying right on time."

My distress twisted into mild panic. I would need to make my peace with flying pretty quick or lose out on seeing my best friend.

"You only think that because you didn't see me on the flights. I didn't overcome my fears, I just didn't faint this time."

"You overcame your fears!"

I laughed, imagining her with her arms raised in victory. "I love you, you loon."

"Love you, too. Now go out there and let that kilted god woo you!"

We hung up on the heels of that tempting advice. I clicked over to my email to see what kinds of crazy-expensive houses Jill had in consideration but found a new email from Lincoln. I opened it up, and all my hopes for a good day turned to dust. He'd sent an update letting me know he'd had to reschedule yesterday's design meeting.

I'd missed the kayak trip for nothing.

What was the Gaelic phrase for wanting to rip your boss a new one?

———

I really wanted some salted caramel anything to help me eat my feelings about my best friend moving away, but muesli would be just as good.

Actually, no, muesli absolutely sucked as a comfort food.

"Are you feeling all right?" Bea looked me up and down. "You look a little peaky."

I shrugged off her concern and sat down at the table. "I'm fine."

I would never admit to her that my friend's good news had

thrown off my morning. It wasn't like I didn't have my own good news. I had a new promotion, too. It just felt…weirdly anti-climactic considering all the work I'd been doing on vacation.

"You have the option of two cycling routes today," Lewis announced. "One amounts to about five miles through town, and the other is twenty miles on the Black Isle. We'll drive you to the starting point and pick you up in the afternoon."

Well, I would choose the longer route. A full day riding a bike around little villages on the island sounded like a perfect distraction. It wasn't really an island, apparently, but it should have plenty of good views, and now maybe I would have a chance to see more of the quaint towns I had only gazed at so longingly from the road.

Conversation swirled around the table while we ate. Spencer relayed a story he'd read about a bicyclist who'd broken his leg in a crash and wasn't found for three days, developing gangrene while he waited for rescue. A bleak start to our morning, not going to lie.

Duncan didn't have much to say, but when I looked over at him, it seemed his silence came more as a reflection of mine than his own desire to be taciturn. I *had* run out on him in the middle of our flirt-fest last night, after all. I didn't want him to think my morning's morose attitude had anything to do with him, so I flashed a small smile. He returned it easily, and that wobbly little something in my stomach flipped over.

*"Let him woo you!"*

Maybe I should.

Our groups divided following our usual pattern: Bea and Rupert opted for the shorter, in-town route with Lewis, while Arnav ferried the rest of us to and from the next village for the longer circuit. After doling out snacks, lunches, and water bottles that we tucked into our backpacks, we set off.

Arnav had driven into town to get the bikes first thing in the morning. Mounted atop the mini-bus, the bikes lent an air of adventure the vehicle had lacked all week. We piled onto the bus, and Arnav took us the short drive to the village of Munlochy.

"All right?"

Duncan watched me more closely than I liked. He seemed to catch everything. Since I couldn't very well say *My best friend is moving away in a few weeks and, oh yes, she thinks I should let you woo me*, I tried to shrug it off. "It's been a weird morning."

Arnav stopped at a turnout on the side of the road and unloaded the bikes and helmets and passed out laminated maps of the area with our planned route highlighted yellow.

"The beginning is the steepest section, but it will bring you to a nice descent along the coast. I'll be back in six hours. That should give you plenty of time to complete the route. My cell number is there in case of emergencies or if you just need a pick up."

He snuck a glance at me, and I scowled back. Sure, fine. Between tumbling around on Ben Macdui and falling straight into Loch Ness, I'd proven myself a bit of a liability. But I rode my bike plenty back home—this would be fine.

Better than fine. I would kick this island's butt.

Standing astride my mountain bike, I strapped on a helmet while I memorized the first three turns of our route. Carlos set off in the lead with the rest of us close behind him. That didn't last. Within minutes, the span between me and the others grew from one block to two, until I stopped trying to catch up. Arnav had warned us, but I hadn't expected the uphill climb to be anything like *this*.

Maybe he'd been right to doubt my abilities.

My breath seared as I tackled the steep grade. I fell so far behind, I could barely see Harlow. Duncan was still somewhere behind me, but that didn't bring me a lot of comfort when I wheezed this hard. Why had I signed up for an adventure tour? I could have found a nice grandma tour like my mom had suggested. You could probably see a lot of Scotland from the seat of a Rascal.

My legs burned with every turn of the wheel, moving my bike up the slope slower than if I'd stepped off and walked. Oh, I was tempted. I kept my eyes fixed on the road, watching for any sign of the plateau that must be coming.

Any time now.

At least I had the coast to look forward to, if the climb up didn't kill me first.

The pain in my legs paled next to my frustration with Lincoln. After the last-minute work I'd put into the mock-ups, he'd canceled the meeting. If I'd been in my office, it would have been just a blip in my day, a mild annoyance he would have smoothed over by sending the intern out for coffee and donuts. In Scotland, that wasted time formed a livid bruise on my vacation, made worse by his indifference. *"Sorry, Molly"* didn't cut it.

"Sorry, Molly" might as well have been my full name, he'd said it so often.

Duncan's bike whirred right behind me, spurring me along. It was both a comfort and a curse that he'd stayed with me. The comfort—well, I didn't question that part. He hadn't left me like the others, which was nice of him, considering he must have had the ability. But it was a little dismaying to know he was right behind me, watching every agonizing pedal of my climb. Forty-nine or not, he was crazy strong. I would have had to ride Queen Anne Hill every day to prepare for this.

I exhaled a laugh even though it took all my strength to keep the bike going. When had I ever been prepared enough for anything? I'd thought I had it all together with my business, and that had crumbled within a year. I'd more than prepared Lincoln for my vacation, but the requests kept rolling in. I'd planned a nice, relaxing trip away from stress and worry, and here I was, falling for a man on the tour.

*No.* Not falling. I mentally slapped myself upside the head. We weren't falling for each other, we were just…getting to know each other. A little harmless flirting. It would be stupid to read anything more into our time together.

So very stupid.

Finally, the road leveled out, and my legs didn't have to work quite so dang hard to keep me moving forward.

"Oh, thank God," I panted. Fingers crossed that would be the worst of it.

Now that I rode at an easier pace, I relaxed a little more, and the clouds darkening my thoughts cleared. It was like my stress-exercising after a weekend of work—I'd burned off my anger along with a couple of calories. All that was missing were the strobe lights and a pumping bass beat.

We reached a junction where the road began to slope down toward the coast, and I could let off my frantic pedaling. Trees surrounded us like we were riding through a fairy woodland, but I would have appreciated the beauty more if my lungs hadn't collapsed several miles back.

Duncan rode up level to me. "How are you doing?"

"I'm going to live." Probably.

I couldn't bear thinking about how I must have looked. Did sweaty swamp monsters appeal to silver foxes? Time would tell.

"Do you want to walk up to the Fairy Glen?"

Our maps showed a short hike to a waterfall ahead. I'd planned to do whatever the others did, but that option had long gone.

"Do you think we have time?" No way of knowing how long it might take me to finish the circuit. If the first leg were any indication, it could be days.

"Absolutely."

God bless this man's optimism. "Lead the way."

A mile or so later, he turned off the road into a gravel car park where we left our bikes. Dismounting eased the soreness in my bum, but my legs shook with every step I took. A twenty-mile ride might not have been the sanest choice I could have made today. Either I would finish my time here with sculpted legs to rival Taylor Swift's or I would never be able to walk again. Sightseeing from a Rascal was still in my grasp.

I was way too tired to convert the sign marking kilometers into measurements I understood. "I hope this isn't far. My legs are jelly."

"Do you need a hand?"

I was about to protest I wasn't that far gone, but then Duncan's big warm hand wrapped around mine and I most definitely *was* that far gone. My legs went wobbly for all new reasons, but no way would I let go.

We walked up a muddy path that cut alongside a stream, crossing it on small footbridges several times as we wound through the forest. Lush trees, flowers, and mosses filled the glen. The air was close and heavy beneath the thick tree canopy overhead, the smell of damp earth and ferns intoxicating. If the color green had a scent, this was where they'd bottle it.

We turned a bend in the path, and the low waterfall laid out before us. Rocks split the wide stream as it cascaded down, forming twin falls that fell in sheets into a little pool.

"This is gorgeous." I could see why it was called the Fairy Glen—it looked like something right out of children's stories.

"I've never seen a better view."

I realized Duncan was looking at *me*, and I rolled my eyes. "You charmer."

"Just speaking truth." He squeezed my hand. "Shall we lunch here?"

We found a log on the riverside and sat down. I couldn't eat much. I was still full from the huge breakfast, and the strain of the ride hadn't helped my appetite. I nibbled at a berry scone and drank some water, watching other visitors come and go.

A dozen people walked through the shady trees to the waterfall while we sat beside the pools. Peace signs were thrown around, photographs snapped, and hikers trekked on. Two children laughed and splashed in the water, making their parents lunge after them when they waded in too deep.

The bike ride had given me some clarity, but the Fairy Glen soothed my heart. The magical place had set my spirits to rights, and the tangle of irritated nerves that had been gnawing at me loosened their grip. I took a deep breath and exhaled like I could clear out the last of my dark thoughts. "This is just what I needed."

Duncan's open, curious look proved dangerous—it could tempt me to bare my whole soul without him saying a word.

"You asked why I decided to come here on vacation? It started when my ex-boyfriend got engaged six months after we broke up."

His eyebrows ticked up. "That's a fast turnaround."

"Yeah. Clearly, he *could* have big, overwhelming feelings, just not for me." I didn't regret our break up, but I'd be lying if I said his change of heart hadn't made me question myself. Wonder if, as Bea suspected, the problem had been me all along. "I don't think I ever felt that way about him, either, for the record. But it wasn't only that. My parents are enjoying a whole new stage of life in their retirement. My best friend just had her first baby, and I found out this morning that she's moving away next month. And I'm just..."

I wasn't really sure how I wanted to finish that sentence. I was treading water while everyone else swam off on adventures. I had a good life, with a good job and lasting friendships. By most standards, I was pretty well-off financially. I had the most fantastic dog around. I wasn't miserable. But a growing piece of me wanted *more*. I just couldn't define exactly what.

"Like I said last night—I've been on autopilot. I needed this trip, I needed *this*." I gestured at the tranquil scene around us. "A little slice of peace, a little break from my everyday."

"What's wrong with your everyday?"

"Nothing. It's perfectly unremarkable. I walk my dog. I get my coffee. I do my job." *And then some.* "It was time I did something special, just for me."

"A big trip is a good choice."

It was, even if I'd needed to be medicated to get here.

"My best friend is always telling me to live in the moment. I don't know how to do that anymore. I'm always overthinking, doing something else in the back of my mind. Work, usually."

A breeze rustled through the ferns casting tiny ripples in the water. He went on watching me, waiting for more, so I went on talking.

"Here, I feel like I'm finally starting to learn how to shut the rest of that off, and just let go. Stop chronicling and experience." He smiled at the reference. "Just enjoy where I am right now."

"Do you like where you are right now?"

He wasn't asking about the waterfall or the views. Looking at Duncan in the dappled sunlight, the atmosphere in the little glen seemed to change. Maybe something inside *me* changed. I hadn't come out here to find him, but here he was, for a limited time only. I could set aside sticking to the plan for a few days. I wanted to know him for however long I could.

"I really do."

He nodded, satisfied. "There you are."

The moment stretched out, waiting for one of us to say or do something more, as though the Fairy Glen weren't satisfied with vague notions and hints. Moving slowly in the stillness, Duncan tucked a stray lock of hair behind my ear. It hardly counted as a touch, but he let his fingers trail along the strand, and my body lit up like he'd caressed my skin.

I would just pretend my hair wasn't coated in sweat.

"I'm sorry I ran out on you last night," I whispered.

"No apologies necessary."

"You're very forward. I'm not used to it."

Maybe more to the point, I wasn't used to the way he made me feel—alive and eager and like my world's axis had shifted.

"I don't see the point in not going after what I want." He paused, his fingers still in my hair. "Unless my interest is unwelcome. I'll stop if you want me to."

"No," I said before he'd finished his offer. I'd never known a man quite like him, but I didn't want him to change a thing. "Don't stop."

His fingers resumed their pull along my hair, finally coming to rest on my shoulder, his thumb spanning my collarbone. I leaned forward, silently asking for more.

He seemed ready to satisfy, when a family with three young children bounded into the clearing. They laughed and talked about the fairy houses they'd seen on the trail to the falls and ran straight into the shallow water to kick up a chilling spray.

That was certainly one way to ruin a moment.

Duncan and I shared a smile.

"Back to the bikes?" he said.

I agreed, and we scrambled down to the gravel lot. I got back on the bike with considerably less enthusiasm than I'd had at the start of the ride, but this trip only went in one direction—I had to keep going forward. I would *not* call Arnav for a rescue.

Thankfully, the road turned downhill until it reached the coastline. Far on the other side of the water lay low hills with billowy gray clouds stretching across the sky above. The bike path hugged the shoreline all the way down the peninsula of the little pseudo-island. To the right, we passed a sculpted golf course green, to the left, the choppy waters of the firth.

Just before we rounded the point of the peninsula, Duncan called for me to wait. I did, and he pulled his bike close to mine.

"Look." He pointed toward the firth.

My gaze followed his, scanning for whatever had made him stop, when a fin broke the water. I sucked in a breath.

"No. Way."

The little girl inside me danced for joy. *Dolphins.* They rose and fell in a cluster, their dorsal fins cutting unmistakable lines in the waves. Others swam farther across the channel, slipping to the surface before disappearing again.

"You got to see them after all," he said.

I grinned until my face hurt, watching the dolphins frolic in the waves. A small crowd joined us, counting the fins and commenting on their every move. A few of them pulled out cameras for quick pictures, and I remembered I needed one, too.

"I almost forgot." I grabbed my camera and offered it to Duncan. "Do you mind taking a picture of the two of us? I don't have any of me in Scotland now."

"Sure."

He accepted the camera and wrapped one arm around me, leaning in close until our helmets clunked together.

"Say 'Lochan Uaine.'"

I burst into laughter as he clicked away, his arm along my back and his hand resting on my shoulder. Maybe the Fairy Glen really had worked a spell on me—I could have stood there all evening with his arm around me and not cared a second about the pictures.

# eighteen

. . .

IF A LIMIT EXISTED for the number of little stone houses I could *ooh* and *aah* over before I got sick of them, I hadn't reached it yet. We pedaled toward the pick-up point, but I had to stop to take a photo of a majestic old church. Duncan didn't seem to mind the delay. I wished I'd had time to stroll through the whole village, but that seemed to be the theme of the trip—always wanting more.

We got going again, but I spotted something that made me bring my bike to a halt.

"What is it?" Duncan asked, a touch of amusement in his voice.

I nodded at a storefront. "I'm required by law to buy something here."

He followed where I looked, and tipped his head in a reverent nod. "I'm not one to argue with the law."

The smell of chocolate overwhelmed my senses in the little sweet shop. The scent hung in the air like a cloud of spun sugar I could almost taste on my tongue. I closed my eyes and inhaled deeply, breathing it in. Heaven.

When I opened my eyes again, Duncan stood close by, his gaze heavy on me.

"You do like your chocolate."

His low voice was richer than the most luxurious dark chocolate. He'd left so little space between us, he could have leaned down and kissed me. I willed myself not to tilt my chin and beg him to do it.

"This is definitely first rate." I didn't mean the chocolate.

"Only the best for you." He let one hand graze over my hip, and my breath hitched. Duncan probably knew a thing or two that could make me forget all about Guylian milk chocolate with sea salt caramel.

Before I could let temptation get the best of me, I darted away to inspect the chocolates. Little bundles of bars in every variety I could think of sat stacked on shelves and displayed on wooden stands. They had a huge glass case full of truffles, candies, and dipped fruit laid out in mouth-watering rows.

I pointed out one section of round little treats and nudged Duncan in the ribs. "Whisky-filled chocolates."

"We need some of those."

We left the chocolate shop with our treasures, AKA, several boxes of handmade artisan chocolates. Before we climbed on our bikes again, we each sampled a whisky chocolate. With all the tang of the liquor and a sweetness that tempered the burn, whisky-filled chocolates were actually pretty incredible.

"Will this count as drinking and driving?" I sucked a bit of melted chocolate from my fingertip.

Duncan's gaze stayed stuck on my mouth, and my heart hammered at the hungry look in his eyes.

"I think you'll keep your head about you."

Pretty sure I'd lost that ability days ago.

The town gave way to a wooded slope leading down to the firth. We cycled through more villages and along the beach, gradually turning back until the road veered uphill again. I stood as I pedaled, using all my weight to keep the bike moving forward. My legs felt almost no pain, they'd become so numb, my hands ached from my fall on Ben Macdui, and my lungs burned on every breath. I wheezed a sigh of relief when we passed back into the country lane we'd started on.

Coasting had never brought on this level of euphoria before.

At long last, we reached the car park where Arnav had dropped us off hours earlier. Carlos, Harlow, and Spencer sat in various states of relaxation on the grass that ringed the gravel lot, their bikes forgotten in an awkward pile.

"There you two are." Harlow strode over as we slowed to a stop. "I was about to call Arnav and have him search the countryside for you."

If she'd been so worried, she might have stopped at any point on the route to wait for us, but I was in too good a mood to say so. "I fell behind right at the beginning, and we couldn't catch up."

"You cut it close." She checked her watch. "We've been here nearly an hour."

For a laid-back yoga instructor, she sure had a secret uptight streak.

"We visited the Fairy Glen waterfall," Duncan said.

"How was it?" Spencer asked.

"A muddy walk, but a pretty picture."

I drew in a breath and turned to Duncan. "I forgot to take a picture."

The smile he wore showed nothing but pride. "You were living in the moment."

That gave me a little glow. Still...*one* picture of the waterfall would have been nice.

Right on time, Arnav arrived and loaded the bikes onto the mini-bus's roof rack. I collapsed onto my seat, my legs absolute mush. For the first time, I sort of wished Duncan wouldn't sit beside me on the ride back to Dingwall. My hair clung to my face, my athletic shirt had been soaked with sweat for hours, and I had no delusions I smelled as good as the chocolate shop had.

He took the seat next to me anyway, stretched his legs out in front of him, and leaned forward to massage his calves.

"Oh, Duncan. You missed a spot with the sunscreen this morning." A bright red stripe of skin peeked out above his shirt.

He tried to look over his shoulder. "Where?"

I lightly brushed my fingers across the nape of his neck. His skin was hot to the touch, but probably more so because of *him* than the sunburn. This wasn't all that personal of a touch, but that tiny graze felt wildly intimate.

He reached up and tested the skin over his neck, wincing when his fingers reached the tender patch. "I'll be feeling it tomorrow."

"I'll be feeling this tomorrow." I swept my hand over my legs. "Expect to see limping."

"Oh no, tomorrow I expect to see you dashing up the Black Cuillins, fueled by those chocolates."

"Tomorrow I just want to stay in bed all day."

He nodded, relaxing back against the seat cushion. "That's far more tempting than those chocolates."

We held eye contact a beat.

"Agreed."

———

The exhilaration of a twenty-one-mile ride was swiftly followed up by a majestic crash into sheer exhaustion. Even Rupert felt the effects of all our activities—lulled by the muted lights in the dining room and the warm smell of roast beef, he dozed off in the middle of dinner. Bea smacked him on the shoulder, but that didn't stop him from falling asleep a second time.

After dinner, the usual suspects retired to the lounge for a nightcap. Duncan and I collapsed onto a banquette, our shoulders propped against each other as we sank into the deep leather seat. Nursing our whiskies, we listened as Carlos and Harlow chattered away the last of the evening's waning light.

"I can't believe you've never seen *Race to the Finish*." Carlos looked from Harlow to me, goggling at our blank reactions to the revelation he worked as a producer on the show. I guessed there was a *junior* somewhere in his title that he'd conveniently left out. He looked to Duncan out of desperation. "Surely you've seen it, it's one of the most popular extreme sport reality shows you can stream."

"I don't watch reality shows," Duncan said.

"I knew you had a flaw," I whispered. He tilted his head closer to mine and bobbed his eyebrows, making my stomach swoop.

Carlos looked like we'd personally insulted him. "You people are a crime." He took a long pull on his beer to shake off his shock. "We shot an episode a few weeks ago in New Zealand dedicated to bungee jumping and abseiling."

I wasn't familiar with abseiling, but I couldn't be bothered to ask questions. I was much too comfortable leaning against Duncan to ask about extreme sports definitions.

"New Zealand is beautiful." Harlow sounded a bit hesitant, as if her Aussie blood prevented her from heaping too much praise on her neighbor. "There's a yoga retreat in the Southern Alps I want to do someday. I've done retreats in Bhutan, Bali, Goa. There's nothing like practicing the timeless art of yoga in such gorgeous surroundings."

I furrowed my brow, unable to find Bhutan, Bali, or Goa on a map. I was totally out of the loop when it came to travel destinations. The Olympic Peninsula, maybe. Anywhere else, not so much.

"We did an episode in Bali." Carlos spoke more to Harlow now than Duncan and me. "Contestants rode jet bikes and went paragliding."

"Paragliding." Harlow said the word slowly as if savoring it.

Carlos nodded. "Take a running jump at a cliffside and just sail."

"Sounds horrible," I whispered to Duncan.

"Not for you?" His voice was a soft purr in my ear. My answering shudder had more to do with his face so close to mine in the soft light than any thoughts of extreme sports.

"No offense, Molly," Carlos said, "but you don't seem like the type to take a running jump at anything."

He grinned like it was all in good fun, but I'd reached my max for shady comments on my personal life.

"No offense, Carlos, but why don't you take a running jump?"

He chuckled softly and downed the last of his ale. "I can take a hint." He stood to go, and Harlow joined him. With a few words wishing us goodnight and a parting wave, they disappeared up the stairs.

Leaving Duncan and I alone together. Possibilities danced through my head.

"I suppose we should call it a night, too," I said.

Yes. Yup. Definitely didn't want to snuggle up in the lounge all night.

He hummed agreement, heaved himself off the leather couch, and held his hands out to me. "It is midnight. Cinderella, and all that."

I put my hands in his, and he pulled me up to standing.

"I'm glad you didn't go abseiling in New Zealand this week."

I laughed, imagining the carnage. This was where I wanted to be. "So am I."

The moment shifted, and we might have been back in the stillness of the Fairy Glen. He traced his fingers along my jaw and up into my hair. My hands found his waist, urging him closer as I waited for his kiss. Finally, he bent down and pressed his mouth to mine.

I made a small sound as my eyes drifted shut, amazed at how quickly he'd left me breathless. My hands slid up his sides and around to his glorious shoulders, holding on like I intended him to stay here a while. His muscles flexed and moved beneath my fingers as his palms glided down my back, spreading shivers like forest fire.

Melting into him, I only knew his warmth, his taste, his beard surprisingly soft against my face. An inferno raged through my body, my thoughts a laser beam zeroed in on Duncan.

First rate, all the way.

When he finally drew back, it was only to a hand's breadth. "No autopilot from here on out."

I exhaled soft laughter. "Agreed."

Only living in the moment, for as long as the moment lasted.

# nineteen

. . .

THE ISLE OF SKYE called to me, urging me to reach the lands that had inspired my vacation as fast as I could. Lewis seemed to heed the call, speeding through villages and past crumbling old buildings that by all rights should have been photographed at least a hundred times. By now, I'd grown used to his cavalier attitude about the views.

I'd grown used to having Duncan beside me on the drives, too. I reminded myself that sitting next to each other on a bus had different connotations for adults than it had done when I was in middle school, but after last night's kiss, I wasn't so sure. Denying our attraction was no longer an option, but just what we would do about that remained to be seen. For now, sitting together chatting while I ogled the sights was comforting enough.

We passed through gorgeous hillsides and hugged the shoreline of breathtaking lochs. Lewis announced the names of each one as we passed but couldn't be bothered to stop at any of them for photo opportunities or exploration. Could I ever become so used to these views that they no longer gave me chills? The ability to breeze past them seemed utterly beyond me. If I'd been in my own vehicle, I would have stopped at every loch, probably several times over, just to revel in the views. Duncan would have laughed at all the pictures I would have taken.

"I can't get over all these lakes."

"It is what we're known for," he said.

I pulled one leg underneath me and leaned back in my seat to face him. "You say you've lived in London ten years, but whenever you talk about Scotland, it's like it's still your home."

"It always will be. It's in my blood. I like London, but Scotland has my heart."

A slow smile spread over my face. "Now you're being unfair. There's nothing like a man talking about his heart to make a woman's melt."

"Then it's all going to plan." His mouth twitched a reflection of his humor, and that alone sent a spark zinging through me.

Honestly, everything about him gave me that zing.

"Do you ever think to come back?" If I lived in Scotland, I'd never want to leave it. I would have time to wander through all the open hillsides, walk on the rocky coasts, and actually experience all the little villages I had only glimpsed.

Avoid every haggis-filled butcher shop from coast to coast.

"The thought occurs, especially on a trip like this." His gaze darted out the window to the lake and back again. "There's a lot to appreciate here. But I don't think I could be so far from my girls indefinitely."

"What are they like? Other than absolutely adorable."

"They are that, aren't they?" He scratched his beard, a sweet smile touching his mouth. "Louisa devours books, especially after bedtime when her light is supposed to be out. She's whip smart and sees right through me. Sophie is a devious little imp, always up to whatever it is I just told her not to do. She's going to be the world's first astronaut princess. Most of our tea parties take place on Saturn."

"On Saturn?" I repeated with a laugh.

"Jupiter is so gauche."

"If she's a princess, does that make you the king?" All my senses said *Yes, indeed.*

"I appreciate that you'd guess that, but no. At best I'm the footman—at worst, jester."

"Aw. Do you have the hat for it?"

He gave a slow nod, and I giggled at the image. Although he would probably wear a jester hat as well as he wore everything else.

"You laugh. You're not the one singing Taylor Swift songs at the mercy of a seven-year-old."

I dipped my head toward him and dropped my voice. "Are you a secret Swiftie?"

"It's no secret. I have two girls—Taylor Swift is the soundtrack to my life."

"Is it too soon to ask for a baritone rendition of "Cruel Summer?""

He laughed. "You don't want to hear me sing, I promise. I was cursed in another life to be perpetually off-key. That's why it's the girls' favorite request."

"They must run the show with you."

"And they know it." There came that sweetness in his expression again, and there went my heart, turning into a puddle. "It's cliché, but I didn't know what love was until they were born."

Well, that was it. My ovaries swooned into a dead faint. Time to just raise the white flag and surrender to the king.

"These little people who are completely dependent on you, who can drive you mad with their antics, yet they hold your heart in their hands. It's like nothing else."

"They're lucky girls. Just listening to you talk about them for five minutes, I can see how much you love them. That's a really special thing."

"What about you?" he said. "Do you want children?"

The simple question came with a bittersweet aftertaste. The answer I would have given even a few years ago felt beyond my grasp now. I'd witnessed firsthand Jill's three-year struggle to get pregnant with Olivia and didn't have any false hopes that I might have an easier time of it if I were to start even later.

"Honestly? I thought I would have had kids by now. I want a family. But I never met the right man to marry, let alone have a child with, and I don't think I'm the kind of woman to do it on my own. I like the idea of partnership."

Going solo had looked even less appealing since I'd seen Jill and Ed in action taking care of Olivia. I would salute all the single moms out there, but I wasn't prepared to dive into that life intentionally.

"It's certainly easier with two. Sometimes when I have the girls all to myself, I feel like I'm barely keeping afloat. Summers, I run them to sports, camps, birthdays, and all of that. I'm more delivery man than dad."

"Don't discount the delivery man. I'm half in love with the guy from the Indian restaurant down the street."

"Oh, my girls don't see it that way. Lately, every time I get us takeaways, I wind up with a lecture about how their stepdad makes such amazing dinners. 'Not from a box,' they tell me, pointing their little fingers in my face. 'Not from a menu.'" He exhaled a laugh. "Of all the reasons to be jealous of another man, his cooking skills are a new one for me."

"I don't know, a man who can cook is pretty appealing." I played up the word, imagining Duncan at work in the kitchen. Oof, I liked that idea too much.

Jester hat totally optional.

"Don't take their side, I'm already outvoted as it is."

"I'm sorry, but I always side with food."

"Molly, we have got to sort out your priorities."

I laughed, ready to tease him about the importance of high-quality food, when something out the window caught my eye.

I gasped and clutched at his hand. "That's it."

Massive stone pinnacles stood out against the hillside, making the harbor town below look tiny. The Old Man of Storr. My breath stalled out and I couldn't do anything but stare. I'd had no idea it was so…prominent. From the pictures, I'd always thought we would have to hike to it, search it out like hidden treasure. But the stones loomed over Portree like sentinels from another age.

Giddy laughter bubbled out of me. We'd finally made it. The reason I'd chosen this country, this tour for my big vacation.

He squeezed my hand. "It's a sight, isn't it?"

At this distance, it really did look like a giant man out there in the clouds, towering over the town. "Is there a place we can stop to take pictures?"

The road didn't even have a shoulder, let alone a place to park.

Arnav turned around with a bemused look on his face. "We're hiking to it tomorrow. You'll take plenty then, I think."

The view dwindled the closer we got, until The Old Man of Storr was completely obscured by the hillside, and ultimately, the town. I hoped Arnav was right about the pictures tomorrow, because I already felt a little sick I'd missed capturing that view.

Tomorrow couldn't come soon enough.

# twenty

. . .

I'D KNOWN the Isle of Skye made for a popular summer destination, but Portree was absolutely stuffed. The streets teemed with people pointing at everything—the buildings, the boats in the harbor, the plethora of gift shops. Tourists had flocked to the shores of Loch Ness, but here, the village felt cramped with so many people wandering around. I'd goggled at the towns we'd passed just as obviously, and I resolved not to look like such a blatantly obvious tourist in the future.

Even if I was currently riding in the most blatantly obvious tourist bus around.

We checked into our accommodation, a cute bed and breakfast a few blocks from the harbor. It looked small from the outside, and I had my doubts it would have space enough for all of us. We passed a cozy but minuscule sitting room before climbing narrow stairs to the upper levels. Lewis handed out room keys and disappeared to help Arnav shuttle some of the gear inside.

Harlow opened our room door and burst into laughter. I peered over her shoulder to see what was so funny.

The room was not just boutique, but *tiny*. After seeing the rest of the guest house, I wasn't sure what else I'd expected, but this room took it to the extreme. Even the two twin beds were narrower than usual. This may have been a trick of the eye due to them being so very close together—the beds could not have been eight inches apart—and graced by a single king-sized headboard.

"If you squint, it looks like one bed," I said.

"I'm a little afraid I might roll out of this." Harlow sat down on one to test its width.

"You can't roll out. You'd just roll onto my bed." Pretty sure we could spoon without leaving our beds.

"I've slept in vans bigger than this."

Lewis popped his head inside our open door. "Everything okay?"

"Yes," I said too quickly.

"It's a little cramped in here, isn't it?" Harlow tried to walk between the beds and pretended to get stuck between them.

"Sorry about that. The rooms are a bit wee for doubles, but it's quite a good lodge with easy access to our activities."

Lewis looked so apologetic, I wished Harlow hadn't said anything. He and Arnav had done everything they could for our comfort over the last week. Complaining about a smaller room seemed a little spoiled.

Although, in all fairness, the room threatened to bring on a case of crushing claustrophobia.

I gave him an encouraging smile. "It will be just fine for us, honestly."

"There's only breakfast and dinner here, so the plan is to have lunch out and meet again in the lobby after for our hike to the Fairy Pools." He nodded once more and ducked back down the hallway.

I picked up a Things to Do card off the small desk. "It looks like we're finally going to tour a castle." Although, given the list, it would be hard for me to choose only one activity here. They had all the usual hiking and kayaking, but also things like otter watching, horseback riding, and axe throwing.

I seriously hoped we wouldn't take a side trip for that last one.

I didn't have a good enough track record on this tour to think I should be holding an axe.

"I don't need to see another castle." Harlow crammed her luggage next to one of the beds.

"I haven't been up close to one yet. I've seen…" I counted on my fingers as I mentally scrolled through the vacation. "Five, I think? They're magical."

"If you like dungeons. My trip to Edinburgh last year, I came with my boyfriend at the time. We toured the castle in the city and a couple of others. It gets real old, real fast." She pulled an exaggerated face. "'Over here, we have a tapestry woven from sheep's innards, believed by peasants to ward off evil spirits. Next to it is a sword made from holy petrified wood passed down through the family MacBeth since Beth MacBeth first carved it.'"

"Beth MacBeth is a national hero."

Both of us turned to find Carlos standing practically in our room, his cheeky grin shining out in lieu of an apology for the intrusion. This guy and open doorways.

"How dare you disparage the good name of MacBeth while in Scotland?" he said.

"I'm just saying, you've seen one musty old castle, you've seen them all."

I guessed Australia didn't have many castles.

"I completely agree. I'm much more interested in current events." His meaningful look showed exactly what he was interested in. "Want to join me for lunch?"

The question had the air of including both of us, but I was no fool—he wasn't asking me along. Harlow picked up her purse and jacket, tossing a quick, saucy look at me as she left. I closed the door behind her before Bea or Rupert could pop in for a doorway chat.

I grabbed my phone and laid down on my bed to scroll through photos of Shatner. I'd never been away from him this long before, and I missed my little guy. I didn't like sitting down without hearing the jingle of his collar as he trotted down the hall to leap up beside me. I missed the snuffling noises he made in his sleep and the way he could only make himself comfortable by making me uncomfortable. He had an impressive ability to turn his twenty pounds into fifty as he pressed against my back.

More than anything else about home, I wanted to stroke Shatner's fur and endure his eager, slobbery kisses.

Jill's photo of the day showed him snoozing atop a pile of pillows like a little prince. My heart squeezed as I stared at his adorable little face.

I checked the rest of my messages, including Mom's daily voicemail.

*"Honey, I'm sure you're having a wonderful time. Have you tried the haggis yet? I'm off to a belly dancing lesson with Monica, Wish me luck..."*

Through some small miracle, Lincoln hadn't messaged yet. I tossed my phone back in my bag, in case thinking of a text would make one magically appear.

A knock sounded at my door. I climbed off the tiny bed and moved the two steps across the room to pull it open. Duncan stood in the hallway wearing jeans and his fleece jacket, once again looking like a very low-key alpha motorcycle man. Unfair of him to be so attractive with so little effort. I'd done nothing to spruce myself up since we'd checked in and wasn't sure it'd had the same effect.

Although, from the way Duncan watched me, maybe I'd misjudged that.

"There's no lunch on-site," he said. "I thought you might like to join me for a bite in town."

Before he could say Meall a' Bhuachaille, I grabbed up my purse and jacket, and followed him out the door. We met Spencer coming up the stairway as we headed down. He looked his usual sad self, but I acted on impulse anyway.

"Do you want to join us for lunch?"

The invitation seemed to startle him out of his gloomy thoughts.

"There's nothing to be had if you stay here, apparently," I went on. "I think I'm pretty okay company. For a while, anyway. This guy…" I nodded at Duncan and made a so-so gesture with my hand. "But joining us would be better than nothing."

He glanced from me to Duncan but shook his head. "I'm not really in the mood right now."

"All right." Honestly, I hadn't expected more, but I had to try.

He stepped past us up the stairs while Duncan and I continued down.

"Just okay company, am I?" Duncan fixed me with a comically intense stare, making excellent use of his Murder Face. He might have been the stuff of action movies but for the glint of playfulness in his eyes.

"No, that was me. You, I said—" I made the so-so motion again, but he stopped the gesture by taking my hand in his.

"Yes, I saw that."

He didn't bother letting go of my hand as we stepped out of the lodge and onto the street. I tried not to revel in the sweet gesture, but my heart did its own thing when it came to Duncan.

"Lewis said there's a chippy just over here." He pointed along the street at a bright blue building. "Fish and chips place," he said in answer to my quizzical look.

"Mmm, yum. As long as the fish are wild caught and the batter gluten-free."

"With organic chips cooked in recycled oil."

We found the restaurant and took a booth overlooking the harbor. I scanned the menu of assorted deep-fried items—deep-fried haddock, cod, prawns. Deep-fried haggis—that was new.

"Deep-friend Mars bar?" I asked. "Is it any good?"

"You'll have to try one."

"Challenge accepted."

The waitress took our orders and hustled off again, leaving Duncan and me alone in a cozy booth, our hands almost-but-not-quite touching in the middle of the table.

It was normal for a kiss to echo over your mouth like your lips were having a delightful dream, right?

Just me?

"I love fish and chips," I said before I could blurt something like *Let's make out!* "Seattle has a lot of seafood restaurants, too, and it was always one of my favorite dinners out with my parents growing up."

"Are your parents in good health?"

I ran a hand over my mouth, covering my smile at his inadvertent *Pride and Prejudice* quote. "Very much so. They both retired two years ago and I think it's the greatest thing that's ever happened to them."

"What are they like?"

"They're total opposites: a brainy engineer and a bubbly music teacher. Dad doesn't reach out a ton, he's just quieter by nature, but Mom keeps me up to date on all their activities. They go out on dates every Friday night and have taken up new hobbies. I'm happy they're enjoying themselves so much."

Even though sometimes I felt like they were the teenagers sneaking off on dates and I was the parent waving goodbye as they spread their wings.

"Everyone should hope for that kind of health and enthusiasm in their advanced age."

He dropped his voice over the last two words and I snorted a laugh at how he'd echoed my teasing. I would never put Duncan in the same category as my parents.

"It's kind of weird, though." I ran my fingers over the tabletop, trying to put my conflicting emotions into words. "I'm an only child. I sort of envisioned myself taking care of them in their old age, but they're out here living it up, traveling with their friends, learning languages. They're doing their own thing. They love my visits, but they don't exactly need me."

Not that I wanted to check them into the nearest retirement home, but they could have let me run errands for them once in a while. Call for my help when their internet got buggy. Ask me to interpret the latest slang phrases. Something.

"I understand. Not being needed is my worst nightmare."

I couldn't imagine not needing a man like Duncan. I wished his wife would have fought for him rather than turn her back on their relationship when he was trying to fix it.

Well...no. I didn't wish that. But someone needed to fight for him.

I shushed my inner Katniss, clamoring to volunteer for the job.

"My parents' second wind is a gift, I know that. But it can be trying, too, in ways I never expected. There are only so many times I can fend off conversations about their sex life." My mother left *nothing* to the imagination.

He winced. "I changed my mind—hearing about my parents' sex life would be my worst nightmare."

"It's either that, or she's asking about mine."

"If they're going to ask, might as well have a good tale to tell."

His wink shimmered through me like stardust and I breathed out a laugh. I had no doubts Duncan would deliver.

The waitress returned with our food and laid out the platters before whisking off again. Two plates of fish and chips, along with the lone fried Mars bar dusted with powdered sugar sat in front of us. The chocolate tempted, but I showed some restraint and tucked into my lunch first.

Next, I cut the Mars bar into pieces. The golden brown batter held a gooey mess of chocolate and caramel. It looked tasty, but just like fried butter back home, that calorie bomb had to have been created on a dare.

Spearing a piece on my fork, I tipped it toward Duncan. "On the haggis scale, how beloved is this dish here?"

He snorted. "I think it's mostly for tourists and children."

I shrugged. "I guess I'm going to get the full tourist experience, then."

I popped the bite into my mouth. The crispy fried batter

melted into the chocolate, and the powdered sugar added an extra —completely unnecessary—layer of sweetness.

"It's surprisingly good. Please, have some of this delectable treat." I scooted the plate to the middle of the table and Duncan ate a square of the gooey chocolate.

The fried batter made a strangely good combination with the caramel center, but I couldn't remember the last time I'd eaten a whole chocolate bar in one go. I struggled between the temptation of delicious, gooey chocolate, and the sure knowledge of an imminent stomachache from sugar overload.

As usual, chocolate won out.

# twenty-one

. . .

I WOULDN'T HAVE THOUGHT a massive, open field could be overrun with tourists, but the Fairy Pools proved me wrong. All the pristine pictures of the empty trail that led into the mountains must have been taken in the off season, because it was absolutely covered today. We'd snagged the last oversized parking spot in a full lot and now scrambled down the walking path with approximately ten thousand other people.

The chaos made me miss the relative privacy of the Fairy Glen with Duncan.

The Black Cuillin range rose into the sky in a series of close-knit jagged peaks, offering protection to the narrow river that cut through the glen to form the pools. Where the Cairngorms had been gentle, rounded domes, the Cuillins were all angles, crags cutting into the blue sky like giants' teeth. Mist crept down the mountainsides, making the scene at once peaceful and slightly creepy.

The path hugged the stream that rushed and foamed from the mountains. We had to pick our way across where the track crossed over, moving from boulder to boulder in wide steps.

"We're lucky it hasn't been too rainy," Lewis said. "This bit can prove a problem if the river's too high."

I could imagine, since the water wouldn't have to rise much to completely cover the stepping stones.

Arnav made slow progress helping Bea across the large boulders. She said nothing, but the process must have unnerved her. She chose her footing on each stone with precision, Arnav's fingers white under her grip. Lewis escorted Rupert, and the rest of us were left to make our way.

Duncan stepped onto the first boulder but turned back and held out his hand to me. I'd have to add chivalry to his list of dreamy qualities. He needed a giant, glaring flaw to counteract everything else that left me a drooling mess. Maybe he was secretly an axe murderer.

Still hot, though.

We passed several smaller pools before we reached the first waterfall—and I took pictures like crazy, thank you very much. The stream here cut through rocks in a narrow fall down to a crystal-clear basin. People at the pool came in two distinct varieties: those dressed in fleeces and rain gear, and those in swimsuits braving the frigid waters. Swimmers splashed in the shallows, daring each other to wade deeper. Rising out of the water, they looked like I'd felt in Loch Ness—freaking cold.

Bea pursed her lips at the young women frolicking on the rocky shore.

"Really," she said to Rupert, but loud enough the rest of our group could hear. "Those outfits don't leave much to the imagination."

Rupert *tut-tutted*, but as usual, paid little attention. I found his perpetual distraction endearing, even if I would rather die than tell him so.

"You'll catch your death of cold!" Bea shouted at no one in particular.

"Not today!" one of the girls shouted back.

"We'll head on up to the higher pools." Lewis motioned for us to continue along the path.

Despite the crowds below, fewer hikers kept on with every

waterfall we passed. The next pool large enough for swimming only had a few people gathered around it.

"The Fairy Pools have become quite popular." Lewis seemed to feel it warranted a vague apology.

"Everyone who comes to Skye wants to see the Pools and The Storr," Arnav said. "They get a fair few visitors."

"The Storr is what inspired me to take my whole trip." I couldn't complain about the crowds when we were all after the same thing.

"I thought it was Loch Ness," Harlow teased.

"Yeah, yeah."

The sun broke through the haze of clouds, shining through the water until I could have counted every rock and pebble lining the bottom of the pool. I took a few pictures of the blue-green water with the imposing mountains behind it, yet another example of Scotland's storybook scenery.

Kneeling at the water's edge, I put one hand into the glassy pool but quickly drew it out again—it felt as cold as Loch Ness.

"Are you testing it for a dip?" Duncan asked.

"If it was hotter out, maybe." The day hadn't warmed nearly enough for me to consider it. "I think I'll keep my clothes on."

"I've never prayed so hard for a heat wave."

Talk about an extreme heat advisory—my insides turned molten. I shook my head at him, but the man was smoldering. Surprised everything close to him didn't go up in flames.

Especially me.

Harlow pulled off her backpack. "I don't know about the rest of you, but I'm going in."

"That feels like a challenge." Carlos grinned, following her lead.

Bea looked on in horror. "Lewis, you can't let them do such a thing. Molly nearly caught her death in Loch Ness. Do you want them to do the same?"

"I didn't nearly catch my death," I said, but Bea went on glaring at Lewis.

"I won't stop them." He frowned as they peeled off their clothes. "Although I'd advise as short a dip as possible, given the temps."

"And the midges," Duncan said.

We'd been swarmed by the tiny flies a few times already. They found every bit of exposed skin, and their bites itched like mad. Becoming a midge buffet seemed a definite mark against wild swimming.

"You're going in with a wetsuit, at least?" Bea said to Harlow.

Spencer laughed at the absurd comment, but she didn't seem to notice.

Harlow stripped down to a bikini, and Carlos wore swim trunks. This obviously wasn't a spur-of-the-moment decision. She leapt across rocks to get closer to the waterfall's spray, and he followed right behind. Easy to see who was trying to impress whom.

Duncan sidled closer to me. "Not tempted to go in?"

"I think I've had my fill of impromptu swims in chilly water."

Although, if I had *this* natural source of heat at the ready, I might not even feel the cold.

"It's deepest closest to the waterfall," Lewis told them.

A worry line creased the center of his forehead, and I wondered how many of his clients regularly went off-script like this. I didn't include myself in that number, since my deviation had been an accident. Normally, I was a very *on*-script woman.

Harlow stood with her toes on the edge of a rock, staring into the waters below the falls. When she finally jumped, pure excitement lit her face, a picture of living in the moment. Something inside me ached for that kind of freedom, like nirvana just beyond my grasp. I hadn't leapt at anything much since my failed attempt at self-employment, but I envied her ability to jump straight into what she wanted.

Carlos went in right after her, and they rose to the surface with huge smiles, cold but clearly satisfied. They only swam for a few minutes before climbing back out.

Arnav high-fived them. "I've been waiting for someone to take a dip!"

Harlow toweled off as casually as if she were at a beach back in Australia. Rupert stood with his back to her, gazing up at the Cuillin Range. I couldn't tell if his ignorance of her near-nudity was intentional or accidental.

"No one's ever tried to swim it before?" Harlow asked Arnav as she squeezed out her hair.

"Not on one of my guides. But I don't always get this trip in the hottest months."

With some careful shimmying behind their towels, Harlow and Carlos pulled their dry clothes back on. They both had a slight shiver to them, but they couldn't stop smiling, either.

That aching sense of longing twisted deeper inside me, yearning for something perpetually out of reach.

Our group continued on up the path, slowly ascending the stony slope. Looking across the glen here was like being transported back in time. I couldn't see a scrap of modern life—no towns or buildings, power lines or street signs—just the untouched beauty of nature. This was exactly what I'd sought out when I planned my trip. The views stunned, but the unfettered feeling of being completely liberated from my usual routine was where the real magic lay.

A shard of regret pierced my view-induced exultation. I hadn't been liberated at all. I'd worked almost every day of my vacation in this wondrous fairyland. Well, not anymore. No more wasting this opportunity to just relax and be at peace in such an ethereal place.

I looked over at Duncan, who seemed equally taken by the scene.

No more wasting opportunities, whatever they were.

We tramped back to the mini-bus for the quick ride to a whisky distillery. I'd been sampling whiskies all week but wanted to see first-hand how the alcohol was actually made. The tour included a short history of whisky told by our host, Andrew. He made the process an interesting tale, but he knew his audience well enough to guess we were more interested in tasting whisky than hearing about it.

He led us to a room where a long table held three whiskies on display. Seven flights had been set up with small samplings of each ready to go, along with glasses of water to cleanse our palates. All we had to do was walk up and drink. Should be easy enough.

Andrew talked us through each one, guiding us on the proper way to drink whisky. It turned out I'd been doing it like an amateur all week. I knew nothing about nosing, swirling, or holding the whisky on my tongue to "listen" for flavors. I'd been to plenty of wine tastings, but I'd never developed a knack for discerning anything particular beyond the main flavors. I had no skill at recognizing notes and tones but could improvise descriptions like nobody's business.

Turned out to be the same for whisky. According to Andrew, the first bottle was a stormy mistress with a taste for spice. Sounded terrible already. Just like he instructed, I swirled the amber contents and sniffed at it as it moved. I couldn't pick up any distinct notes beyond the harsh scent of malt. I took a sip, and my nose crinkled automatically. This was nothing like the whiskies Duncan had picked for me. All smoky heat, with none of the light, sweet undertones of the others.

To be fair, the others had been plenty strong, too, but this took it to a whole new level.

My eyes watered as the drop of whisky burned its way down my throat. I chugged a glass of water, but it couldn't wash away the fire.

Duncan watched me as he swirled his glass, a small smile playing on his lips. I made an exaggerated face but said nothing until Andrew had moved on to Bea and Rupert.

"Dear God," I whispered, "and I thought gin was awful."

"You don't like gin?"

"Gin is like drinking perfume. This is like drinking plague."

My mouth fell open as he took another sip of his whisky. "Do you like it?"

"It's not an everyday whisky for me, but it's good." My grimace only made him smile wider. "You have to work your way up to peaty Scotch."

"I think half my taste buds just died."

He consoled me with a pat on the back, letting his hand linger on the curve below my waist. Looking up at him, his closeness was almost enough for me to forget I'd just swallowed a corrosive liquid that was probably melting my insides.

The second whisky proved as bad as the first to my untrained palate. All burn, no flavor, full-throttle gross. Still, I smiled and nodded politely when Andrew walked by.

"At least give me a Coke to wash it down," I whispered to Duncan.

"Blasphemy. You'd be drummed out of the distillery if you said that out loud."

"And drawn and quartered, I suppose."

"All manner of things."

His voice went sinfully low, and my belly tumbled as I wondered what other punishments he had in mind for me.

The last whisky on offer was at least sweeter than the others but still retained the heavy, smoky flavor that made them all too strong for me to do anything more than take a sip and try not to flinch. No offense to the dedicated whisky distillers, but I'd rather set it on fire than drink this stuff.

Andrew came by to get my opinion on their single malts.

Yeah…I would need a minute to come up with something believable.

I couldn't flat out lie to him—my tongue still tingled from the whiskies' burn, and my throat constricted, desperate for me to cough out the last of the offending liquid. At least I hadn't choked on them in front of the whisky expert, but I couldn't be sure he hadn't caught my grimaces.

"They may be a little too bold for my taste." I'd barely sipped at each glass and I wanted to rip my tongue out. I couldn't imagine actually drinking the stuff.

"You're not the first to say so." Andrew's gracious smile let me know he'd taken no offense. "Our flavors here are particularly peaty and smoky, heavy notes that aren't for the faint of heart."

"Oh, I'm certainly faint of heart. Very timid and unadventurous."

Duncan kept his eyes on me as he drank another sip of that godawful whisky.

Okay. Maybe not *completely* unadventurous.

———

Dressing for dinner had always sounded like such an old-fashioned habit, but on an active tour that had us sweating through our clothes every day, it was the only way to ensure we could bear sitting next to each other at the table at night.

I'd just changed into fresh clothes and re-braided my hair when my phone buzzed inside my travel bag. It wasn't likely Jill—she had already texted her Shatner pic of the day, a shot of him mauling a chewy treat. My mother had left another cheery voicemail and a picture of her belly dancing friends.

One guess who was calling.

How could business be this crazy while I was out of town? I considered ignoring it. Just leave Lincoln's demands until after dinner when I could devote myself to it. But it'd be better to get this out of the way now, rather than let dread spoil my whole evening.

"Lincoln." The false cheer in my voice grated on my ears, and I hated it had already become my default Head of Design persona.

"Molly." He said my name like a lifeline. "Good, I caught you. I need your help."

The promise I'd made myself at the Fairy Pools echoed in my mind. *No more work.*

"We're finalizing the Bradbury site, and I need all hands on deck."

"I turned those storyboards in before I left."

"I know, but the dev team is busy with another account, so we really need you to do some of the front-end coding to help us keep on schedule."

"Coding?" Even on a regular day, I much preferred the design side of my job to the development side. Not that he didn't ask me to code anyway, but here and now it felt crazy to even consider it.

"Molly, you know how it is." He typed away in the background, probably working up code while we talked. "It's a fast-paced business."

I did know. Deadlines shifted as clients changed their minds on layout or page specifics. Some demanded short timeframes and early site completion, shaving weeks off of schedules. Even with all hands on deck, something could always go wrong. None of that had anything to do with one important point.

"I'm on vacation." Even as I said it, the glimmer of my plans for the evening faded away, replaced by rounds of mind-numbing code. Coding wasn't strictly part of my job description, but I could do enough that Lincoln had come to rely on me in a pinch.

I just hadn't expected to get pinched in Scotland.

"I hate to say it, but this is a bad time for you to be on vacation, Molly." Lincoln managed to sound casual and threatening at the same time. "Everyone else is working overtime as it is. Maybe you should cut your trip short so you can finalize this site."

The idea made me queasy. "That's impossible."

"Look. I want you for this Head of Design position because your work is flawless, you're dedicated to the team, and I can rely on you no matter what. Was I wrong in thinking that?"

Anxiety unspooled in my stomach. *Team* was one of Lincoln's favorite keywords. Team effort. The team needs you. Don't let your team down. Amazing how much guilt teamwork could create. I broke into a light sweat, glancing around the room. What was more important, a few hours of vacation time, or everything I'd worked for in the last ten years of my career?

"You weren't wrong," I said. "I can do a few hours' worth to get the group started."

Every word came out a groan of defeat, but Lincoln would never hear it.

"That's our Head of Design."

His praise twisted the knife, as though I were sacrificing my vacation time out of the goodness of my heart rather than giving in to his vague threats. For the first time, I wondered how many more hours I would have to put into the business once I got back and fully settled into the promotion. I didn't have a lot of spare time left as it was.

I hung up, mentally scrubbing the rest of my evening. Nothing ever went to plan, but doing code on vacation was the worst of all possible plans. My one consolation was that the day's activities were already done—although, truth be told, I'd started looking forward to my evening activities with Duncan more than the actual tour.

I would just have to put off those hopes for tonight.

# twenty-two

. . .

I NEEDED COMFORT FOOD.

My vow at the Fairy Pools not to do any more work in Scotland vanished in the face of Lincoln's threats, my high over the exquisite sights demolished. I hated that I'd given in—but I couldn't completely regret it, either. I couldn't risk my job, not when I had so much on the line.

So—food.

I ate two whisky chocolates before I went down to dinner, hoping the sugar kick would perk me up. Dinner was hearty— potatoes and red meat—but at least nothing was fried. After my lunch of fish and chips with a deep-fried Mars bar chaser, my stomach had turned into a lump of congealed grease. I didn't want to see anything coated in batter for the rest of the trip.

Any ill-effects from chocolate would be completely forgiven.

Bea and Rupert announced their intention to set out on another hill walk after dinner. It was already past six, but this far north in the summer, the sun didn't go down until closing in on eleven. It might be perpetually shrouded in clouds, but Scotland didn't lack for daylight hours.

I had to admire just how active they'd been every day of the trip. They could have easily chosen a senior tour built around visiting museums and castle gardens, but they'd opted for activity and adventure. I appreciated their spirit, even if I had no intention of tagging along on this particular walk.

"You're all welcome to join us," Bea said. "It's quite invigorating."

"I'd be happy to join you," Lewis said, possibly due to contractual obligations.

"I'm off to the pub," Arnav said. Lewis shot him a warning look, but he raised his water glass. "For the ambience, of course."

I guessed there must be a stipulation that the guides couldn't drink on-tour. They'd encouraged everyone else to drink whatever we liked, but I hadn't seen them drink anything stronger than cola.

"Where's the good pub, Arnav?" Carlos asked. "Harlow says she can drink me under the table, and I aim to prove her right."

Harlow rolled her eyes. "I said I'd have one drink."

"As if anyone goes to a pub in Scotland and has just one drink, especially an Aussie. Live up to your stereotypes, woman."

"Live up to yours. Aren't you supposed to be a charming Lothario?"

His eyes widened. "That's offensive. I've been charming the hell out of you."

She rolled her eyes, but the wash of color on her cheeks said he wasn't wrong.

"The pub's easy enough to find," Arnav said. "Head out the door and turn left. It's three buildings down, big black sign says Olde Man and Skye. Can't miss it."

"Molly? Duncan?" Bea hadn't given up her quest for companions. "Care to join us?"

Duncan seemed to be waiting for me. Questioning all my decisions, I cast an apologetic look at him before I turned to Bea. "I need to go up and do a bit of work."

"They've got you working from Scotland?" Carlos said. "That's dedication. Me, I said no calls until I'm back in the office."

None of his work tales had included anything like a nine-to-five environment. Shooting footage from the back of a speedboat didn't sound like anyone's office routine. "Do you even have an office?"

He smirked. "Not this week."

Envy for Carlos. That was a new experience.

"Are you in for the night, then?" Duncan didn't show a trace of judgment.

"I said I'd do a couple of hours."

"And after?"

I probably smirked as wide as Carlos. "Pub?"

He nodded. "Pub it is."

———

I silently raged against the poor WiFi connection in the lodge. If I had any idea where they kept the router, I would have moved closer to it, but I wasn't in the mood to wander around with my computer open searching for full signal strength.

The work itself wasn't the problem. I could create a good-looking, functional website even if I did it under duress.

No, the problem was I shouldn't have to do it at all. As gratifying as it was Lincoln had chosen me for Head of Design, it didn't mean as much when I saw how easily I could lose it. What a crummy position to put me in. Would he have rescinded the offer if I'd refused to help out tonight? Neither answer brought any kind of comfort.

Lincoln enjoyed playing up his company's reputation as a fun office with a game room for blowing off steam, weekly *Take Your Dog to Work* days, and a casual dress policy. The part he never detailed in his many online profiles or to prospective employees was how much overtime was a given, and that vacation days meant nothing.

This wasn't the first vacation he'd ruined over the years, just the first international one. Between cranking out lines of code, past vacations danced through my thoughts—a handful of glorified long weekends which I had also worked through. A few hours on the beach, followed by several on my laptop, rinse and repeat.

The intrusions hadn't been so noticeable closer to home, as though proximity to the office had blurred the lines between what was or was not an acceptable request. Typing away in a cramped lodge in Scotland with spotty WiFi was a siren blaring *You should not be working!*

I didn't finish the coding until past nine. It was inelegant, but I'd at least laid the foundation for the development team. I sent it off, renewing my vow to enjoy the rest of my vacation. No more work. No more after tonight.

Ready to make a beeline to the pub Arnav had mentioned, I stopped in my tracks at the bottom of the stairs. Duncan sat reading in the glow of a tartan-shaded lamp.

I grinned like a fool. "I thought you would have gone ahead with Carlos and Harlow."

"I thought I'd better wait for you," he said, closing his book. "Can't have you going off and getting lost on the way to the pub."

"Is it possible to get lost in a town this small?"

"If one set their mind to it."

He sounded like he was up for the challenge. What I wouldn't give to get lost somewhere with Duncan.

He stood to join me. "Ready?"

Just as we opened the front door, Spencer came downstairs. His gaze was fixed on the door, as though he might pass us by without so much as a hello.

"Spencer, are you going to join us at the pub?" I knew the answer, but I couldn't stop asking anyway. I still held out hope that somehow, something would get him to enjoy the trip.

"No, not tonight." He sounded as though he wished he were somewhere else.

"So, some other night?" I asked brightly.

"Probably not." He ran a hand down his face, looking more disheveled than ever. Hair askew, beard unkempt—and I thought

I recognized the shirt he wore from yesterday. "It's nice of you to keep trying when I'm…" He threw a hand toward his face. "This."

His eyes glistened with tears.

"Oh, Spencer, are you okay?"

"I'm all right!" His voice went a little too high and his watery grin wasn't all that convincing. "Just the little problem of my fiancée leaving me right before the trip. Three years together and then—"

He threw his hands in the air. "Gone. But she's doing well, don't worry. I just found out she's moved in with someone else. So, you know, a week on from our break up, she's having no troubles."

"I'm so sorry." That put my experience with Sean into perspective. Guilt cascaded through me that I'd ever thought myself wronged in some way.

"I'm tempted to go back to nonstop crying the way I did the first week after she left, so I'm probably not the best man for a fun night at the pub."

"I know what that's like."

Although…did I? When I broke things off with Sean, I binged Star Trek movies the whole weekend, but I didn't shed a tear. Okay, I cried when Spock died, I wasn't heartless. But I didn't cry over Sean. I'd cried more on this trip than I had over my last break up. I wasn't sure if that said more about that relationship or me.

"Anyway," Spencer said. "I thought a walk might be good."

"With Bea and Rupert?"

"Not a chance. Bea talks to me nonstop about the benefits of marriage and companionship." He blew a raspberry. "The woman can't read the room."

At least she was consistent.

"I really am sorry how things turned out. You deserve better than that."

He gave a stout little nod and a brave smile. "Enjoy the pub."

With that, he walked out the lodge doors into the night.

"Poor guy," Duncan said softly.

"I guess that explains his unhappiness."

We trailed him down the front steps. Spencer slouched away, putting as much distance between him and us—and probably everyone else in this country—as quickly as he could.

"Yet you're always trying to win him over," Duncan said. "Why is that?"

I shrugged, watching Spencer turn down the side street behind the lodge. "I guess I just hate the idea of anyone being so miserable here. We're in the most beautiful place on earth, and none of it seems to be reaching him."

I understood why now. He'd probably planned the trip with his ex-fiancée. Everything I found so exhilarating just twisted the knife for him.

My concern for Spencer's heartbreak dimmed a touch in light of the pleasure that shone on Duncan's face.

"You think it's the most beautiful place on earth?"

"I really do."

He took my hand and raised it, pressing a kiss to my palm. "You do know how to capture the heart of a Scotsman."

# twenty-three

. . .

ARNAV, Carlos, and Harlow sat together at a large table, drinking ales and laughing up a storm. It looked like most of the tourists and college students who had lined the village streets by day now crowded inside the pub. A small band played music in one corner, and drunken youths from the nearby hostel danced between tables.

"What'll you have?" Duncan asked me.

"Whatever you're having."

He raised an eyebrow.

"Within reason. None of that turpentine stuff, please."

He shot me a disapproving look. "The *please* is the only thing that's saving you."

He went to the bar, and I took a seat next to Arnav, who gave me what little room he could.

"How was work, Molly?"

I put on my cockiest grin even if I didn't really feel it. "I slew that beast."

"Where's your drink? You should celebrate."

"Duncan's getting me one. And I don't know if I should celebrate doing work on vacation."

"I do it all the time."

"It seems like this would be a pretty great job to have." Leading the witness, but still.

"It's got its perks. Great views, always outdoors, meet loads of new people." He took a long drink from his glass of what I assumed to be plain cola. "Better than being in an office any day."

I couldn't argue with that. I hadn't been out here very many days and already dreaded going back to my office. Actually…that dread might have started long before my vacation had.

Duncan joined us and placed two small glasses of golden whisky on the table. He sat down across from me, his knees pressed against mine. A sparkly little something flared to life in my chest at the contact.

"That's not the table leg," I said.

"I know." His saucy look sent me soaring even without a drop of alcohol.

Arnav gestured at my drink. "You're coming around to the water of life, eh?"

"I'm learning from the best." I raised my glass in toast to Duncan and took a small sip. This whisky had a citrusy taste on my tongue, but it still had a bite going down. Wasn't sure I'd ever truly get used to that. "This isn't bad at all."

Still watching me, Duncan raised his glass to his mouth. My eyes followed every tiny movement of his lips until I looked away, jealous of the glass.

Arnav leaned over the table, staring into the crowd that danced around the band. "No way! It's one of my mates from uni. Excuse me."

He grabbed his cola, stepped over me, and crossed the room where he greeted a sunburned young man with disheveled hair. Their enthusiastic reunion raised the decibel level in the pub by several points.

Carlos and Harlow didn't seem to notice the noise. Leaning close together in conversation, they might as well have been alone. It seemed she'd finally succumbed to his charms.

And me? Calling myself immune to Duncan's charms would

be a brazen lie. I found his charms quite charming, in fact. Those blue eyes, that beard, those hands—

"Do you often work while you're on vacation?" he asked.

Now that question pulled me straight out of my admiration. On the surface, it might have been casual curiosity, but a hint of disapproval lurked in his tone. I wasn't sure if the disapproval was for my boss because he'd asked, or for me because I'd accepted.

Probably both.

"Yes." No sense in hiding it now.

"Is that why you missed kayaking the other day?"

I nodded. "But I don't take many vacations, so at least there's that."

"Why not?"

Duncan had said people in the U.K. weren't often immediately forthright and direct, but his simple question sure got right to the point.

I scrambled for an answer. How to convince him I wasn't married to my job even though I kind of was? I had no good way to write off Lincoln's constant interruptions of my vacation time, so why did I keep doing it?

"My line of work can be pretty time consuming." Flimsy but true.

"Still wouldn't hurt to have a break now and then."

"It's not that easy."

"Doesn't have to be so hard, either."

My exhale settled close to exasperation. "What's it like being a man? Are you coated in magic bubble wrap that keeps you from feeling pesky emotions?"

"I prefer to think of it as an emotion-repellent forcefield. That sounds more manly."

I laughed, wishing such a thing existed. *"'It doesn't have to be so hard,'"* I echoed, doing my best to mimic his accent but only managing to sound like a tipsy pirate. The whisky deserved all the blame—the drink had already filled my chest with warmth and set me at ease.

Duncan's smile was too knowing. "The forcefield that repels emotions also works on guilt."

"It isn't guilt," I said automatically.

He called out the lie with a simple look.

My shoulders sagged, confirming everything. "It's some guilt. I have a promotion on the line. I thought it was a sure thing, but now I don't know."

"If you take your holiday time, no promotion?"

I splayed my hands on the table. "Maybe."

Lincoln's threats might have been all talk, like a parent counting down from three with their unruly toddler, unsure what they would do when they reached one. Or...he could follow through and pull the promotion from me. There were no good options here. Empty threats would be bad enough, but acting on them? I couldn't think of it.

Duncan watched me with that unreadable, impassive expression he had sometimes. It wasn't unfriendly, but the close scrutiny unnerved me, like he'd found something in me even I didn't see. Times like this, I really wanted to know what was going on in his head.

"You don't think to find something better?"

Fear pricked at me just thinking of it.

"This is a really good company. We're top in the industry. We get more work requests than we can handle." I'd suddenly turned into a PR rep in my quest to justify my choices. "Lincoln is constantly being interviewed and profiled in tech magazines as this golden child success story."

"Is that your boss?" he asked. I nodded. "And what does he tell them about all the hard work *you* put in? He mentions the rest of your coworkers, yes?"

I slumped a little more, mentally scrolling through the articles I'd read. The rest of the team were never mentioned by name. We were all lumped in with *Lincoln and JBQ.* I'd never thought much about it, but maybe that was just one more facet of the problem.

"So you're breaking your back to build his reputation." Duncan's voice wasn't unkind, but the truth of his words hit me right across the face.

Once, I'd thought I would try to build something for myself. Instead, I'd spent nearly ten years furthering my boss's image. I'd been paid well enough I never thought to complain, especially after that dark year when I was flat broke, but was the money really the only thing I wanted?

What had happened to those dreams of being known for eye-catching websites and promo materials? What about my goal to create a business people sought out because they loved my work? I'd let those dreams get swallowed up by practicality. Safety. The sensible path of corporate work.

Duncan leaned against the table, and I mirrored his movement, closing the distance between us.

"I was once where you are. Worked my arse off for someone else—evenings, weekends, and all the rest—thinking it was good enough. But I reached a point where I wasn't satisfied with 'good enough' anymore. That's why I took the leap and started my own company. I had a rough first year of it and questioned it a hundred times. But I wouldn't go back now. I couldn't be satisfied with just good enough when I could have the best."

I shifted in my seat again, replacing the slight distance between us. Just good enough wasn't such a bad thing when *the best* risked the very real possibility of *the worst*. Sometimes when you step out into the void, all you do is fall.

"Not everyone can start their own company." Sounded a little pathetic even to me.

"Why not?"

"Is that your motto? *Why not?*"

His mouth twitched in response. Where did he get his relentless confidence? And could he bottle up some reserves for me?

"You need more than just naked enthusiasm," I said. "You need clients. A business plan. Marketing know-how. A way to differentiate yourself from everybody else. A buffer of savings to keep you afloat."

He raised his glass. "There's your to-do list."

Ugh. The pub was entirely too hot and cramped for this conversation. "Going off on your own takes work and planning. It's not something you just jump into blindly."

Not again, anyway.

"There's no gain without a little risk. I think you have the capability."

I laughed at his unfounded optimism. If only he knew. "I also have an apartment I don't want to lose and an elderly, arthritic dog who needs medication."

"Is he unwell?"

"He has a slight touch of kidney disease." We'd kept it mostly in check with medication so far, but that would only last so long. The question of how long pinched at me. But talking about Shatner's declining health bummed me out even more than talking about my job. "He's just old. He's gone all gray around the muzzle. He's ten, so that's like, I don't know, forty-nine in human years."

Duncan's mouth tipped up delectably at my little jab, and his knee knocked against mine. "Ancient."

"Exactly." The warmth of his touch almost made up for all the talk about work.

He took another drink of whisky. "So. Your business plan."

*No.* I did not need him joining my mother on the sidelines of my life, waving pom-poms and cheering me into self-employment. I'd already taken that road and found a dead-end. More like a cliff, and I'd careened over, *Thelma & Louise* style.

"So you do have a flaw. You're pushy."

He looked thoroughly unsurprised by the assessment. "I like to think of it as assertive."

"Bossy."

"Bold."

I shook my head at him. Honestly, I liked those traits when it came to how he pursued me, but I needed to shut down his desire to guide me into another round of ill-advised entrepreneurship.

"Do you have any idea how many web designers I know who valiantly struck out on their own and are now tending bar in some dive just to scrape by? It's a lot." I could have given my personal experience but telling him of my failure in the face of his success was too much right now. Impulsive and destitute didn't go so well with bold and assertive. "Can we talk about something else? You are literally killing my buzz."

"If you like. But I'll say that the woman whose boss calls for help from five thousand miles away sounds like a woman who can handle things on her own."

# twenty-four

. . .

A SECOND WHISKY LATER, and I was *not* handling things on my own. I'd finished the first too quickly just to stop thinking about Duncan's casual assessment of my job, and his mistaken belief I could run my own business. I'd downed the second whisky trying not to think about his hands, his mouth, his eyes, and everything in between.

Now, I casually clutched the edge of the table to stop from spinning, pretending at an air of normalcy I definitely didn't feel.

"After my father died, I knew I had to change things." Duncan's quiet somberness sounded strangely loud in the riotous pub. "Losing him made me finally realize I needed to take a step back from work. Clock out on time, delegate tasks, take vacations. My marriage was over by then, but I make sure nothing comes before my girls now."

He was being so wonderful, confiding in me about his feelings over his father's death, and I could hardly concentrate on what he said for fear I might topple over.

I altered my facial expression to convey concern but must have missed the mark. He blinked hard at me, looking me over.

"Are you feeling all right?" He glanced down at my empty whisky glass and back to me. "Too much?"

"A bit." I'd heard someone say drinking whisky was like being wrapped in a warm blanket, but right now I suspected whisky was about to smother me with a pillow.

"Come with me." He stood and held out a hand. "You'll feel better outside."

I stood, but the pub tilted and I swayed on my feet. Nope. Not good. Probably best if I just crawled beneath the table to sleep it off.

"I've got you." He wrapped an arm around me and held my hand as he led me through the pub doors.

Add it to the list of his wonderful qualities: he could make taking care of a drunk woman look romantic.

"I saw a little store just down here," he said.

The cool night air came as a relief after the stifling pub, and I gulped it in. The sky hadn't yet darkened fully, leaving the street in a hazy evening glow. The light didn't stop me from stumbling just a teensy bit as we walked, though.

Maybe more than a teensy bit.

Duncan kept a firm grip on my waist to keep me upright. Every few feet, the ground pitched beneath me, and I clung to him harder. I didn't want to think too much about the poor impression I was making here, but I couldn't have walked back to the lodge by myself if I'd had the whole night to do it.

We made a quick pitstop at the corner store, and then he led me down to the bay's edge until he found access to the shore. Smooth rocks littered the beach, and I had a hard time keeping my footing. I picked across them like I was moving over a frozen lake, afraid I'd go down any minute. The air was cooler, though, and punched a small hole through the whisky haze that enveloped me.

"Let's sit you down." He helped me lower onto a rock right on the waterline. "Take off your shoes and socks."

Too far gone to question his instructions, I tugged at my laces, slipped off my shoes, and pulled off my socks, baring my feet in the fading light. I frowned at the chips in my turquoise nail polish. A pedicure hadn't seemed like a necessity for the trip. My shoes were supposed to stay firmly on my feet my whole visit here.

That was probably a metaphor for something.

"Put them in the water," he coaxed.

I dipped one toe and sucked in a breath. He reached over me, took my calves in each hand, and pressed my feet all the way into the water.

"That's freezing!" I screeched.

"I know," he said, still holding my legs. "It will help."

I didn't know how dunking my feet in ice water would help sober me up. Right then, all I knew was that his hands were on my legs. Their warmth edged off the cold that already crept up from my feet. He turned to face me, so close I couldn't think of anything but our kiss. His eyes dropped to my mouth as though he was thinking about it, too.

Instead of moving in closer, he eased away from me like a perfect gentleman. I must have been too drunk to kiss. I wasn't sure I agreed with that one, but I wasn't so far gone I would beg.

Yet.

He let go of my legs and rummaged around in his plastic shop bag to present me with a gigantic jug of bottled water. "This will help, too."

Then he shook out two tablets from a little container. "And these. Paracetamol for your head."

Even with my feet dipped in the freezing Portree Bay and a steady stream of water to heroically battle it out with the whisky I'd consumed, my brain still didn't feel attached to my body. At least the worst of it was in my head and not my stomach.

*Please stay in my head and not my stomach.*

"I'm sorry to put you through all this."

"Don't be. I should have done a better job looking out for you. Never should have got you that second." He smiled, and in my weakened state, the affection in his eyes just about knocked me over. "I've been funneling whisky to a novice."

"Maybe this was part of your plan."

"My plan wouldn't have been so circuitous." He had my legs in his hands again, pulling my feet from the water and into his lap where they left dark wet patches on his jeans.

I wiggled my toes to check that I still could. They moved, even if I couldn't feel them much.

"Don't want you to get too cold." He rubbed my feet between his hands, getting the blood moving through them.

As methods of sobering up went, this one wasn't so bad.

When my feet were sufficiently warmed, he opened a bottle of orange liquid. "Have one of these."

"What's this? *Irn-Bru*? Those aren't even words."

"Drink up. It's juice. Fizzy drink. What do you call it? Soda-pop."

He said the last with a distinctly flat, generic American tone that made me laugh.

I took a swig from the bottle but winced. "It's so sweet."

"That's Irn-Bru for you. Full of sugars, and the fizz should help your stomach. Between that and the water and the shock to your system, you should come right."

The drink was sugary the way Old Tarty was decorated: garish, grotesque, and should probably be outlawed. Addictive, too—I didn't love the taste, but I couldn't stop taking sips from the bottle.

We sat for a few minutes listening to the water lap the rocks, Duncan's hands moving over my feet.

"It's not like I've never thought about starting my own company," I said out of nowhere, suddenly ready for the conversation I'd chickened out on earlier. "I did, once."

"What happened?" His fingers worked lovely little circles on my toes.

"I completely tanked." Saying the words out loud stung, but freedom came with them, too. I'd tried so hard to move on and pretend that year had never happened, maybe I needed to admit the truth. "I worked for a big, sterile firm out of college where I did a lot of lifeless work for faceless accounts. What you'd call 'just good enough'—soul crushing, but with steady pay."

He watched me with those blue, bare-your-soul eyes. Caught between them and his hypnotic foot-rubbing skills, I kept talking. "I'd seen coworkers take the plunge and start their own businesses. I had this dream of marrying my art with the web, creating logos, designs, and sites that were more than just functional. Kind of a one-stop branding shop. And I did it. I quit my job with starry-eyed expectations for my future."

That thrill of stepping out on my own still burned in my memory, a rush of adrenaline that I'd been certain would carry me to success. "I am *practical*, Duncan. You have no idea."

His expression was like pure sweetness washing over me. "I might have some idea."

"With this, I followed my heart. I had so much enthusiasm and drive, and I just knew everything would work out. I thought I had it all planned." I exhaled bitter laughter. "I got a few clients. I created some gorgeous websites, and a few logos I was really proud of. But it wasn't enough. Enthusiasm only got me so far. Then it was all scrambling and grasping and clinging to hope."

Hope became desperation, and desperation finally despair.

"I didn't know how to market myself, I didn't understand my competition, and I probably undercharged the accounts I had. I scraped by for almost a year, burning through all my savings and then some. I moved back in with my parents. Sold my car for the cash. When it was all over, I had *nothing*. So. That was that. No more blind idealism."

My stomach rolled with the memory of the lowest of my lows. I'd come through it with a more cautious approach to personal finances, a willingness to endure unreasonable amounts of overtime, and an aversion to the cheap ramen noodles I'd lived off of during those long months.

"And then I finally got this job. It's a really good job at a really good company. Maybe there are parts that could be better, but total failure is worse. I took a leap and landed on my face."

"Nothing is ever one hundred percent certain."

"Thanks, Callum MacZen." I knocked my toes against his fingers and immediately regretted it when he let go of my feet.

"You've learned from your mistakes. You know what to do differently next time."

This man and his confidence. Maybe that should go into the flaw category, too.

"Next time? Are you listening? Sure, I want something more, but not when it comes with a chance of losing *everything*. I can't do that again."

"Molly, I ruined my marriage. I didn't take time for myself, let alone for my wife or our daughters. I was so dedicated to my business, I neglected the most valuable thing I had. I was selfish and short-sighted, and my priorities were all wrong. I paid the price, and my family fell apart." He tucked a lock of hair behind my ear, trailing his fingers along my neck. "Does that mean I should stop trying to find lasting love? Should I give up and become a hermit?"

*No!* I wanted to shout. *Don't stop trying for love!* Not when I sat right in front of him.

"Or," he said, his fingers lightly working their way over my shoulder and down my arm until they intertwined with mine. "Should I learn from my mistakes and try again?"

This man and his charm had me turned upside down even worse than the drink. I wasn't sure if I wanted to call B.S. on his enthusiasm or lean right into it.

"Seems a bit of a stretch to compare the two," I said softly. My failed business didn't seem nearly so crushing as a failed marriage, no matter how it had felt in the moment.

"Probably. But I hate to see you let one failure stop you from ever trying again."

Hmm. I saw his point, even if I didn't necessarily agree with it.

He watched me like I had a spotlight on me. "Did you enjoy the work you did when you were on your own?"

I sucked in a breath, every word of argument crumbling away.

"I loved it. All the custom work, the creative freedom, the connection with my clients. Before things fell apart…I was really happy."

Not just happy but satisfied. Content with my work in a way I hadn't managed to capture again. Nothing I'd done for Lincoln compared.

He ducked his head to catch my eyes. "I don't think anything that makes you glow as bright as you are now should be set aside forever."

Maybe not. But I'd played it safe so long, I wasn't sure how to get back into the business of taking risks.

"Are all Scottish men so wise?"

"It's all in the MacZenmaster handbook."

Somehow, he'd made sobering up by starlight both a romantic moment and a weirdly reassuring career pep-talk. Still, I wasn't in a state to make any major decisions. Not when I was this tempted to throw myself all in with this Scot.

# twenty-five

. . .

THE SUN WAS TRYING to kill me.

I curled up in bed and pulled the blanket over my eyes, blocking out the offending light. Despite the aspirin I'd taken and Duncan's unique assistance, my head throbbed in angry retaliation for all the alcohol I'd consumed last night.

Eventually, I'd sobered up enough for him to guide me back to the lodge, his arm wrapped around my waist so I wouldn't lose my balance. Outside our rooms, he'd given me the last of the jug of water, followed by a sweet kiss goodnight on my forehead.

After all his talk about trying for love again, I would have wanted more than just a forehead kiss to seal the evening—if I hadn't been worried about suddenly seeing the contents of my stomach all over the hallway carpet.

Now, I only wanted to lie in bed as still as possible and make empty promises to never drink again. Our group would finally hike to the Old Man of Storr, the sight that had inspired me to come to Scotland in the first place and had teased me with glimpses every time we drove in and out of Portree—and just opening my eyes felt like cruel and unusual punishment. How was I supposed to actually *reach* it?

I finally ventured downstairs, taking delicate steps the whole way, and found Duncan on the landing.

"Harlow said you were on your way down. How are you feeling?"

I groaned. "I think I need new blood. That's a thing, right?"

"Only if you're Keith Richards."

"Then I guess I'll have to tough it out." That, or crawl under my bed and moan all day. I could go either way. "Thanks again for last night. I still feel foolish."

He put a hand on my back in consolation. "Whisky'll do that."

Bea and Rupert came down the stairs, sweeping us into the dining room with them. Almost as soon as I sat down, someone put a plate heaped with food in front of me. The Scottish fried breakfast shone up at me in all its glory: fried tomato, fried round of blood pudding, a sausage, a messy pile of haggis, a flat scone, a fried egg, fried mushrooms, and—unbelievably—baked beans. Now that was one item I hadn't expected to see in Scotland, and certainly not on a breakfast plate.

My head throbbed a vicious beat, but my stomach growled a reminder I'd had nothing but whisky, water, and Irn-Bru in the last twelve hours. Mostly confident I wouldn't lose my breakfast, I tucked in.

I made short work of the egg, sausage, mushrooms, and tomato. The scone tasted weirdly bland, which made sense when Bea pointed out its primary ingredient were potatoes. This left the haggis, baked beans, and blood pudding on my plate, two of which I was willing to at least try.

Before I had a chance to change my mind, I took a bite of the haggis. It turned out tastier than I'd thought, even if the peppery spices overwhelmed. My mind shut down the voices reminding me of the contents—it couldn't be that much worse than a typical American hot dog, which were also packed full of questionable meat and sprinkled with delicious flavorings.

Next, I cut a small bite of the blood pudding. I looked at the piece of sausage speared on my fork a long moment before I popped it in my mouth. The flavor was coppery, as Duncan had described, and the texture mealy, but it wasn't the worst thing I'd ever eaten.

The baked beans wallowed untouched in their brown juices. I hated them as a summertime side dish and wasn't any more inclined to eat them at breakfast, even in Scotland.

Rupert leaned toward me kitty-corner across the table. "What do you think of the haggis?"

"It's not bad." It wouldn't go into my permanent meal rotation, but I didn't find it horrifying, either. The meat had been ground so fine, it had no real texture to it, and the spices overpowered the underlying organ flavor.

Duncan shot a little look of pride my way and I had a strange feeling I'd passed some sort of Scottish hazing ritual. Did haggis really matter that much to people? I didn't go around pressing mayonnaise and bologna sandwiches on strangers back home. Then again, I did encourage everyone I knew to get their burgers at Red Mill, so maybe it wasn't all that different.

"It's just like I told you about men, dear," Bea said as she sliced her mushrooms.

Unfazed but uncomprehending, I nodded. "Yes, I was just thinking that men are like haggis."

"We're better when we're fried?" Carlos suggested.

"Better after a stiff drink?" Duncan said.

"Better avoided altogether?" Spencer offered.

"Unexpected," she said briskly.

*Unexpected* had been the theme of the trip. For liking plans and lists, I had to admit, the surprises hadn't been all bad. Case in point: the man across the table from me. He went right on looking at me in a way that made my stomach tumble. Anyway, I hoped it was because of him, and not the blood and entrails I'd just eaten.

"Well, I'm still not trying it." Harlow pushed around the different meats on her plate with her fork, her face scrunched up as though she'd been offered something scraped off a shoe instead of something scraped out of a sheep.

"Cavemen ate meat," I pointed out.

"Not the entrails."

Spencer laughed. "You think primitive peoples didn't eat entrails, brains, and organs? I'm pretty sure cavemen weren't as choosy as that."

Harlow glared at him. "It's mixed with oats, and I can't eat that, either. It's not healthy."

The edible portion of her plate consisted of fruit, vegetables, and eggs, but even that seemed a bit of a stretch. Didn't most fruits and vegetables require cultivation beyond cavemen's abilities? Hard to imagine cavemen carefully tending their tomato starts in the Neolithic.

"I saw a documentary about this. Most cavemen died from dehydration caused by diarrhea. If you want to call that healthy..." He shrugged and went back to eating his breakfast.

I couldn't tell if Spencer's comments on death by dehydration meant he was feeling better or worse.

Spots of color appeared on Harlow's cheeks and her eyes narrowed like she wished she could set him on fire. "I'm going to finish getting ready. Excuse me."

She stood and left the table.

Carlos shot him a look. "Well done. You must be a delight at parties."

"What?" Spencer didn't have an ounce of apology in him. "I'm not the one trying to hook up with her. Fad diets are all scams anyway."

"I quite agree," Rupert said. "People these days with all their no-fat, no-carbohydrate oddities."

He blinked hard and shuddered, apparently realizing he'd just insulted his own wife's dietary oddities.

"Although," he said slowly, "sometimes there is merit to such things."

Bea pursed her lips and set her napkin on her plate. "I think I should get ready, too." She pushed away from the table in the same way a cruise ship gets underway—slowly and with a great deal of drama.

Carlos turned to Rupert. "Forty years of bliss, huh?"

Rupert stood from the table and patted the younger man on the shoulder. "When you find the right one, you learn to overlook the little things."

I felt he'd taken that adage too far, but I liked the sentiment anyway.

---

The Old Man of Storr loomed magnificent and mysterious on the hillside, making me completely forget my hangover.

Okay, I hadn't forgotten it at all, what with my head still pounding and my limbs aching as though I was coming down with something. But the sight out my mini-bus window dimmed my post-drunken misery to tolerable levels.

I'd caught glimpses of the Storr in the last two days, but the closer we got, the more I buzzed with excitement. I left the coach ready to sprint up the path to reach it.

I did *not* sprint, just to be clear.

The first section of trail formed an easy footpath that led through green, windswept grasses. The morning was mild, with heavy clouds streaking across the sky. The air smelled crisp and and fresh, and everything around us seemed to say "You are in Scotland."

I couldn't stop grinning at everything. The dirt path? Glorious. Rocks and stones? Delightful. Even Bea's pinched expression looked good up here.

Massive stone slabs crushed together to form an imposing horizon. Behind us lay rugged slopes leading down to a loch, and beyond that, the Sound of Raasay, shining in the morning sun.

I sparked like a live wire, thrilled I'd finally made it.

Bea and Rupert trundled along, hardly looking around as they chatted away. Carlos and Harlow raced up, engaged in a friendly, if slightly dangerous, competition to the top. Spencer stayed in his own world, trudging up the hillside as if the clouds had come out just for him. Lewis and Arnav seemed long used to Skye, and while they remained as friendly and enthusiastic as ever, they'd seen it all several times over.

Only Duncan seemed to see the same views I did. His gaze held the same reverence and awe that filled my heart as we looked across the isle. He was right there with me, reveling in the gleam of the lochs, the smell of the winds carrying over the hillside, the tumultuous sky that went on forever. I didn't need to try to imagine him in some long-ago time—he belonged here, now.

I took a few pictures and then stood and tried to burn these images into my memory so I could take them home to cherish. Duncan stood at my side while I gazed out at the deep green lake shining so bright beneath the sun I could hardly stand it.

"You're crying again." His low voice wrapped me up in a gentle hug. "No one's died here." He paused, looking around. "I take that back. People have most certainly died here."

I laughed, wiping the tears from my cheeks. "It's this place." I gestured as though I could take in the whole of the view, the moment, the history all at once. "It's just…"

Magical? Beautiful? Home?

"Come here."

He opened his arms, and I tucked myself against him like I belonged there, letting him shelter me from the buffeting wind. I shut my eyes, and for just a moment, it was magical. Beautiful. Home. I pressed my cheek against his shoulder, inhaling his delicious scent, lost in the soothing sound of his breathing.

For as much as this man thrilled me, he brought me peace, too. I didn't have to keep scrambling for security. I could finally relax and just be.

He pulled back and ducked his head to examine me, seeking confirmation of something. The wind whipping down the glen sent my hair swirling in the air like a tangible version of the electricity that crackled between us. The smile we shared felt significant, as though we'd decided something profound with just a look.

Did that really happen outside of romance novels and Bea's university train ride? Whatever it was, I wanted to run with this surety and trust in it instead of examining it for flaws until it faded away.

"Everything okay down there?" Bea's voice carried to us on the wind.

"We're all fine here," Duncan called back without breaking eye contact with me.

"She's so helpful," I said softly.

His mouth quirked. "Always looking out for you."

We continued up the pathway together, which must have satisfied Bea, who returned her attention to her own footsteps. Hopefully soon, she would get far enough ahead she wouldn't feel the need to turn around every five minutes to see what the stragglers were up to.

"It's unspeakably beautiful out here." I went back to the conversation I'd been trying to have with Duncan before it had dissolved into smoldering stares and longing silence. "It gets to me."

"There's nothing wrong with that. I've been overwhelmed a time or two this week, myself."

The cheeky look he shot my way lit my chest with sparklers like a Fourth of July celebration. *Hard same.*

Had I ever had *this* before? I wouldn't have described my love life as boring—although Jill would have gladly called it worse—but I'd never known anything like this rush of excitement, this eagerness to know everything about someone. I couldn't be sure it wouldn't all burn up in a moment like flash paper, but I wanted to enjoy the flame while it lasted.

Distance had made the craggy rock outcroppings look almost small from the car park, but as we drew closer, they towered even higher above. The hillside grew rockier, and the wind chilled my exposed skin. I slipped on my rain jacket to keep the cold from seeping through my fleece and pulled my wool hat on. The path stayed a struggle to the last, and my legs burned with the effort, but nothing could have convinced me to turn back.

We reached a small section of trail where a dozen other hikers had stopped to look behind and snap photographs. Once I made sure of my footing on the sloped path, I turned, too. The sight obliterated my breath, pushing out every other thought as it demanded my full attention.

This was it. The view in the photo that had led me here. The Old Man of Storr, a rock crag standing apart from the cliffside, with the sound in the background and rugged peaks on the horizon. *Isle of Skye, Inner Hebrides.*

I wanted to sear this view into my memory, breathe it in and store it in my lungs. I wanted to swallow it whole and carry it around with me forever. I pulled out the camera and took photos but slipped it away again. Shaken by the wind, I hugged myself and tried to simply live in the moment. Be fully present. Experience the now.

Bea and Rupert perched together on a low rock, Carlos and Harlow shared a quiet conversation, and even Spencer seemed struck by the sight as he gazed into the distance.

Duncan came up behind me, resting his hands on my shoulders. I leaned against his chest, and he wrapped his arms tight around me. His warmth soaked through my skin down to my bones. Now *this* was a moment I could live in.

"Is it everything you'd hoped?" he murmured in my ear.

This view, this trip, these experiences—my answer was the same.

"Better."

Eventually, we returned to the path that climbed up and around the crags until we reached the summit of the Storrs. As though seeing its cue, rain fell in heavy drops, splashing against our jackets and welling up in puddles on the trail. The clouds blurred down from the sky into sheets of rain over the mountains, making the view that much more enchanting. Lewis pointed out places of note, but I couldn't take it all in. The Trotternish Ridge, the Isles of Harris, Raasay, Rona—it was all too much to keep straight just then.

The downpour discouraged us from lingering too long as we walked down from the ridge line. I kept my focus on the rocky path, desperate not to slip. Bea and Rupert pulled retractable walking sticks from their packs and navigated the way down as nimbly as prim mountain goats. Whatever else I sometimes thought about them, they sure seemed to know what they were doing. I kept my footing, but it was slow going.

"I know you said your legs would give you trouble after that bike ride, but I didn't expect it to be this difficult for you to walk."

Duncan's voice came from right behind me, and if the trail hadn't been so muddy, I would have turned around to catch the smile I knew he wore.

"I'm trying not to take the quickest route down on my backside." Baby steps, I kept telling myself, baby steps.

"You're right, your backside should be protected at all costs."

His laughter buoyed me, even if I didn't pick up the pace. The path looked slippery as hell.

"You know," he said, that ruffle of playfulness in his voice, "Bea and Rupert have half a kilometer on you."

I looked up to see the older couple far below. They'd managed the return path just fine, meanwhile my heart jolted with every wobbly step.

"I'll half a kilometer you," I mumbled under my breath. That made him laugh harder, a rich low rumble I wanted to sink into. How could I fall with his deep voice to catch me?

I briefly skidded on stones and sucked in a breath. I had to stop a second to find my balance again. I would *not* have a repeat of Ben Macdui. "You could be helpful."

He took my hand, his grip firm and warm, keeping me steady. Outwardly, anyway. Inside? Nothing but a tangle of giddy emotions.

"That was a steep go there at the end," he said once we'd put the worst of the path behind us.

Why did he sound so surprised? I hadn't been inching down the path for my own benefit. Well. Actually, it *had* been for my own benefit. Still.

"Next trip, I'm buying a walking stick. Or two."

"There's already a next trip, is there?" He squeezed my hand, the tilt of his mouth one hundred percent smug.

"Definitely."

# twenty-six

. . .

BACK IN THE LODGE, the time had come to face the call I'd been putting off. But I needed to do it at least once. I arranged myself on my tiny bed and tapped my mother's contact on my phone.

"Honey! It's so good to hear from you!" She sounded like it had been a year since we'd last talked instead of only a few days.

"I'm sorry I didn't call earlier. I've been busy in the evenings."

"Busy evenings aren't a bad thing." She sounded so saucy, I had to roll my eyes. "Are you having a good time?"

"Yes." I could fit whole worlds into that tiny answer. "I'm in love with this country. Everything is as green as you think it's going to be—and greener. The towns, the architecture, the history—I can't do it justice. And I'm never going to recover from the food."

She laughed. "You must be having the time of your life. I can hear it in your voice. You're relaxed."

I caught a glimpse of myself in the bathroom mirror and hardly recognized the woman I saw. Rosy-cheeked and seraphic, I'd become Our Lady of the Highlands. My smile seemed etched on permanently. How could I be so totally at ease when I'd spent every day in Scotland finding new methods of total exhaustion?

And yet, I wasn't sure I'd ever felt so at peace. It must have been some magical convergence of the fresh air, the grueling physical feats, and close proximity to one particular Scot.

Duncan definitely had restorative properties that required further research.

"I think I actually am relaxed."

I genuinely couldn't remember the last time I'd been anything close to this relaxed. Of course, I hadn't had anything close to this much of a vacation before, either.

"I'm so happy for you. How are the people on tour with you? A good bunch?"

"They are." Two seemed the right number of words here. Gabbing about Duncan with Jill was one thing. She might give me a hard time, but she would keep it to sane levels. Mom would start planning a Highland wedding as soon as she caught on to my inclinations.

Although, seriously, a wedding in the Highlands would be gorgeous, wouldn't it?

No. I needed to escort that *extremely* premature notion out ASAP.

"I'm glad to hear it. Does this mean you'll start flying more often?"

The less I thought about planes, the better. I didn't need to preemptively ramp up my anxiety. "I'm still in denial about the return flights."

Her gentle laughter made me weirdly homesick.

"At least you tried. You wouldn't want to go your whole life without one big trip."

*One big trip.* That homesickness turned into plain old sickness. Was that all this was, then? My one big trip before I settled back into my old routine? I wasn't sure I wanted to completely let it go. But that was the trouble with vacations—at some point, they had to end.

The ache in my chest amplified like someone had cranked a dial in my heart. I couldn't think about going home yet, either.

"How are things on your end?" I asked before I could slip too far into my sad little thoughts.

"Oh, we're the same as always. Although, your father is so delighted with the belly dancing lessons, he's been having me put on shows for him—"

"Okay Mom, I have to go down for dinner. It's been good talking to you." Let's just nip that conversation in the bud right now.

"You, too, honey. Enjoy the rest of your trip. Soak it up."

"I plan to." For as long as I could.

———

After dinner, Carlos, Harlow, Duncan, and I met up at the nearby pub again, where Carlos bought us a round of ales from a local brewery. The ale made for easier drinking than the peaty whiskies we'd sampled, thank goodness—although I would pace myself more appropriately than I had last night.

We settled in at a table where the sides of Duncan's leg pressed against mine. Seemed like we had more room than that tonight, but I couldn't complain. Give me all the coziness.

"I didn't think you could drink that," I said to Harlow. "The grains and all."

"The occasional drink won't hurt."

Her fervor for her diet seemed to come and go. She turned back to Carlos, who pretty obviously delighted in her attention.

I couldn't feel bad about being edged out when that left me on my own with Duncan.

"Tell me about some of the houses you've restored," I said.

He ticked his head to the side as though considering my request.

"The most recent renovation was in Kensington, restoring the house to suit its 1920s history. We gutted the first level, expanded the kitchen and bathroom, and resurfaced all the hardwood floors."

"Do you do any of the actual work, or are you more like the foreman?"

"Do I do any of the actual work? Do I look like the numbers man?" With his elbows still on the table, he flexed his biceps, and I laughed at the way they danced beneath his shirt. I wanted to grab one in the worst way.

"Well, you look like you could boss people around pretty well."

"My crew would agree, although I don't. Do I seem tough to you?" He stared me down with his fiercest glower.

If he'd looked at me that way the first day we met, I might have dropped out of the tour entirely. Tonight, it did something magical to my insides, lighting me up and fanning those flames. I knew more of the man behind the stare now and feared no ill-intent.

Pretty sure I would like all of Duncan's intentions.

"Very tough," I confirmed.

"I'm safe as kittens." His glower disappeared, and his face relaxed. "I have a good crew. I couldn't do anything without them. I get to do what I enjoy and still have the freedom to travel and meet fascinating women in the process."

Hmm. *Women.* Plural. My brain wanted to ask questions, but my body said *Let it slide.*

He watched me with an intensity as though he saw me in a way no one else did. His eyes were so bright and so blue, they reminded me of the Fairy Pools. I could get lost in them and never want to find my way out again.

Hey, look at that—I'd already finished my ale.

Harlow touched my arm, bringing me out of the crystal pools of Duncan's eyes. Ugh, I was far gone.

"Carlos and I are going for a walk," she said. "It stays light out so long, and we don't want to waste it. See you later."

Carlos saluted us and ushered Harlow from the pub. A strange pang of regret corkscrewed through me. I'd intended to see as much of Scotland as I could, and here I sat holed up in a bar. For all I'd joked about cozy gardens and sitting rooms, I really did want to make the most of this trip.

"Are we wasting our time here?" I asked Duncan. His brows tugged together, and I realized that question probably wasn't as direct as it had sounded in my head. "I mean, should we be living it up, going to look at the…" I waved my hand around in the air, searching for the word. "The scenery?"

"I don't think we're wasting our time, Molly." He seemed to be talking about more than just the one evening. "Anyway, you're getting a feel for local culture."

"That does sound better than saying I'm just sitting around in a bar." Pub. Whatever.

Determined not to have a repeat of the drunken night before, I got up to stretch my legs and get a glass of water from the bartender. Pubman. Publican? The place was so packed, I had to wait just to ask for water. Back home, people crowded around the bar and shouted over each other to get the bartender's attention. Here, it seemed to be done through eye contact with the bartender. No shouting, no pushing, he just chose a person and took their order.

I wasn't sure I was even in line.

After a minute or two, I realized a youth-hostel-looking sort of guy stood next to me.

"Having a nice night?" he asked.

Everything about him reminded me of Arnav—he looked young, a little rumpled from his travels, and his face flushed pink from alcohol.

"Yes, very, thanks."

His eyes went wide. "Are you American?"

"Yes?" I couldn't tell if his surprise was good or bad.

"That is brilliant!"

I'd never seen anyone so excited to meet an American before, and it felt like a bit of a trap. "Thank you?"

He gestured at the back corner of the pub. "My mates and I usually see American women on our backpacking trips, but we've had no luck this round. But here you are! Do you want to join us?"

"Thanks, but no. I'm with a tour group."

"Oh yeah? What have you seen?"

I rattled off a list of things our group had seen and done in the last week. Listing them out, it made for an impressive set of accomplishments, even if I didn't quite have all the pictures to prove my part in them.

The young man stepped closer to me. "What brings you to Scotland?"

I shook my head, unable to give one set answer. I'd wanted to see the sights but found more here than I could explain to a stranger in line at a bar. "I just wanted the adventure."

He seemed to take that as an invitation, and he leaned even closer. "I lost my number. Can I have yours?"

"Can you—?" I needed a second. No way did he just try to pick me up using that tired line. Maybe I'd downed my ale too quickly or maybe I'd spent the last week with a man who put this boy to shame, but the stale pick-up line struck me as hilarious. Laughter burst out before I could stop it.

His leer collapsed as I broke into a fit of uncontrollable giggles. Covering my mouth didn't help. The laughter just kept coming until my sides ached and tears sprang to my eyes. Nearby pub patrons turned to see what was so funny.

"I'm sorry," I managed between giggles. "I've never actually heard that one in the wild, and I..."

I kept laughing, is what I did.

He summoned whatever pride he had left and ignored me as though he had no idea what was wrong with this crazy woman. The poor guy got the bartender's attention, paid for his drink, and beelined back to his friends, leaving me giggling at the bar. I asked for my water, still grinning.

"Now that was brutal."

I turned to see Duncan sidled up close to me. He didn't seem big on personal space these days. I had no complaints.

"It's been a long time since I've seen someone shot down so totally."

Chastened, I stifled my laughter. "I did tell him I was sorry."

"The boy's ego may never recover."

"He's young. He'll be fine." I took my water from the bartender and sipped at it, small bursts of laughter still rippling through me. *Can I have yours?* Amazing.

"Clearly, his skills aren't as good as he'd hoped. It's a terrible line." Duncan glanced from the corner where the youth hostel guys were and back to me. "He never should have tried such a thing on the likes of you."

"Seriously. To think I came all this way only to fall for such an awful pick-up line. I'm affronted."

His mouth twitched. "I can tell."

"Does that line ever work?"

"I've never tried it, so I couldn't say."

"No, you wouldn't use a line like that." I looked him over. "What lines do you use?"

"And give them all away?"

"Oh, please say that Culloden thing wasn't a line. I really liked that."

"Oh, no. That came from the heart."

Every time this man talked about his heart, mine went a little wild.

He ordered a whisky, although not a turpentine one. Say what he would about the peaty ones, I didn't intend to work my way up to them. Our table had been overtaken in our absence, so we made ourselves comfortable on a pair of barstools, snugged close together. I leaned one elbow heavily on the bar and rested my chin in my hand. My skin burned like a little inferno where our legs pressed together, but no way would I move.

I gestured at his glass. "What is this whisky?"

The answer sounded more like a sneeze than a name. I couldn't have repeated or spelled it for my life.

He slid the glass closer. "Have a taste if you like."

I sniffed at it, the aroma surprisingly pleasant. Hyper-aware of every movement of my lips as he watched me, I took a sip. The rich flavor warmed my tongue and lingered even after the burn. Still strong for my tastes, but not bad.

"That's really good," I said, sliding it back. "You know your stuff."

"It's my national duty to know my whisky."

"Obviously." I wondered what it would be like to taste the whisky on his mouth. I could imagine its spicy heat on his lips. I took a long drink of cold water to try to head those thoughts off before they could take hold. Nope, no chance. They'd already stuck in my mind.

"I wish I had a few of the whisky chocolates right now."

Sure. *That* was what I wanted.

"They are good," he said. "Chock full of calories, though."

"Yes, you need to get this whole thing under control." I made the *wax-on* motions in front of his chest. "I didn't want to say anything, but you've really let yourself go."

He laughed modestly, no doubt well aware of what excellent shape he was in. Fifty or not, he could have bench pressed the kid who'd just come onto me. The thought did nothing to chill the heat coursing through my veins.

"How do you do it? Do you work out every day?"

"Yes."

"Ugh, I couldn't do it. Too much work."

I did spin classes once a week if I was feeling dedicated, but I wouldn't pretend I managed much more than that. A little bit of strength training while I watched reality TV, but daily cardio? Not interested. I didn't want a better booty *that* badly.

"Mmm, you're plenty sexy just as you are." He looked liked he was thinking about something *delicious*.

Funny, well read, and thought I was sexy as-is? What dream world had this Scottish silver fox descended from?

"Fifty looms," he explained after a pause. "Working out every day helps me fight it off, at least figuratively."

"You're definitely winning the fight." Was he ever. I might have sighed as I looked him over. "No Viagra for you."

His eyes went wide, his whisky glass paused halfway to his mouth. "Viagra?"

Oh crap, I'd said that out loud. What was the matter with me? If it were possible to die of shame, I'd be six feet under right now and spared from cringing under his shocked gaze.

Maybe the pharmaceutical gods would smile on me, and it wasn't called that here? But no—from the way he stared at me, he knew exactly what I'd referenced.

He set his glass on the bar as though throwing down a gauntlet. "I do just fine on my own."

"It popped out. I don't think you *need*—" Nope. Definitely not finishing that sentence.

"You're on a roll tonight." Amusement tugged at his lips. Maybe he wasn't truly offended, but sweet merciful heavens, what a thing to say.

I played with the cuff of his fleece, letting my fingers trail along the top of his wrist. "I am going to blame this on all the Scotch."

"From yesterday?"

I gave him a hopeful smile. The glint in his eyes reassured, but I still wanted to crawl into a hole somewhere.

"You were telling me about your workouts." I tried to look engaged, as though our conversation hadn't been interrupted by me blurting out humiliating nonsense.

"I wasn't."

Truly, I had no graceful way to recover from this. "Pretend?"

He exhaled a low laugh. "I have a personal trainer who keeps me motivated for my workouts. By myself, I'm limp and listless, but he gets me up and keeps me up. Although, if I'm ever up for more than four hours, I should probably call a doctor."

---

Somehow, the pub only grew more rowdy as the evening wore on. We'd leaned in close, our faces almost smashed together just to hear each other. Not a terrible place to be, but not conducive to carrying on a conversation. We called it a night and set off for the lodge hand in hand.

The little harbor town glowed auburn as the last of the sunset faded away. We had plenty of light to see our mini-bus in the lodge's drive, although I suspected that eyesore was visible from space.

I looked up, but all except the brightest stars were drowned out by the light of the town. "I wish we were staying someplace more remote. I bet the stars up here are incredible."

"I wish we were staying someplace more remote, too."

Duncan's impish tone made my stomach tumble. Of course his thoughts would turn that direction. Not that mine were so far behind.

"But it is beautiful up here," he went on, pausing outside the lodge. "My father took us camping a lot when my brother and I were little, and we'd sit out beneath the stars, failing to memorize all the constellations he pointed out to us."

"Those sound like good memories. I was too far gone last night to say so, but I'm sorry for your loss."

He gave my hand a gentle squeeze. "Thank you. It was sudden. It's been three years, but nothing's quite the same."

"You were close?"

He nodded. "It's why I started traveling these last few years. He might not have gone farther than the borders of the U.K., but he loved exploring. I feel I owe it to him to see what I can of the world."

"That's sweet." So sweet, my heart started dancing a jig over all the sweetness. "Do you still go camping?"

"I have a few favorite spots outside of the city where I take the girls. We toast marshmallows, and I tell them the names of all the constellations."

Oh, this man had me tied up in knots, turning me as gooey as a perfectly roasted marshmallow.

"I like camping, too. Shatner is an excellent tent-mate." I hitched a shoulder. "Aside from the occasional fumes."

He roared with laughter. "Sounds deadly."

Inside the lodge, a lone lamp illuminated the empty sitting room. We crept up the narrow staircase to the second floor, shushing each other on the creaking steps like two drunks in a bromance movie.

We paused at my door, squaring off in the low light. His hands moved to my waist to pull me closer, and I pressed mine against his chest, trying to memorize everything at once. His gaze slid from my eyes down to my mouth, and my breath stilled as I waited.

He moved toward me in slow-motion, seeming to savor the moment in a way that tortured as much as it thrilled. His mouth hovered over mine, and he inhaled deeply, as though I were a rare whisky and he intended to relish every taste.

His lips finally reached mine, but he still moved at that languorous pace, taking his time over every touch until I couldn't handle it anymore. I wrapped my greedy arms around his shoulders and tugged him closer.

Just when the kiss started to get good—so very good—snickering interrupted us. A grim sort of laughter lit Duncan's eyes as he pressed himself away from me to face our witnesses.

Carlos and Harlow stood behind us on the landing, hands clasped.

"I guess that explains a few things." Carlos's giant smirk looked all too knowing.

Not that we'd left all that much mystery tonight.

"Nothing happened." I didn't need to explain myself to him—with a pathetic lie, no less—but his *I know all your secrets* look irritated me.

"A little more nothing would have been preferable," Duncan added.

I couldn't contain my grin, stupidly pleased by how direct he was. I hadn't been with anyone who'd just come right out and said what he wanted—at least not when it came to me.

Carlos turned to Harlow. "Should we spare them more misery and say goodnight?"

"Probably for the best," she said.

They split up, and Carlos walked the ten feet or so to the room he shared with Duncan, while Harlow shot me silent sass before she disappeared into our room. Once the hallway had emptied again, I looked up at him.

"How much nothing are we talking?"

Suddenly, his hands were in my hair, his mouth on mine. We were a rushing frenzy, a tangle of mouths, hands, and heated breaths, like we only had seconds to spare before someone else stumbled upon us to spoil the moment.

The speed with which he made me forget my name was truly impressive. Slow and methodical or dashing and intense, Duncan knew how to light me up like a beacon.

He pulled back, his eyes blazing, his smile delightfully crooked. He was so handsome. Simple but true. I wanted to run my hands over his scalp, kiss every inch of his gorgeous forehead, and nuzzle in his beard. We hadn't done nearly enough nuzzling yet.

"I should probably…" I pointed toward my door.

Not that I was totally against making out in the hallway, but it seemed a dangerous business.

"Probably." He gave my waist a gentle pinch and slipped away. "Goodnight, Molly."

I went to bed on a glorious high, toes tingling and heart tapping an urgent rhythm against my rib cage. Living in the moment had definite benefits.

# twenty-seven

. . .

HARLOW WAS REALLY PUSHING it with the smirking. She'd flashed knowing looks at me all morning as we switched off positions in front of the ensuite mirror, but her silence wormed under my skin. I could only handle so many sneaky looks before I had to speak up.

"Out with it."

That smirk just widened. "You and Duncan, eh?"

Seemed a vague accusation to lob at someone—although, whatever she was charging me with, I was one hundred percent guilty.

"You and Carlos?" I lobbed back.

She shrugged. "I like him. He's made this trip more fun than I expected."

I couldn't disagree. Being with Duncan had added an unexpected thrill to my vacation, the shot of whisky in my glass of Coke.

The most delicious whisky, FYI, not that grease-cleaner stuff.

"But what happens after the trip?"

Whatever casualness I'd tried to pretend, I needed her answer for myself. Lying in bed last night, my skin still buzzing from our goodnight kiss, the question of what would happen once this adventure tour ended had replayed in my mind. Anything? Could I be okay with nothing?

"He wants to keep in touch." Harlow twisted her blond hair into a neat braid. "I've learned not to trust in empty vacation promises."

"You've been burned by that before?"

"I grew up in a tourist town. I'll believe he's coming to Dublin to see me when he shows up on my doorstep. Until then, I'm not counting on anything beyond today."

My stomach lurched over that grim reminder. We *were* on vacation, after all. Expecting more would just be greedy.

Even if I was growing greedier by the day.

"Anyway, I kind of thought Duncan was too old, you know, but whatever floats your boat."

She flashed a playful grin, but still—rude. "He's only forty-nine."

"Wow. That's pretty old." She bobbed her eyebrows, clearly enjoying goading me.

"Says a girl who hasn't cracked thirty."

"And his beard is so gray and scraggly."

Teasing was all well and good, but that hit below the belt. "I like his beard."

"Oh, that's your thing, is it?" Her grin grew wide as she opened the door to head down to breakfast. "I'm not judging you. We all have our kinks."

I followed her out into the hall. "Liking beards is not a kink."

"I am sorry to hear that," Duncan said.

I squeezed my eyes shut, utterly frozen. *Of course* he had just left his room. I opened my eyes again, and the sight of him sent all rational thought fleeing from my mind. Did they do good morning kisses in Scotland? If not, could we make it a thing?

"Does your timing have to be so perfect?" I asked once I'd dragged my mind away from those delectable thoughts.

His mouth tipped up. "We Scots will take you by surprise."

"So I'm learning."

He waved me on ahead of him, looking far too satisfied.

I couldn't bear to indulge in all the meat offered in the Scottish Fry again and stuck with muesli. The big breakfasts carried me well past lunch, but also left me bloated and just a little bit disgusted with myself. The deep-fried Mars bar days ago had only added to the disgust. Delectable, but with lasting effects.

"The rest of you have really been missing out." Bea heaped sugar onto her porridge. "Our evening hill walks have proven to be some of the loveliest stretches we've seen on the whole tour. You might want to join us tonight."

"We saw a golden eagle last night," Rupert added.

Bea frowned. "It was a grouse."

"I think not, my dear."

Bea straightened, turning away from her husband. "The grouse-viewing is first rate, and the views of the sound make for some lovely photo opportunities."

She glanced meaningfully my way, no doubt thinking to tempt me.

"Maybe." My first choice of temptation would be spending the evening tucked away with Duncan at a secluded table at the pub. Well, maybe that was second choice. Third. It was somewhere on the list. Either way, my ideal evening on Skye wasn't grouse-watching with Bea and Rupert. "Spencer, how have your hill walks gone? Seen any wildlife?"

"The walking's good. The midges, not so much."

We'd spent every day on Skye slathered in assorted bug repellants and oils. I had horrible itchy spots in several locations, but only Bea had come out totally unscathed. She reported each evening that she still had yet to receive a single bite. I had to conclude that her blood was so awful even the midges knew to avoid her.

"Our activity for the morning should keep us pretty well protected," Lewis said. "You'll still want to use the sprays on your face and hands, though."

We were slated to kayak on the Sound of Raasay today.

Missing out on kayaking with dolphins at Cromarty Firth for no good reason stung like a sliver under my skin. Hopefully, a nice kayak on the sound would soothe that.

"Rupert and I have no interest in kayaking." Bea spoke to Lewis as though she were scolding one of her children. "I'd hate to think we have to sit around the lodge until we leave for Dunvegan Castle in the afternoon."

"Of course not," Lewis soothed. "You're free to choose an alternate activity. If you're tired of the hill walks, there are boat tours that leave from the harbor. We should be able to get you last-minute tickets."

She seemed to consider as she ate.

"You get a good view of the islands and usually some wildlife like otters, seals, and golden eagles," Arnav said. "Maybe even grouse."

Bea looked to Rupert. "We might like that. What do you think, dear?"

"I'll do anything you like, my love, anything you like. As long as I'm not in a rickety little skiff that's about to topple over, I don't have a care in the world." He wiped his mouth with a napkin, eyes shining at me. "But Molly knows all about getting toppled over, don't you Molly?"

Was I happy or disappointed he'd overcome his skittishness around me? "It is one of my specialties."

"The rest of us will head down to the harbor," Arnav said. "As long as the weather holds, we should spend a few good hours on the loch, maybe even reach the Isle of Raasay before we turn back. We should set off as quick as we can, though. I'll be waiting out front as soon as you're ready."

We went our separate ways to make our last preparations for the morning's activities. Knowing how the wind whipping over the water would chill me in a kayak, I'd meant to go to my room for another layer when Duncan pulled me aside.

"What do you say to taking a seaplane ride with me this afternoon? My treat."

*Seaplane*? His invitation sank through me like a double-edged sword, all flattery and horror. I couldn't even find my voice for a minute, his offer freaked me out so much. "That...wasn't on the itinerary, was it?"

"No, but a sight-seeing tour over Skye can't be missed. I'd like to have you join me."

Excitement whirled through me at the idea Duncan was asking me out on a date. Was it a date? It sure sounded like a date.

On a plane. Because *of course* he would invite me onto a plane.

"I don't know. I'm not the world's best flier." World's worst would have been closer to the truth, but I wasn't ready to tell him so and completely spoil the invitation. "Are you sure you wouldn't rather tour the castle? In the spirit of reclaiming your roots?"

"I feel my roots have been duly reclaimed. I'd just as soon spend the afternoon with you, flying over the Black Cuillins."

His compliment filled my chest with fireflies and simultaneously made me want to throw up. I had the feeling he was asking me to say yes to him and not just the tour, which I found more compelling than the not-to-be-missed sights.

Struggling over what could potentially be a life-and-death decision, I hesitated. Narrowly avoid death by seaplane, or spend the afternoon with Duncan?

The question shouldn't have been so hard to answer.

"I understand if you'd rather see the castle," he said.

Hard to believe, but that wasn't the problem. Spending time with Duncan won out, no doubt—it was just the tricky business of where we would be spending our time. But...I could do this, right?

Bare minimum, I *wanted* to.

"Okay, yes." It would be the most incredible date ever, or an epic disaster. Fully memorable either way. "But I can't let you pay for me."

His eyebrows ticked up. "Why not?"

"Because of the..." No one had ever asked me this before, men just let me pay when I offered. "Because of feminism. Equality and all that."

He looked like he was battling a smile and barely winning the fight. "All right, in the name of feminism. It's twenty pounds."

I glared at his lowball number. "There's no way any sight-seeing tour costs twenty pounds."

"This one does." The sparkle in his eyes said I wasn't going to get much more equal than that.

This was definitely a date.

"I'll go make a few calls and be right out to Old Tarty."

He winked as he walked away, but the zing of excitement it shot through me quickly turned to dread.

Why did he have to choose a seaplane?

---

We walked down to the harbor to find our kayaks, my stomach churning over the idea I had a date on a seaplane with Duncan in just a few hours. A seaplane, offering two exciting means of grisly death. While I was taken with the idea of spending the afternoon alone with the man, I was less enthusiastic about crashing into the side of a mountain with him.

The tiny packet of valium in my makeup bag crossed my mind. But I couldn't do that. Valium might make me more amenable to the flight, but it would also make me more than amenable to anything that came after. Not that I needed any help in that department now, but I wanted to be reasonably alert for this…whatever it was.

Date. Deathtrap.

Arnav led us to a section of dock loaded down with kayaks, canoes, and associated gear. They kitted us out with life vests, and we climbed into the kayaks one by one. I slipped into mine, sealed myself up in the rubber skirt to keep out as much water as possible, and paddled away from the docks.

I hadn't been in a kayak in years. On calm waters, it wasn't much harder than canoeing—and I'd already proven myself disastrous at canoeing. Loch Portree was protected by two peninsulas before it opened out into the Sound of Raasay, but it rocked with waves from the Atlantic Ocean. Arnav had lectured us on the walk down about riding perpendicularly across the waves so nobody would roll their kayak. He'd made particular eye contact with me, as though falling from things was just what I did now.

"And no one needs to jostle anyone else's kayak, either," I said. "*Carlos.*"

He gave me a sheepish grin, but he'd pretty well lost his remorse over the Loch Ness incident.

Once we were all kayaked up, Arnav took the lead. Our game plan was to cut across the loch and the sound, heading toward the Isle of Raasay. A few fishing and pleasure boats moved around in the loch, reminding me of the very reason I didn't often kayak. In Seattle, boats of all sizes constantly criss-crossed Lake Union, sending heart-racing wakes rolling through every few minutes. Loch Portree, at least, had lighter boat traffic and more exotic views, but I gripped my paddle so tight my fall injuries hurt all over again.

My body fell into the rhythm of paddling, and my thoughts drifted. Really, they didn't so much drift as zoom straight to Duncan: the man, our kisses, our imminent afternoon on a seaplane. I fretted just a little over what our time together meant to him, what it meant to me, and most importantly, when we would have an opportunity for more of those kisses.

This was *so* not part of the plan.

Something broke the water close to my kayak, a smooth body rising and diving again before I fully realized what had happened. My heart jumped into my throat, and my mind filled with images of Nessie and mysterious creatures of the deep.

"What was that?" I didn't like the thread of fear in my voice, but I had *no idea* what I'd just seen. A little fear seemed warranted.

Arnav laughed. "We've picked up a few friends."

The water's surface broke again, and I turned in time to see a seal gliding alongside us. Another came up on my other side, and the two rose and fell as I paddled. Amazing to see them so close… but also a little nerve-wracking.

"Is this safe?" I called out to Arnav.

He laughed again. "They're only dangerous if you're a fish."

A third seal swam farther out in the loch, seeming to watch over the others as they dove back and forth among our kayaks. The one closest to me glided lazily along, watching me with bulbous black eyes as though wondering what I was doing in his loch, and why I was riding in that plastic thing.

"Does this make up for missing dolphins?" Duncan called out.

I nodded, grinning like a kid. It more than made up for it.

On my other side, something else caught my eye.

"You're smiling!" I jabbed my oar toward Spencer. He paddled along, watching the seals with such a look of wonder, he didn't seem at all the man I'd known so far on the trip. He actually had unseen levels of joy beneath his misery.

"I'll try to tone it down," he called back, but didn't manage to do it.

"Don't you dare!" So. His weakness was animals. If I'd known, I would have found a puppy somewhere to shove in his face and get him smiling from the very first day.

After a while, the seals found something more amusing to do than trail after kayaks and swam away. We'd nearly paddled to the Isle of Raasay, where green slopes tumbled down to meet the rocky shore, when Arnav instructed us to turn around. The paddle back went easier, since the Atlantic's waves gently eased us home.

The man from the kayak hire waited at the docks to help steady us as we climbed from our boats. Even just a few hours on the water had made my legs wobble when I climbed out. I couldn't even think about my noodle arms.

"You got yourself wet there." He pointed out the huge swaths on my pants where water had crept under the boat skirt and pooled.

"This is nothing. You should have seen me after Loch Ness."

———

Back at the lodge, I took a quick shower before I needed to go down to meet Duncan. It was early yet in Seattle, but I checked my phone for Jill's daily update on Shatner anyway. I found a photo of my dog stuffed into one of Olivia's onesies like it was no big thing, with the note *I have been assimilated.*

Regret twisted through me, thinking how Jill would be moving in just a few weeks, but I crammed those feelings aside. I would get through this vacation, get back home, and spend as much quality time with my best friend as I could before she became a Californian.

Lincoln, of course, refused to be pushed aside so easily. My eyes narrowed as I read through new emails, my blood growing hotter with every word. He'd asked me to storyboard a website for a brand-new account. The rest of the design team was busy on other assignments, leaving only me available for the work.

I could have powered up the bicycle ride on the Black Isle fueled by my rage at his casual dismissal of my vacation. I was in *Scotland,* and one hundred percent *not* available.

I zeroed in on one line. He'd closed the email with *I know I can count on you, Molly.* He never mentioned the promotion. He didn't need to. It poked and prodded in every word.

Reading through the client's requests and throwing together a bare-bones storyboard would take up my entire afternoon, and possibly the rest of the weekend. The idea of climbing onto the seaplane with Duncan left me sick inside, but it didn't compare to the idea of *not* doing it because of Lincoln. No client expected this kind of quick turnaround on a site, especially on a Friday. The dire urgency had to have come straight from him.

Would I lose the promotion if I refused? I paced a few steps in the tiny bedroom. Surely his request could wait until I got back Monday morning. Head of Design or not, the kind of timeframe he wanted was steep. If I'd been in Seattle, I would have hunkered down for the weekend and created the storyboards without a second thought. But I was half a world away, not just down the hall. Work would still be there Monday. Scotland—and Duncan —would not.

My fingers flew on my phone as I typed in a brief reply.

*I am on vacation. I will do this on Monday.*

I paused, my index finger hovering over the little icon that showed the email speeding its way through the atmosphere. Lincoln might take it badly, and I wasn't at all sure what the fallout would be. Even so, I needed to draw a line. I only wanted a few more days. He could take all the rest when I got home.

I tapped the icon, and a tiny fear skittered through me.

*Message sent.*

Taking slow breaths, I silenced my phone and tucked it into my dry bag. Not that it would do much if things went sideways on the seaplane ride.

Seriously, a *seaplane ride*? What was I thinking? Sure, Duncan was funny and sweet and had biceps from here to the Outer Hebrides, but the man wasn't worth dying for. Then again, dying in a tragic seaplane accident would probably cut down on my workload.

I found him in the sitting room, looking as normal as he had ever done—jeans, T-shirt, black fleece jacket. Not that I'd expected to find him in a full morning suit with top hat and tails, but the date, if it was a date, felt significant.

He walked over to me, his eyebrows pulled together. "Everything all right?"

"Yes."

He hesitated drawing any closer. I exhaled a sigh. I'd heard it —I sounded snippy and out of sorts. I could feel the crease in my forehead, embedded there by Lincoln's continual requests and my own complicity in working through this vacation.

I tried to look less murderous. "No. My boss wants me to do some design work."

"Ah. You won't be joining me today."

His resigned disappointment hit harder than outright bitterness would have. For the first time, I saw just how skewed my priorities had been. He expected me to drop everything for work—because I'd been doing exactly that this entire trip.

I curled my hand into the crook of his elbow and smiled up at him. "I'm still going. I sent him an email saying I'll do the work when I'm back in the office on Monday."

A slow grin lit across his face, even as my own spirits plummeted. Monday and all it signified left my heart hollow.

I only had two days left in Scotland.

# twenty-eight

. . .

WOULD RUNNING from the dock screaming kill the vibe of this date?

Duncan and I walked hand in hand down to the harbor for the seaplane tour that he'd magically managed to book last-minute. I'd hoped to find a sudden storm had blown in to prevent the flight, but no such luck. The day was calm, with azure skies and light clouds that could hardly be considered ominous.

Fickle Scottish weather.

My heart thumped at a terrifying speed and my stomach had turned into a hard ball of dread, but I tried to look composed. Casual. Not at all like fear was about to splinter my brain into a hundred pieces.

"Have you ever flown in a seaplane before?" I asked.

"No, but when I saw the listing on the website, it sounded too good to pass up. I reserved our spots before I asked you—they'd had a cancellation just this morning. Lucky me, you agreed to go."

"Lucky you."

But that was Duncan all over—see an opportunity, take it, and hope for the best. I was more the type to see an opportunity, take a hundred pictures of it, and think back on it as a fond memory. Maybe I needed to take a little more action in my life. Taking action had brought me here, and I wouldn't trade this trip to Scotland for the world.

Then again, taking action had landed me on the dock about to board a prop plane on pontoons. Seemed a hit or miss deal.

I spotted the bright yellow seaplane long before we reached it. Apparently, it was some sort of bylaw that every dedicated tour vehicle in this country needed a hideous paint job. A few people stood around on the dock, eagerly looking at the plane as though they couldn't wait to get going.

Psychopaths.

I neared the plane like a death row inmate approaching the electric chair. Duncan kept glancing at me, like he could tell something was off, but he wasn't sure what. Maybe the way I'd gone kind of stiff and couldn't seem to relax. Maybe it was my wide, fake smile. Pretty sure he couldn't hear my weird, labored breathing.

I could have just confessed my fear of flying right then. I would have plenty of time to run back to the lodge before the prop engine even started up. But I didn't want to keep leaving opportunities behind, even if this one freaked me the heck out.

We reached the others on the dock, and Duncan checked us in. The pilots-slash-tour guides introduced themselves as Scott and Brodie, both of whom looked like they'd barely graduated high school, let alone successfully completed pilot lessons. Their youth unsettled me, but to be fair, I wouldn't have been any more at ease if they'd both been Rupert's age.

"We've got ninety minutes to show you the best of the Isle of Skye, and we don't think you'll be disappointed." Scott grinned as though no one among us could possibly be five seconds from a breakdown about flying in a small hybrid aircraft.

Brodie opened the plane door and motioned us aboard. The layout turned out to be a more cramped version of our mini-bus, with seating for nine in groups of one and two. We'd fill the plane, and I wasn't sure how I felt about that. I'd read an article once that said planes that crash are usually not at capacity because some small percentage of travelers cancel their flights at the last minute. The article insinuated the people who'd changed their minds might have had some kind of ESP that wound up saving their lives.

I couldn't remember just what type of magazine I'd read that in, and it probably hadn't been the most scientific, but Duncan's last-minute booking didn't feel so lucky now.

We piled on, and he offered me the window seat. He had no idea how it pained me to take it. I would hardly need a window with my eyes shut tight. Still, I slid onto the seat and buckled in, tightening the strap several times. I put on the headset that hung on the back of the seat in front of me, presumably so I could listen to the pilots give their spiels about scenery.

My hands twitched as I checked my seatbelt again.

"All right?" Duncan had a casual air, but just like on the bus after my tumble into Loch Ness, he watched me too closely. Any minute now, he would figure out my panic, and I wanted to delay that as long as possible.

"Yup." I flashed a bright smile, thinking about the money he'd spent on this excursion. Now that I'd strapped myself into the plane, I would have gladly paid my fare and then some to get off again. I couldn't decide where to turn my attention—looking around inside the plane was no good because the pilots and their instruments were *right there*. Looking outside was no good, because we were either going to die a gruesome death when the seaplane sank tragically into the bay or die a gruesome death when it tragically crashed into the Black Cuillins.

The pilots shut the door and locked it for good measure.

There it went. My last chance to escape this awfulness without causing a scene had just gone. A light sheen of sweat covered my skin. I sucked in a breath, but it rattled like a sob. Blissfully unaware of my rising panic, the pilots climbed into their seats.

I tried to distract myself but couldn't think of anything more pressing than imminent death by seaplane. Brodie flipped a switch, and the motor revved to life. The propellers sped up, and the noise grew, sending my fear thrashing around in my chest like a caged animal. I tried to take deep breaths, but they were coming a little too quickly for any real relaxation.

I should have just taken the valium. Coherence was overrated.

The pilots pulled the seaplane into the middle of the harbor, motoring past pleasure boats and a few bigger commercial types. I moved my arms around, touching my legs, my elbows, my stomach, reminding myself this wasn't a nightmare. It was all real. We picked up speed until the plane tilted back, and we took off.

I turned my face from the window, shut my eyes tight, and clasped my hands. Every change in engine noise made my ribcage crumple a little more in on itself. This was a terrible mistake. We were going to die.

Duncan covered my hands with one of his and held them tight, gently brushing his fingers over mine. A nice gesture, but it couldn't move my fears. Everything inside me screamed at the climbing sensation, and it was only a matter of time before I let the scream out.

He slipped the headphone off my ear so I could hear him.

"You're safe, love."

I couldn't get enough of his soft, encouraging voice, but I did *not* agree. "Mm hmm."

I stayed where I was, eyes shut tight, jaw clenched to hold back tears. After all of this, I couldn't start crying, too. I was a grown woman, dammit. People did this all the time.

*I* didn't, but people out there did.

"I know you're scared, but you can get through this. I'm right here." He squeezed my hands tighter.

Why, *why* did he have to be so soothing? Like his calm could battle my panic and actually win? I opened my eyes to see his blue ones looking back at me with all the confidence of a man unafraid of being in the sky in a tiny metal tube.

"You're safe," he said again.

I nodded, not at all sure.

"Look out the window."

He nodded over my shoulder, but I really didn't want to look. I would take his word for it. I could just stare at his face for ninety minutes. I'd pay twenty pounds for that.

He smiled and nodded again, indicating *whatever it was* outside. Fine. *Fine.* I took a deep breath and looked.

*Oh.* Incredible. We'd already left the harbor behind and were flying south over Skye, low enough that every loch and crag appeared crystal clear. Terrifying, but breathtaking, too. I gave him a surprised little smile and pressed my face close to the window again.

In the near distance, the Black Cuillin mountain range were sharp peaks rising up through the low-lying mist. As much as I'd loved the views from our mini-bus as we drove across Scotland, this vantage gave the roads serious competition. More dramatic, no question. The threat of death made the views that much more spectacular.

We glided over the island, and my terror eased its grip, replaced by naked awe. I still struggled to push my worries from my mind, but the fact that I could at all felt like a major win. Maybe I'd absorbed Duncan's confidence by proximity, or maybe it was just that I could enjoy being with him anywhere, even ten thousand feet in the air. He had one arm around me, pressing close against my shoulder so he could see out the window, too. I consoled myself that if the worst should happen, dying in Duncan's arms wouldn't be such a terrible way to go.

A small, clear voice said living there wouldn't be so bad, either.

Our young guides pointed out lakes and rivers, mountain peaks and film locations. Sooner than I would have thought possible, they made a wide turn to head north again. The plane banked toward my window, and the wide-angle view of the ground it gave me made my stomach roll over. I turned away from the leaning sensation and wound up wrapped in Duncan's arms.

He pulled me close and caressed my back, my face pressed against his neck. There in his arms, I found protection from the fear of falling from the plane, but a new sense of falling enveloped me. It would only take a little nudge for me to go over that edge, and what would happen if I fell?

Duncan could catch himself, sure, but could he catch me, too? Or would I belly flop all over again?

The plane righted, and the spike of panic ebbed. I leaned back enough to see Duncan's face, our arms still tangled. For a while, we just looked at each other. No words, just eye contact. And... yeah. I could have stared into this man's eyes for longer than I'd ever thought likely or normal.

He trailed his fingers across my cheekbone, stroking my jawline with his thumb. A sexy move—but full of tenderness, too. Affection cascaded through me, a typhoon ready to wreck my heart in its aftermath.

So many choices had led us to this place. One small change, and I never would have met Duncan Stewart. Never would have heard his low laughter, seen those blue eyes, or felt so known. I wasn't sure what would happen when the trip ended, but I would thank my lucky stars the rest of my life we'd had these days together.

After a long, long while, we turned our attention back to the window. The Outer Hebrides lay far in the distance, nothing more than dark blurs on the horizon. Exploring them would have to be the work of another vacation. The pilots rattled off names of everything in sight, but I didn't worry about whether or not I would remember them, or if I should take pictures of the view. I just enjoyed the moment for what it was.

Until it came time to land.

The engines whined and the plane's nose tilted down just enough to notice, and panic roared through me once again. I gripped Duncan's hand tighter, the fear I knew so well choking out all other thoughts. But in another minute, we'd landed on the loch and returned to the harbor, safe and sound.

Once we'd fully stopped and the engines stilled, I exhaled a huge sigh in gratitude we hadn't died. I side-eyed Duncan, smiling sheepishly. He smiled back but shook his head as though he couldn't believe me. I'd made my biggest fear painfully clear.

I climbed down from the plane, shook hands with Scott and Brodie, and thanked them for the safe flight. Only once we'd left the other tourists behind did Duncan speak up.

"If I'd known you hated flying that much, I never would have suggested it." He sounded sincerely sorry, and yet his apology carried a touch of scolding, as though I shouldn't have accepted his invitation in the first place. "I didn't intend to push you into something you didn't want to do."

After the hard time I'd given him the other night about his assertiveness, I guess his regret made sense, but I didn't blame him.

"I heard it was not to be missed." I had no good explanation that didn't reveal more than was necessary. *I just wanted to be with you.* Although, after all that intense eyeing each other on the plane, I think he knew. "Maybe I went a little overboard in making the most of my vacation."

"So paragliding is next, then?"

"One terrifying thing at a time, Duncan."

# twenty-nine

. . .

RATHER THAN RUSH TO try to make suppertime at the lodge with the others, Duncan suggested we have dinner in town. I agreed, unsure how to label the evening. What was a first date that couldn't lead to a second? That thought stayed small enough it couldn't blind me to the important point—how much I enjoyed his company for however long I had it.

The restaurant he chose wasn't nearly as crowded as the pub had been. Although known for its seafood, visitors to Skye seemed more interested in its beers and whiskies than the catch of the day. The neat little building sat right on the waterfront with views of boats coming in and out of the harbor.

"It must have taken every ounce of strength in you to climb aboard that seaplane," he said.

I cringed just thinking about my wild-eyed panic. "I was pretty bad, wasn't I?"

"White as a sheet, twitching left and right like you wanted to burst through the window. I thought you might get sick."

"I can't hit all the indignities this trip, Duncan. I need to save something for next time."

"Yes, maintain the intrigue." He laughed but then paused,

eyes stuck on me. "About the next time. What do you say to coming to London?"

"London?" My laughter died away as I realized what he was asking.

"London has a few crumbling old buildings of the kind you so admire. I'd drive you out into the countryside to gawk at the scenery as much as you like. Grant you easy access to plenty of chocolate."

I smiled at his teasing. "That does sound tempting."

He placed his hand over mine where it rested on the table. "I don't like missing opportunities."

"I've noticed." What would it be like to have everything a visit with him promised? *Life-changing.* "I would love to visit you in London, but I don't know when I could."

I'd told him there would be a next time, and I wanted to believe it would happen, but time off for another vacation like this was months in the future or more. Lincoln had barely tolerated my time away, and I wasn't even Head of Design yet. My schedule would only become busier after we made everything official.

"Maybe it's soon to talk about it, but I've been around long enough to know what I want, Molly. I think we have a shot at something here. This isn't an empty bit of fun for me. I don't want this to end just because the vacation is over."

Warmth unfurled in my ribcage like a cozy blanket around my heart.

"I don't either," I said softly. For a moment, I let myself imagine what it could be like to have all the time I wanted with Duncan. Long conversations over dinner, laughter over private jokes, sultry kisses that never ended. *More.* Everything that had been tangling my thoughts these last days made real.

He intertwined his fingers with mine and held on tight. His eyes sparkled with confidence, but a shadow of vulnerability hid there, too. "You've made me laugh like no one else. You're glorious in your euphoria, whether you're kayaking with seals or reveling in your truly abysmal archery skills."

I snorted a laugh, thinking of everything else he could have added to that list. Falling out of canoes, tumbling down mountains, and getting absolutely smashed on whisky—but I'd loved it all.

"No man could resist the way you glowed on Ben Macdui," he went on. "You soak up every experience. Being around you is like carrying a little piece of the sun in my pocket. I don't know how I'm going to do without you."

His words shone a light into all the little empty spaces inside me until I ached from it. I'd never thought of myself as sunshine before. I seriously loved that he would see me like that.

"I feel the same way. You glower a little bit more than you glow," I conceded, squeezing his hand. "But I don't want this to end either."

I could almost see that dream world with him happening.

*Almost.* On the heels of the most romantic thing anyone had ever said to me, all the reasons I couldn't possibly be with him crashed into the moment. Under the weight of reality, my heart shrank back down to normal size. My job, Shatner, my home, Jill, my parents—my life was in Seattle, not Scotland or London. The thought of never seeing Duncan again left me heartsick, but what else could we do?

"I need some time to think about it."

His eyes glinted as he caressed my hand. "The invitation stands. Now. Today. Tomorrow. Come as soon as you can."

It was a flattering, incredible offer, but one I couldn't realistically entertain. For now, I would have to be satisfied with making the most of the trip I was on. That would have to be enough.

———

We strolled through Portree as the evening sunlight shone its golden rays on the loch, making the water sparkle like jewels. A few fishing boats skimmed slowly through the harbor, and a kayaking group set out toward the mouth of the loch for a paddle.

"It's a glorious day." I leaned against a railing, gazing into the harbor.

He nodded assent, looking me up and down. "Where's your camera? Shouldn't you have taken forty pictures by now?"

"I left it in the lodge." The arch look he shot me said he doubted I could have parted with it so readily. "Really, you can check my pockets."

"Check your pockets? Don't mind if I do." He pulled me close, the weight of his hands perfect on my waist.

I hugged his sides, laughing against his neck. "I don't have it."

"Best if I do a thorough inspection."

Our mouths found each other like we'd been waiting for this all day. This kiss was luxuriously slow, as though Duncan had all the time in the world to explore me, and not a single care that we were on display in the little harbor town. I couldn't remember ever being so bold.

It was glorious.

Last night, he'd joked about getting lost in Portree. I loved the idea of being completely alone with him somewhere. Anywhere. But for now, I would take what I could get.

"Do you want to get a drink?"

His answer was immediate. "Absolutely."

The pub still crawled with tourists. It must stay like this all through the high season as hikers explored Skye in the warmer months. Did it die down in winter, when snow might blanket the island and only locals made their way in for a dram of whisky to warm them?

Actually…a trip to Skye in the winter with Duncan sounded perfect. A little snowy wandering by day, a lot of warming up by night.

We sat together at the bar, where he ordered his ever-present whisky, and I ordered a glass of cabernet.

"I take it you don't do much traveling," he said after his first sip.

"Not by air." As if my clarification made his statement any less true. I shrugged. "I don't do much traveling."

"No Tahiti for you then?"

"Not likely. Jill and I took a trip right after college—to Disneyland, of all places—and I kind of freaked out on the plane. I passed right out. It was pretty awful." Coming to in a cold sweat with multiple people fussing over my supposed medical emergency? I don't recommend it. "We had to rent a car and drive all the way back to Seattle. After that, I just resigned myself to not flying."

I gestured absently with my hands while I talked, brushing against his in the process. I pulled back, but he moved his hand closer until the backs of his fingers lightly played against mine. Warmth unfurled inside me at his soft touch. Nothing about his gaze was coy or sensual. I might have thought he didn't realize we were touching but for the subtle movement of his fingers on mine.

"This is the first time I've tried to fly again," I said, catching back up to my thoughts.

"Then I can count myself lucky."

The curve of his mouth was a distraction. I needed to stop staring at it...but couldn't seem to do it.

"But it isn't as though I've never gone anywhere," I continued, speaking too fast as though that could somehow slow down my heart rate. "I go to Vancouver, British Columbia sometimes. Or Portland. Boise."

If I stopped talking and focused on his hands, and every little aspect of how they felt on mine, then, oh, *then* I wasn't sure what I might do. Or rather, I knew what I would do, I just didn't have the guts to do it. So I rambled.

"Actually, I do a lot of camping. I think I mentioned that before. That's actually a sort of travel." *Yes, say* actually *a few more times.* I sounded sixteen years old. "All around the Northwest."

He turned my hand over and moved the pad of his thumb in small patterns across my fingers and palm. It didn't seem like a forward gesture, just a comfortable one, and that easiness electrified me more than anything else.

"That's what drew me to this tour. We aren't camping, but we're spending every day outside, trying something new. I like that."

I wasn't sure if that last sentence was about trying something new or the way his fingers stroked mine.

"I don't think you're as buttoned-up as you make yourself appear," he said. "I think you like adventure, but you've told yourself you need to be more practical."

*Bingo*. How had I traveled five thousand miles to find this man who looked straight into my soul? Nobody else had ever seen me so clearly before. I felt like I couldn't hide anything from him, but I didn't want to anymore, either.

"Practical is safe," I said softly. It had protected me from so much these last several years. Business failure, financial instability, embarrassment. Heartache.

"Adventure can be safe, too," he said. "With the right person."

His voice enveloped me like a full-body hug, warm and comfortable and achingly perfect. I liked the idea that *adventure* and *home* could be one and the same person.

*Him.*

"I've never had that," I said softly.

"Doesn't mean you can't," he returned.

I adored this man's certainty. Staring back into his eyes, it was hard to doubt.

"Do you take trips like this often?" Only a half-hearted attempt to maintain the conversation, really. All the nerve endings in my body might have existed entirely in the one hand he touched.

"Not quite like this one. I went to Italy for a week in the winter, and last summer I went to Australia." He smiled to himself. "That one was also a guided tour. I didn't want to die alone in the Outback."

"That probably would have been a downer for your vacation."

"Not the high note you want to end on."

I finally stretched my fingers out to lock with his. My glass of wine wasn't quite empty, but I felt as light and giddy as I had done from the whisky. I could have stayed at that pub all night, drunk on his touch and talking about anything.

"Why did you take a guided tour this time? Not much chance you would die alone in the Highlands." If I just kept talking, I could distract myself from thinking about what was happening with my hands, and even less about what was happening with the rest of my body. Definitely ignore the inferno in my belly, and the flames that reached higher with every word he said.

"I enjoyed my trip to Italy, but I was alone. Mealtimes, sight-seeing, exploration—I was always on my own. There's a lot to be said for solitude, but companionship certainly has its merits, wouldn't you say?"

His thumb moved along mine until I shivered.

"If I had come here on my own, I might have spent the whole two weeks holed up in a hotel in Edinburgh."

"That doesn't sound too terrible to me." His mouth quirked up delectably at his teasing.

I meant to laugh, but it came out a soft sigh. "Not terrible at all."

"I feel like Tahiti is still in your future."

When we finally left the pub, the evening twilight had faded to a blue sky streaked with purple. We let ourselves into the lodge and walked up the stairs in silence, my hand warm in his. On the landing, I turned to say goodnight and was instantly in his arms, taking up where we'd left off on our last kiss.

No one had ever kissed me with such surety. Purposeful but not insistent, content to drink me in at any pace. Every touch held a mix of sweet and spice, a tenderness rough around the edges. I ran my hands up his arms and shoulders, grazing the firm muscles beneath his jacket. Resting one hand at the nape of his neck, I lightly stroked the stubble on the back of his head. His hands were warm on my back, locking me against him.

The kiss was a little like the day—it lingered on until I lost all track of time.

When at last he drew away, I didn't want to let go. My heart had shifted into overdrive, butterflies whirled wildly in my chest, and my skin seemed alight with flame. I needed a minute to compose myself.

Hard to do when he kept pressing quick kisses to my mouth.

"How much time do you have in Edinburgh?" he asked.

I hated to even think it. "Just the one night."

"Then we should make it count."

# thirty

. . .

MY EMOTIONS TANGLED into a knot I couldn't work free. One minute, I felt light and airy over Duncan, and the next, a weight dropped into my chest knowing the tour was nearly over. Just when misery threatened to sink in, I'd push those thoughts away and focus on the memory of our kisses, leaving my toes tingling all over again.

I rolled onto my side, grinning to myself, toes absolutely going wild.

Harlow had already dressed for the day. "Looks like you had a good night."

I sat up in bed and stretched, hoping I could mask some of my incriminating happiness. "I did."

"Where did you go? Unless you can't go into details."

"We went on a sight-seeing tour on a seaplane. Then we went out for dinner and the pub." It didn't sound like much when I told it like that, but my memories of the evening seemed to last for days.

"How was the seaplane thing?"

"Incredible. I hated it, but I loved it." That I'd gone at all still shocked me. That I'd survived it and enjoyed myself? A Duncaninduced miracle. "I never would have done anything like that if he hadn't asked."

"What else would you do if he asked?" She chucked her pillow at me, and I threw it right back. "Seriously, it's great to see you guys go all mushy for each other. It's nice that older people can get a chance at love, too."

My mouth fell right open. Now I knew how Duncan must have felt when I said he was *of a certain age*. "I'm probably only ten years older than you."

"Yeah. And you're rocking that middle age thing."

Oh, sweet baby Jesus, she did not just say that. "Let's try to end things on a positive note, Harlow. I don't want to have to throw hands with my roommate on the last day of the trip."

She laughed but tried to look placating. "My point is, I'm happy for you. It's cool."

I guess if I could ignore all her middle-age talk, I appreciated the gist of it.

Unable to delay the inevitable, I checked my phone to see how Lincoln was handling my refusal to step in and work on another site. His email simply said we would discuss it on Monday. I would have laughed if it didn't sound so ominous. My boss wanted to discuss my resistance to working through my vacation?

Maybe researching labor laws would be an interesting way to pass the return flight.

At breakfast, I inched my chair closer to Duncan's, needing to be as close as I could for as long as I could. I was being ridiculous over him, but my goodness, did I feel amazing.

"Did you sleep well?" he asked.

I couldn't look at him—I had a terrible poker face. Sleep hadn't come easily last night, and the trace of a smirk on his mouth said he knew it.

"Yes, thank you." Now, I grinned like an idiot. "Did you?"

"No. I was plagued by vivid dreams."

I shook my head at him, unable to focus on my breakfast. I wanted to hear about those dreams.

"You know," Rupert said, jabbing his spoon in Duncan's direction, "our dreams most often represent our unfulfilled desires."

Harlow snorted but had the decency to cough into her napkin right after.

"Sometimes," Rupert went on, "they're portents of the future."

Duncan nodded as though this were perfectly rational. "God bless those portents."

He rested one arm behind my shoulders while Lewis described our last day. We would be in the bus for most of it, driving back to Edinburgh. He assured us that the views through the Trossachs would be spectacular, even passing through them at sixty kilometers per hour.

"We'll stop for lunch and a short hill walk, but we'll still have plenty to see on our return," he said. "We'll end the tour with a ceilidh in the city and send you off with happy memories of your time in Scotland."

I glanced at Duncan. *Memories.* That's all this would be, all anything between us could ever be. Nine days had passed too quickly, leaving me reeling from all I'd seen and done and aching for all that remained undone. A quick drive through the Trossachs didn't seem like it would live up to climbing Ben Macdui or accidentally swimming in Loch Ness.

A morbid, premature sorrow settled deep in my chest, proving just how much I would miss Scotland. It had been an incredible adventure, but my real life waited for me back in Seattle.

Duncan gave me a quick side-hug, reminding me the trip wasn't quite over yet. Just a few things left to do, but I had a feeling we'd saved the best for last.

———

Scotland had so many lakes, any road we traveled on was bound to skirt one eventually, and the winding road back into the heart of the country provided a prime view of several scenic lochs. We'd had no opportunity for pictures, and I tried to just enjoy the experience as we sped south through the Highlands.

Duncan and I had reached a silent agreement to throw out all concerns for personal space and sat with the sides of our legs pressed together, our shoulders bumping with each jostle in the road, his hand resting lightly on my leg. The ride back to Edinburgh seemed stuck on fast-forward when I wanted time to slow down so I could enjoy this closeness.

"What is that?" I squinted at a dark shape in the distance.

He leaned forward to peer out the window, pressing close against me. "That's Eilean Donan castle."

The shadowy shape grew sharper as we drew nearer, revealing a castle set on the edge of the lake. Unlike the flooded castle on Loch an Eilein, this one looked in perfect condition, or as nearly so as a thousand-year-old stone building could be. The walls weren't crumbling down, at any rate.

"It's been rebuilt," Arnav said out of nowhere. "It's not nearly so old as the other castles we've seen."

I guess that explained its fresh out-of-the-box appearance. "How many castles are there in Scotland?"

He turned around in his seat to face me. "That depends on your definition. Some are ruins, some are nothing but the ground they stood on. Others, like this one, are relatively new. So to answer your question: a lot."

"Thank you, Wikipedia."

"I grew up here, you know. I had to write plenty of school reports on castles, and yes, I made free use of Wikipedia."

Almost as soon as we passed the castle on the lake, green slopes rose up all around us. These mountains were neither gradual like the Cairngorms, nor spiky peaks like the Black Cuillins. They made me think of The Storr on Skye—rough, rugged, and rocky.

"Does everything in this country have to be so beautiful?"

Duncan smiled at my wide-eyed question. I knew I had that

gobsmacked look on my face again, but I couldn't get enough of the views.

"I could show you a few pubs in Glasgow you wouldn't call beautiful," Arnav called back.

"Pubs are man-made. They don't count."

"You've been mooning over the castles, and most would argue that those are man-made." Spencer made his presence known with his usual brand of negative commentary.

"Those are historically beautiful. They count."

"If you can get past all the people who have died in them."

"You need to watch a different kind of TV show."

"I've got a suggestion for you," Carlos called. "Do you like extreme sports?"

I looked at Duncan. "Do I sound like an idiot, going on and on about how green and gorgeous everything is?"

"Your enthusiasm is endearing."

I cut him a stern look. "You didn't answer the question."

Tenderness lit his eyes, and my stomach dipped, swooped, soared.

"I came here to reconnect with my heritage, but I think you've done a better job at connecting with Scotland than I have. Believe me when I say it's endearing."

Well. I could accept a compliment like that.

He leaned forward and pulled an iPad from his backpack. Calling up a photo gallery, he passed it over to me.

"You asked about my company." He nodded at the tablet. "You can scroll through photos of some of our renovations. If you like."

I took it and opened one of the gallery folders. The first few photos showed a nice but outdated home that, from my experience with BBC TV shows, seemed vaguely British by its prominent radiators and the washing machine in the kitchen. The photos after showed a total refurbishment of the kitchen and dining rooms, giving the home a new yet vintage appearance.

"These are beautiful."

He smiled at the praise. He knew his work was good. I loved that confidence he had, the sense of self that said *I'm damn good at this and deserve to be complimented.*

I opened the next folder and found similar remodels of outdated homes Duncan had beautifully upgraded. I happily swiped through the photo galleries, making little comments now and then about the dramatic results. He had enough fodder for several seasons of an HGTV show. *Reno Addict: London.*

"Do you want to see some of my work?" I asked. "From when I was on my own?"

"Please."

I pulled my laptop out and opened a folder I'd left untouched for years. I showed him the sum total of *Molly Clarke Designs*, from the light and airy branding and design elements I'd created for a custom paper goods shop, to the dark and broody work I'd done for a local brewery. It wasn't a long trip, but wandering down memory lane dragged into the open something I'd tucked away and forgotten.

Pride and satisfaction swirled through me, along with a stark thread of regret.

"These are good, Molly. You have talent."

"I had fun while it lasted, anyway." I snapped the laptop shut and put it away. "I tried to create something special for each client, but I don't know how much of a difference I made."

"Trust me—in a world where cookie cutter work is cheap and easy, true skill will always be valued."

I smiled at that. He could have been talking about himself, too.

"Well…the paper shop closed not long after I did, so they might have wished they'd chosen cheaper cookie cutter work."

He shook his head at my self deprecation, but I looped my hand around his arm. Resting my head against his shoulder, I watched the views go by out the window. "I will keep your point under consideration."

We stopped in Glencoe for lunch and to stretch our legs. The hill walk wasn't much more than wandering around for an hour, but the views still stunned. A heavily wooded lochan sat tucked away among the imposing hillsides, and we traced its outline on a gravel path. Lewis told the tale of the massacre at Glencoe, when unsuspecting Highlanders were slaughtered by the English military they'd hosted in their homes.

He sure knew how to kill a mood.

I stood with Duncan on a little pier that jutted out over the lake, trying to take everything in. A single brown mountain peak loomed above the treetops, appearing in hazy reflection on the lake's surface, and a light breeze blew across the water, sending waterlilies bobbing.

The last day of my trip would have been bittersweet on its own, but the curling, stretching feeling in my heart went beyond regret. Whatever I'd thought this vacation would be, I hadn't expected it to feel like this—as though everything I wanted waited on the other side of a door I couldn't open.

I nuzzled against Duncan, and he wrapped his arms around me. I bit back my thoughts, afraid of saying too much or too little, everything and nothing. Time pressed in on us like a tangible force—I had twenty-four hours left in Scotland.

It seemed Duncan could read my mind. "Is there no way to extend your trip?"

I choked back bitter laughter. "I'm expected at work on Monday, if not sooner."

He pulled me as close as he could, resting his chin on the top of my head, his whiskers tickling my scalp. "I hear Seattle is nice in autumn."

I smiled into the softness of his fleece jacket, holding him tight. Even if I couldn't come back to see him anytime soon, maybe he would visit me. That was a *maybe* I wouldn't mind holding onto. "I'd love to show it to you."

We stood wrapped up in each other's arms, until we had to

leave Glencoe. We were in the slow, lingering twilight of our vacation, and although it might seem like it could go on endlessly, night would eventually fall.

But what a night it would be.

# thirty-one

. . .

THE FORLORN LOOK of our Edinburgh hotel came as a rude awakening. Gray cinderblock couldn't compare to sweet stone guest lodges.

Arnav helped us with our bags, and as I grabbed my luggage handle, a strange kind of homesickness coursed through me. I wouldn't ride in that hideous mini-bus ever again. I'd grown used to the old thing, garish tartan overlay and all.

"I think I might cry."

"Over this old thing?" Duncan said.

"I'm going to miss Old Tarty." I patted the bus's frame. "I've grown quite attached to her."

"I have to say, that puts your tears at Culloden in a new light."

I jabbed a finger at him. "Those tears were real."

Our hotel sat in the heart of the city, smack in the middle of crowded buildings and bustling streets. I'd grown so spoiled by small, friendly lodges that walking into the spacious lobby through doors that opened themselves felt impersonal and wrong. The decor was all clean lines and sleek modernity that not even the occasional pop of tartan could make homey.

The staff wore suits and name tags, and although they were just as friendly as the many hosts I'd met in the Highlands, it didn't have the same effect. We were no longer staying in Grandma's Perfect Highland Lodge. Back to stark reality.

"Remember everyone," Lewis said before we sprang off into all directions. "We've got about an hour before we meet back here for dinner and then the ceilidh."

We checked in and were handed sleek key cards instead of the actual keys I'd grown accustomed to. I turned mine over and over as Duncan and I stepped onto the hotel elevator. This, too, came as a weird culture shock.

"I feel a bit like Rip Van Winkle waking up in the future."

"You'll get along all right in time," Duncan said as we stepped out of the elevator. "Modern women have really made strides since you fell asleep."

We agreed to meet downstairs in an hour. Despite the melancholy of the day, I looked forward to experiencing traditional Scottish music and dancing at the ceilidh. A party was just what I needed to keep myself from crossing the threshold over into tears and ruining the last few hours of my trip.

At least I had the room to myself tonight. Harlow had opted for her own room since she had a few extra nights in the city. A week ago, my first thought would have been to throw on pajamas, crawl into bed, and flip through my options on BBC. Now, I wanted to crawl into bed all right, but not the pajamas or the BBC. I just wanted one particular Scot.

After a long, hot shower in which I conceded that big cities had a few benefits after all, I looked over my meager clothing options. Lewis had said ceilidhs had no dress code, that people would turn up wearing everything from jeans and a T-shirt to formal kilts, but I still worried I'd be underdressed in my travel-friendly skirt and blouse. I hadn't brought much makeup but put on what I had. After going the last week wearing nothing on my face but sweat and tears, putting on mascara and blush made me look like some kind of goddess.

I hoped, anyway.

I'd just set off down the hall to find Duncan when his door

opened and out walked a kilted god in the flesh. He wore a tight, lightweight black sweater and a gray tweed kilt, along with a plain black sporran and the clunky hiking boots he'd worn all week. Seeing him like this, I was ready to shove him against the wall and kiss his face off.

You know, like a middle-aged woman would do.

He held his arms out as though asking if he had my approval. Did he ever.

"This isn't fair at all. I had no idea you were going to kilt up."

"No reason to spoil the surprise. You like it?" He did a shimmy, kicking up the kilt's hem.

I applauded the show. "You look so good."

"So do you." He looked me up and down, unashamedly taking me in. "You look damn fine in a skirt."

He took my hand and led us downstairs, my heart hammering the whole time. We found the rest of our group in the lobby, each one decked out in various states of festivity. Arnav was also in full kilted glory, but unlike Duncan, he wore what must have been a clan tartan, resplendent in blue, yellow, and red.

"Duncan, that is a stellar kilt, mate," he said.

"Yours, too."

"I like to throw it on for the ceilidhs. Show a little pride for my nan. Plus, it always confuses people to see a brown person in a kilt."

"I've got a bit of tartan on, too, you see." Rupert flipped up the end of his plaid tie. "A little nod to our neighbors to the north."

"I see." Duncan looked over the tie. "Which clan is it?"

"Well…" Rupert seemed unprepared for the question. "Do you know, I can't recall?"

Duncan took it in stride. "I'm sure we appreciate it all the same."

We followed Lewis the four blocks to the restaurant. I kept shooting sideways glances at Duncan, etching that kilt into my mind like I could will it into a core memory.

"This isn't your clan tartan, I'm guessing." The fabric looked nothing like Arnav's or the brightly colored versions we'd seen hanging in the many souvenir shops across the Highlands.

"It's a dress kilt. Family loyalty aside, my clan tartan is rather too festive for my taste."

"That bad?"

"Think Old Tarty levels. Bright red and green, so it's always Christmas in the Stewart tartan." He pretended to shudder.

"Isn't there some sort of kilt police whose job is to make sure you're wearing the proper tartan?"

"Yes, but they're all in the pubs just now, so I think we're safe."

"Well, you look very handsome."

He smirked over at me. "I suppose it's better than saying I look surprisingly not awful."

"I'm not surprised you look so sexy."

"Sexy?" He laced an arm around me. "Now we're getting somewhere."

———

The restaurant turned out to be more of a dining hall, and had such festive decor, Duncan must have broken out in hives just looking at it. Tartan or a stuffed stag's head covered every square inch—sometimes both at once. Hints of wood paneling peeked out from behind huge bolts of tartan fabric that lined the walls, and the massive tables were covered in twelve-foot lengths of plaid. We could have parked Old Tarty in the foyer and the clientele wouldn't even look up from their haggis.

The menu was the same for everyone, a Scottish roast dinner served in multiple courses throughout the evening. Roast chicken and roast beef were the stars, with appearances by mashed potatoes and turnips, smoked salmon, and every kind of roast vegetable known to man. I couldn't take that much food seriously, but I sampled everything. It was good, if not on par with some of the home-cooked meals we'd had along the tour.

I tried haggis again, only to discover a slight variation in the recipe left an unfortunate aftertaste.

"You're off to Ireland then, are you Harlow?" Bea asked.

"Not until Tuesday. I have a few more days here before I fly over."

"Good thing, too," Carlos said. "She's convinced me to go bungee jumping with her tomorrow."

Murmurs of surprise went around the table. Duncan raised his eyebrows at me, an unspoken *Are you interested?* I shuddered a firm *No*. Death-defying would remain firmly outside my comfort zone.

"He did a whole television show devoted to bungee jumping, and he's never done it." Harlow dished up caveman-approved foods onto her plate. "I told him we needed to fix that."

"There's still a lot of me that needs fixing, you know." He had those big puppy eyes going again.

"Oh, I know."

I wondered if they really would keep in touch, or if, as Harlow had said, Carlos would forget about her as soon as his regular routine kicked back in.

"And you, Spencer?" Bea asked between bites. "Back to…New York?"

It seemed she hadn't gleaned much else from their brief conversations.

"Back to New York. To my apartment. Going it solo." He crumpled lower in his seat with every addition.

"Maybe you could think about getting a pet," I suggested. "A dog or a cat might help."

He needed something to get him through this gloom, and animals had done the trick out here. For a minute or two.

"Animals have a short life expectancy."

I knew it all too well. "But the love they give you is worth the eventual goodbye."

He hitched a shoulder at my heartfelt endorsement. I wouldn't dare hope I'd convinced him.

"We all know where Molly's off to," Rupert said.

My stomach lurched, fearing they were all imagining Duncan and me escaping off somewhere. They wouldn't be wrong, I just didn't want them imagining it.

"She's going back to work," he finished.

"Oh," I said with a half-hearted laugh. "I suppose so."

Had I ever really left work behind? And what did it say about me that my life could be summed up so succinctly?

*Molly, 38, married to her job even in the middle of vacation.*

"Don't forget what I told you, dear." Bea winked theatrically. "About men."

I had to suppress a laugh. As though I would forget her helpful hints. "I won't."

I looked at Duncan, thinking about all of Bea's rules I intended to break.

"Back to the daily grind, eh, Duncan?" Rupert said.

He nodded, but his eyes never left me. I suspected rule-breaking was on his mind, too.

"As for us, Monday is our anniversary," Bea said, earning a round of applause. "Our oldest is planning a big do, the whole family will be there. We met in college, did we mention?"

She recapped the serendipitous meeting she'd described to me in Dingwall.

"Best decision of my life," Rupert said. "Imagine what would have changed if I'd never gotten on that train."

They shared a look full of heart-eyes and kissy faces. They were honestly kind of adorable.

The sumptuous feast passed in a blur of food and conversation. I tried not to think too much about saying goodbye to everyone in the morning. I did my utmost to push all my worries, aches, and longings away, focusing on now instead of what might have been. Focusing on Duncan.

I looked at the kilted god beside me, determined to enjoy this night. I could deal with all the rest on the plane home.

———

We walked into the dance hall to find the ceilidh in full swing. A mass of people in all levels of formal and informal dress circulated around the huge room, dancing, laughing, and drinking. A band featuring three bagpipers and half a dozen drummers played to their enthusiastic audience.

Dancers moved around in waves, following a caller's instructions. A spacious bar covered one length of the room where revelers stopped for drinks. It was a friendly, loud, raucous good time, just the thing I wanted to send off my Scottish vacation.

We watched the dancers go through the motions of a reel. Women spun lightly on their feet while the men marched around them, a barrage of kilts swinging in time to the drumming music.

Arnav came up to Duncan and me, grinning like he'd already partaken liberally from both the bar and the dance floor. Not a bad way to celebrate being off the clock.

"Have you danced yet, Molly?" he asked.

"Ah, no. I don't really know how—"

"There's nothing to it, just do what the caller says. Come on." He offered me his hand. "Have a go."

I looked to Duncan, who nodded me on, apparently eager to watch the show. Well, he'd seen me do some pretty embarrassing things on this trip—might as well add dancing to the list.

I put my hand in Arnav's and followed him to the dance floor where couples stood in rows, men facing women. The band struck up a faster song than I would have liked, and the dancers buzzed and whirled around me. I heard the caller but couldn't make out what he said, and what I did hear made no sense when I didn't know the moves. Mostly, I tried to copy the women around me without stumbling into anyone.

I laughed over my missteps when the couples came together again. Arnav held my hands as we moved back and forth, apparently unconcerned I had no clue what I was doing.

"I hope you've enjoyed your trip with us, Molly." He shouted just to be heard over the band.

"It's been the time of my life." The stupid grin on my face and the lightness in my heart proved the truth of every word.

The couples moved apart again, and I swung around a different man, improvising shuffling steps as I went. When the dance finally ended, I was out of breath and probably as rosy-cheeked as everyone else. Arnav thanked me for the dance and stepped away to find another partner, so I made my way back to Duncan.

He watched me with a touch of pride. "You're a natural."

"I am nothing of the sort." I laughed, pushing my hair away from my face where it clung in sweaty strands already. "I turned the wrong way every time and stepped on some poor man's toes. I'm a failure."

"A failure? The only failure is in not trying again." He held out his hand. "Shall we?"

Somehow, I hadn't actually expected him to dance, but I jumped at the chance to witness it. We stepped onto the dance floor in time to catch the next number. The moves proved no more intricate than the last, but I had no more success with them, either. I bumped into the ladies on both sides of me and even a gent as I passed him, but I didn't let it get me down. I laughed the whole way, not caring how badly I messed up the moves.

Duncan had an easier time of it. His athleticism made him graceful, clunking along in his hiking boots. We made eyes at each other, hooking elbows and spinning in circles, never pausing even when I got lost in the shuffle and my next partner had to come running to find me.

After our first dance, I wound up paired with Rupert. Duncan bobbed his eyebrows at me over Bea's silver hair. I caught glimpses of him nodding and cheering my way, watching me with undeniable affection through dance after dance. In this tiny space of happiness within this small, perfect vacation, it didn't matter that we'd just met—I knew this man. He had sparked a flame inside me, and I wanted to reach out and grab my life with both hands.

At last, I spun back into Duncan's arms, and we laughed as we held tight to each other. He leaned in to kiss me as naturally as if it'd been part of the dance. We were in a room crowded with strangers, but I returned the kiss with all my heart.

When he pulled back, I blurted out the first thing that came to mind. "Do you want to go back to my room?"

"Hell, yes."

We laughed all over again as he took my hand and led me from the dance floor. Rushing through the streets of Edinburgh, we hardly noticed the people we passed, our attention was so taken up with each other. Duncan's smoldering gaze showed me no mercy, and I kept on grinning at him like a lovesick fool.

Wait, lovesick?

I pushed that thought away for later. No time to stop and wonder at it now.

As soon as the hotel elevator's doors closed, Duncan's mouth met my neck, kissing his way up to my ear. I inhaled slowly as he nibbled on my earlobe and moved across my jaw. Just before his lips could reach mine, the elevator doors opened at our floor.

I fumbled through my purse for my room key. He stood behind me, his hands resting on my waist. He pulled my hair aside so he could kiss the nape of my neck, his breath sending fiery tendrils across my skin. Locating the slim key card was no easy feat with distractions like that, but I finally unlocked the door and we stepped inside.

I almost expected to find Harlow on the second bed, but the room remained blissfully empty. I tossed my purse onto the chair and faced Duncan. He watched me with that calm, controlled look he had that I just loved, like he was imagining every little thing he wanted to do to me, but he could be patient until I came to him.

So I did.

Held in his arms, the same sensation I'd had on Storr washed over me, like I'd come home. Like I belonged right here. I filed that away, too, as something to ponder later. Right now, I just wanted to experience him.

His hands moved over my back and waist, his eyes never leaving mine as he mapped me. His touch was purposeful, firm but gentle. There was nothing timid about him, but he wasn't too forward, either. We might have been together for years instead of days.

I glided my hands along those majestic biceps to his shoulders. One hand went to the nape of his neck, the other to the hollow at his throat. Finally, I moved my fingers up to run them over his beard, and he made a sound like an engine purring to life.

I leaned closer, placing a chaste kiss on his mouth. Then another. Again and again my soft kisses fell until I lightly bit his lower lip. He held my face in both his hands and took control, sending my thoughts spinning with every touch. How could a man both ground me and overwhelm me so thoroughly?

He pressed kisses across my jaw, up to my forehead, down my nose. His mouth turned up on one side. "Are you sure you wouldn't rather have chocolate?"

I sure couldn't speak for all men, but this one? He just might be worth everything.

I lightly pinched his side even as I tugged him closer. "I'm choosing you."

# thirty-two

· · ·

HAD I really said I would give up men?

I woke to hazy gray light streaming through the hotel window, Duncan's hand resting on my side. I'd been keenly aware of him beside me all night, like a wiggly tooth I couldn't stop touching. Every time I woke in the dark, I snuggled against him, and in his own sleepy state he'd drawn me closer.

Last night replayed in my mind, and my stomach swooped low. If any man qualified as first rate, Duncan did. He'd wooed me slowly, sumptuously, knowing exactly where we were going but content to take every side trip along the way, unwilling to miss a single moment. He'd shamelessly obliterated the memory of every other man I'd ever known.

His fingers moved on my waist, letting me know he'd woken. I rolled over to face him and snaked one arm up his broad back. His eyes were still closed, but his mouth tipped up in a sleepy smile. I liked seeing him up close in the morning light, relaxed and happy.

"Good morning." I tried to angle my breath away from his face. As comfortable as I was, he didn't need to endure my gruesome morning breath.

"Mmm. I could get used to waking up like this." He moved his palm along my back, his voice gravelly.

"I could get used to falling asleep like *that*."

"Yes?" He peeked open one eye and hugged me closer until no space remained between us. "Now I'm awake."

Morning breath was no longer a deterrent.

Doggedly refusing to think about my flight home, I focused solely on Duncan for our last few, marvelous hours together. We called up room service and had breakfast in bed. We shared an indulgent, soapy shower. We made love like we were at the beginning of everything instead of the end.

"You're missing out on Edinburgh castle," he teased, propping himself over me. "A lot of photos to be had there."

I pulled him back down to me. "Photos are overrated."

Eventually, sobered by the late hour, we had to leave our cozy cocoon. I gathered the last of my belongings and stuffed them into my luggage, trying not to think about my flights. I pulled on the *I Heart Scotland* shirt I'd bought my first day, the only real souvenir of my adventure. The only tangible one, anyway.

Duncan had slipped down the hall to his room to change back into jeans. When he returned, he had a brown paper box in his hands.

"What's this?" I asked.

"Open it and see."

I took it from him, my heart already doing little skips as I wondered what it could be. Beneath the lid lay a bundle of green and red tartan. I plucked it from the box, and it unraveled to reveal a fine cashmere scarf. I wrapped it around my neck, running the soft wool through my fingers. "Where did you get this?"

"On Skye."

I snuggled my face against the soft wool, telling myself not to cry. It was a generous gift—I didn't even buy cashmere for myself. The bright red would be striking in Seattle's gloomy winter rains, a much needed reminder of our time here. "Is this Clan Stewart?"

"Oh, aye." He laid on his thickest brogue for me, my Scottish GPS. "So everyone will know which clan you belong to."

I might have turned into a fluffy cloud, all soaring softness over the idea of this man claiming me with a bit of tartan. I thanked him with a kiss, which turned into several kisses, until I grew too hot for the scarf and had to peel it off.

Duncan cradled my face in his hands, resting his forehead against mine as though we could communicate everything in that touch. My heart ached, and my eyes pricked with waiting tears. He'd said no more of London or Seattle—this morning was only about now.

We rode the elevator in silence, our fingers laced together. The airport shuttle would arrive soon.

Bea accosted me in the hotel lobby. "Must you go so soon, dear?"

The simple question hit hard. Must I go? Plastering on a polite smile, I said I must. "My flight leaves in three hours. I don't want to miss it."

I glanced at Duncan, who gave me the grimmest of smiles. I *did* want to miss it, but my real life was pulling me back home.

"Well, I'm sure you'll be back. Scotland does grow on a person." She air-kissed my cheek and trundled off again.

I didn't see anyone else from the tour in the lobby. Bea would be my only goodbye.

Except for Duncan.

A bright blue shuttle pulled up outside the hotel's glass doors, and my heart dropped even lower.

"That's your ride." Duncan walked me out to the curb, my hand held tightly in his as though he didn't want to let me go.

The shuttle driver tossed my bags inside and settled back onto his seat, waiting.

I looked over the shuttle. "No tartan."

Seemed a lost opportunity.

Finally, I faced Duncan. I fought back tears—if I started crying now, I wouldn't stop.

"You're sure I can't convince you?" he said softly.

No pushing, only a gentle request.

Heartache rose in my chest like bile. Everything I wanted fought against everything I already had. "I can't miss my flight."

"I know how you love to fly."

"I'll—" No. I wouldn't tell him *I'll keep in touch*. So much less than what I wanted, it would feel like a watered-down goodbye.

I threw my arms around him and pressed my face to his neck. "I'll miss you," I whispered, my lips brushing his skin, my eyes squeezing back tears.

He held me tight. "We'll see each other again."

I clung to his confidence like a buoy. Holding my face in both hands, he kissed me with all the tender sweetness of an *I love you*. Oh, I wanted to believe in that kiss.

He scrutinized my face and nodded once. I almost wished he would have railed against my choice, but he understood me better than I'd realized. I had to go, and he wouldn't push me to stay.

We had one last, all too brief kiss before I climbed onto the shuttle. Duncan stood in front of the hotel, one hand sunk in his jeans pocket, the other raised in farewell as the shuttle pulled away from the curb.

I got about one block from the hotel before the crying started. Not sad, stoic tears running nobly down my cheeks, but huge, blubbering crying that shook my whole body and covered my face in snot. My heart hurt and my stomach rolled and I hated myself just a little.

Maybe a lot.

"All right, Miss?"

The shuttle driver watched me in the huge rear-view, his brow furrowed as his sole passenger had a nervous breakdown. A red and green tartan ribbon wound around the rear-view arm. I might have asked if it was Clan Stewart if I could have mustered up interest for anyone but myself just then.

I gave him a pathetic wave and resumed my crying, going full-bore crazy in front of a stranger. It *was* crazy to think Duncan and

I could have anything more than this vacation. We weren't Bea and Rupert, randomly running into each other on our way to the same place. We were grown adults with lives half a world apart. Trying to create something real meant phone calls at odd hours and full-day plane trips and snippets of togetherness cobbled from vacation days.

Leaving felt like running my heart through a shredder, but I couldn't see how long distance would work.

Only…Duncan hadn't asked me to be in a long-distance relationship. He wanted *me*, now, with him. Didn't I want him, too? *More than anything.* His confidence, his unflagging encouragement, his laughter that felt like home. I wanted it all. But I couldn't make a rash decision like that. I needed time to think about it. Maybe when I got to Seattle and cleared my head.

I sagged against the seat as Jill's words came back to me. *"'I'll think about it' means 'I'm going to drag my feet until it's too late to do anything about it.'"* After my spectacular work failure, pondering and deliberating had become my go-to until whatever it was I wanted had long gone. Would I really let Duncan pass me by?

Or would I find a way to trust in this feeling that swallowed me up whole, telling me I was meant to be with him, no matter what it took to get there?

My phone buzzed, and I fumbled for it with shaky fingers. Maybe Duncan knew I needed a gentle push, after all. My excitement shattered when I saw who it actually was.

Well, I couldn't possibly feel any worse. Might as well answer. "Lincoln."

"You sound awful, Molly. Were you sleeping?"

"No, I wasn't sleeping." My voice was thick from crying and my nose had clogged with tears, but I wasn't sleeping at noon on a Saturday. "Shouldn't you be?"

"It's on my list. Look, I need you to get that storyboarding done that you put off Friday."

He rattled off details on the new client, but on top of everything else going on, I couldn't process his demands.

"I'm about to get on the plane home."

"You can do some workups on the flight back. I need them tomorrow."

I laughed through my tears at how casually he could ask me to give up what little remained of my vacation time. "Tomorrow's Sunday."

"Molly, I can't tell you what a headache it's been having you gone." He sounded exhausted, although given the time difference, he should. "You're my strongest designer out of all of us. No one can cover for you."

"It doesn't sound like anyone has covered for me at all. This is the same work you asked me to do two days ago. You *did* have the others pick up the slack, right?"

"Moll, who do you think is going to pick up the slack when you're Head of Design?"

For a minute, relief bloomed to life that I hadn't blown the promotion. But then a vision of what it would be like when I had the job played through my mind. Nights in the office, weekends at my laptop, no vacation even in the middle of one. Would I have any time free from Lincoln's constant demands?

"I'm not sure I want to be Head of Design." I trembled a little as I admitted the truth that had troubled me for days. The title and the raise would be gratifying, but I would have to sacrifice everything else I wanted in order to get them. That didn't seem like such a good trade anymore.

"Molly." Lincoln sounded like he was talking to a child. "I chose you for this. I'm giving you a gift, here. This could be a turning point in your career. You don't want to miss this opportunity, do you?"

"What?" I froze, my voice loud in the empty shuttle.

"This is big, Molly. I don't want you to throw it away on some kind of vacation high."

He went on scolding me, but I couldn't hear him. My chest constricted until I felt like I had fallen into Loch Ness all over again. This *was* big. What was building between Duncan and me, what I wanted for my work life, for my home life—I wanted a *life*. Life wasn't something to think about fondly and file away as *what might have been*, it needed to be lived, savored, and loved.

I'd been standing on the edge for so long, afraid to risk failure again, but were my safe choices really any better? I couldn't let my life pass me by. I needed to leap into the unknown.

"You're right," I said, cutting him off. "I can't miss this opportunity. I quit."

He hesitated on the other end. "Molly, what is this power play trying to achieve? You just had two weeks off."

"Did I? You had me working almost every day." I'd accepted it out of habit and obligation, but that didn't make it right.

"That's part of the deal, Molly."

"Not anymore. I can't keep doing this. I want more than just good enough—I want the best." Every word I spoke gave me strength, like I'd found some untapped well of badassery I hadn't known existed.

"You can't just walk away." His voice rose, hitting a mix of anger and fear.

"You'll find someone else, Lincoln. I'll send you an email and make it official."

"Molly, think it over. We need you."

"I'll detail my grievances in my resignation letter, but for now, all you need to know is that I quit."

"Molly—"

I hung up and tossed my phone into my bag. Blood rushed in my ears, and the aftermath of making such a huge decision left me a little giddy, but none of it felt wrong. Taking a stand for my future felt like long-overdue *rightness*.

Now to claim the rest of the future I wanted.

"Stop!" I stumbled up the aisle to the shuttle driver. "Can you turn around?"

"Turn around?" His eyebrows bobbed at me in the rear-view as we charged ahead. "Forget something at your hotel?"

"I did, and I need it, desperately. Can you turn around?" We were who-knows-where in the city, and I had no idea how far from the airport, but I had to go back. Now.

"I can't. I run a loop: hotel, airport, hotel, airport. Can't turn around."

"How long will it take to get back to the hotel?"

He shrugged. "An hour."

I had wasted so much time already, another sixty minutes felt like a lifetime. "There's no one else on the shuttle. Please, won't you go back to the hotel?"

"I'm supposed to run the loop."

"It's so important, please." I looked around, needing to find a way to convince him to bend the rules. "Will you do it in the name of love?"

He made a face like he didn't believe in love. Not enough to risk his job, anyway.

"Will you do it for Clan Stewart?" I waved my scarf in the air, proving it matched the one on his rear-view. He sighed but shook his head. I looked out the windshield at the buildings rushing by, every block we passed taking me farther from the only man I wanted.

The man I loved.

I checked my pockets. "What about for forty-seven pounds?"

At the next signal, the driver flipped on the blinker and made a series of turns to take us back to the hotel. I could have kissed him, but I'd acted crazy enough already. My heart felt lighter now that I was headed the right direction. I'd let life carry me along on its waves for too long. It was time for me to take charge. I knew what I wanted, I just needed to reach for it.

When we pulled up to the hotel curb, I pressed the bills into the driver's hands.

"I'll take the forty-seven quid," he said, tucking the money into his pocket. "But I did it for Clan Stewart."

I grabbed my luggage, leapt off the shuttle, and rushed into the lobby. Bea, Rupert, and Lewis stood at the front desk looking at train schedules when I blew in. They shuffled over as I made a desperate search of the lobby and restaurant.

"What are you doing back again, dear?" Bea asked. "Did you forget something?"

"Yes, and I need to find him right away."

She processed that with a slight jolt, then smiled as though everything had gone according to her design.

"It's just like I told you, all you needed was to find the right one. It's like Rupert and I." She smiled at her husband, and they went right back to making heart-eyes at each other. "We were strangers when we got on the same train in Edinburgh, and by the time we reached London, we were in love."

"Yes, but have you seen Duncan?" I'd already heard this story twice over and didn't need the replay. I only wanted to find my man.

"He said he was walking up to the castle," Lewis said.

"How long ago was that?"

"Right after your shuttle left, I guess."

"Thank you." I shifted, ready to run out the doors, but I couldn't pull my luggage all through Edinburgh. I turned to Bea. "Could you?"

She put a hand on my luggage. "Leave it, dear, leave it."

"Thank you," I said again. I dashed out the hotel doors, Rupert's rallying cry of *Go, go!* ringing in my ears.

Only, I didn't know where to go. I looked up and down the street, hoping Duncan might still be close by. I couldn't see him or the castle from this vantage and wasn't quite sure where to go. I went straight to a man selling newspapers on the corner and asked for directions to the castle.

He pointed along the street, and I sprinted that way. Dashing by beautiful stone buildings like the ones I'd admired so often, I didn't have time to take anything in. I kept an eye out for Duncan, and avoided the cars on High Street. It was too busy, too crowded, too much of a long shot, but I had to try.

I reached a barricade where vehicle traffic ended and the lane narrowed, but I kept on. I'd begun to doubt the newspaper man's directions, but the castle finally rose up in front of me.

I paid my admission and accepted a map, then jogged through the gates. People crowded all around, gazing down at the city from the high vantage, reading bronzed signs set into the castle's stones, and taking pictures of themselves standing on an ancient rock. Any other time, I would have happily joined them, but just now the views meant very little. I only had one thing in mind.

Finding him wouldn't be easy. The castle wasn't a single building but a series of them, and he could have been inside any one. Too late, I realized I had no way of knowing if he'd even gone inside the gates.

I followed a circuit to the top, and found a massive cannon surrounded by dozens of tourists. Still no Duncan. I sagged against the outer battlements, my heart racing from running six city blocks in as many minutes. I hardly saw the city below.

Finally, I did what I should have done as soon as I got the shuttle driver to turn around. I pulled out my phone and found the contact Duncan had put there this morning. Ignoring the list of new voicemail notifications from Lincoln, I pressed the button.

He answered on the second ring.

"Hi," I said, out of breath and unsure how to start.

"Hello." His voice sounded somehow deeper than usual through the telephone. "I'm flattered to think you miss me already."

"I do, Duncan, so much. I think leaving was a mistake." Only, I didn't want to have this conversation over the phone. I needed him in front of me. Indefinitely, if I could swing it. "I'm *here*. I'm at the castle looking for you."

"You're here?" His voice rose a touch. "Where are you?"

I looked at my map, but my poor brain couldn't process it all. "I don't know. I'm by a cannon, kind of at the top."

"One cannon, or a lot?"

"Just one."

"I'll be there in two minutes."

I grinned like a madwoman as I listened to him breathing, and by the sound of his footsteps, I guessed he was running through the castle grounds just as I had done.

Any second now.

Any. Second.

"Molly!"

*Duncan.* I might have turned into a supernova. He climbed the last set of stairs to the upper level, looking a sweet mix of surprised and delighted. I threw myself into his arms, and he caught me up so my feet dangled above the ground. I kissed him hard, stamping this moment on my heart.

Core memory unlocked.

He had just as much enthusiasm, kissing me back with a passionate fire until I grew dizzy from it.

*Mine. All mine.*

I had to break the kiss, if only for a moment, and he set me back on the ground. "What are you doing here? I thought you didn't care about the castle."

The affection in his eyes hit me straight between the ribs, coloring my heart like it meant to dye it permanently.

"I was taking pictures to send to you. The real question is, what are *you* doing here?"

I flashed a crooked smile. "I had an opportunity I didn't want to miss."

A glint of satisfaction danced in his eyes, and then he kissed me thoroughly. He held me close against him like he would never let go again. I fit alongside him so perfectly, it was crazy to think I had ever thought I could leave him. I was completely lost for this wonderful, unexpected man.

I tried to look stern but couldn't pull it off the way he did. "I've decided I need a new business plan, after all."

"And a visa I think, but we can handle that."

We held each other, gazing out over Edinburgh below.

"I love you." I craned my neck to look at him. Scary to say those words so quickly, but undeniably true. "Is that crazy?"

"Not crazy at all, since I love you, too."

Yeah. That required more kisses.

"Do you like tea parties?" he asked after a minute.

My heart went soft all over again at the thought of one day meeting his adorable little girls. "Yes, especially on Saturn. Do you like dogs?"

His laugh came out low and gentle. "Yes, especially pugs named Shatner."

"Then I think we're all set." I pulled his face down to mine to kiss him again. I never wanted to stop kissing him and talking to him and just being with him. I wanted *him*, for years and years.

"Are you certain?" he asked softly.

I stood on tiptoes to look him straight in the eye. "Nothing is ever one hundred percent certain, but I'm sure this is worth the risk."

# epilogue

...

One year later

**THE DELICIOUS SMELL** of Belgian waffles filled the house, all warm and sweet and cozy. Any minute now, Duncan would wander downstairs to see what I was up to, so I had to work fast. He rarely slept in—if this had been a girls' weekend, they would have ensured he was up long ago—and I hoped to surprise him with a little celebration before we set off to explore a castle this afternoon. I'd sugared a bowl of strawberries and just pulled the melted chocolate from the double boiler when I heard footsteps on the stairs.

These feet took their time, alternating steps in a steady cadence. My guy still had a lot of energy left in him, but he treated the stairs with care. He was getting up there in years, after all.

As soon as Shatner reached the first level, he bounded over to me, curly tail wagging.

"Good morning, my sweet little guy." I stroked his forehead and kept my voice low in an attempt to keep Duncan unaware of my plan for as long as possible. "Your breakfast's in your bowl."

Shatner sat at my feet, using his cloudy brown eyes on me like the world's most powerful hypnotist. He wasn't about to settle for dry kibble when special waffles were on the menu. I couldn't blame him.

"Like you're not going to get a bite."

The tip of his pink tongue peeked out. He knew he was spoiled rotten.

I went back to my breakfast preparation, and pulled the waffle from the iron. I got out the tray and set to plating up strawberry waffles with chocolate sauce. My drizzle technique wasn't elegant, but chocolate really only had to taste good.

"What are you—"

I shrieked, heart pounding, as I spun to face Duncan. I must have been too focused on getting the chocolate just right to hear him come downstairs.

His mouth tilted to the side. "Doing?" he finished.

He looked past me to the food on the kitchen counter, his eyes brightening as he took in the scene. Meanwhile, my eyes were glued to him. He stood there in a black T-shirt and blue athletic shorts, barefoot on the cherry hardwoods, and he still managed to look like he'd stepped right out of one of my romance novels.

One with a slightly older, take-charge home remodeler who swept unsuspecting women off their feet on whirlwind tours through Scotland. My very favorite kind of romance hero.

"I made you breakfast in bed." I met him in the middle of the kitchen, our hands going to each other's waists automatically. "Well, it was going to be in bed. We can eat at the table."

"Oh no, we're going back to bed."

He leaned down and kissed me, letting his hands travel along my back and up into my hair. He set me on fire with his attentions —his sizzling kisses were the best way to start my day. I nestled against him, calculating whether we had time for anything more before the waffles went completely cold.

We didn't—but that wouldn't stop us.

Shatner's whining finally broke us apart. We held onto each

other but looked down at my old pug who really didn't like all this unnecessary waiting.

"He's upset about delayed waffle gratification," I said.

"I don't like delayed gratification, either."

I moved both my hands to the back of his neck and stroked the stubble on his head. "That's hardly ever a problem. You usually get what you want, don't you?"

He snuggled me closer. "I don't have much more I could want now."

"Nor have I." I loved the way his blue eyes sparkled at me. "Not since we met a year ago today."

He threw his head back as though basking in sunlight. "Ah, blessed day."

I laughed at his silliness. "It was. I'll never stop being grateful for that day. This last year has been…"

It'd been hard turning my life upside down for a trans-Atlantic move. It'd held a great deal more flight anxiety for me, with our trips back and forth to see each other before my entrepreneur visa came through in England. And it'd been emotional leaving family and friends behind in the States.

But it had also seen the return of *Molly Clarke Designs*, where I was able to do the kind of work I loved, with more requests coming in every month. It had ushered in sweet relationships with his daughters, too—tentative and awkward at first, but through the magic of Taylor Swift singalongs and binge-watching cheesy tween movies, they'd made space for me in their lives.

And it had given me the most passionate, most genuine, most vital relationship I'd ever had. The more time we spent together the more *right* everything between us felt. We didn't agree one hundred percent of the time, and we'd weathered a few arguments, but we always talked things through. Always kept seeking each other out.

The last year had been a wild ride, but none of it had been on autopilot.

"I've never been happier. I love you so much." My voice

cracked, and his eyes seemed to soften as he watched me. I tapped his chest over his heart. "You are my favorite adventure."

"My Molly." He scooped me up so my feet dangled, burying his face in my neck. His beard tickled my skin as he kissed me once, twice. He set me down again, eyes bright. "Let's get married."

My breath stilled in my lungs, my eyes wide. Maybe I hadn't heard him right? "What?"

"I love you. I want to marry you, and have you be my wife, and I want you to stay with me always. Let's get married."

Shatner whined behind us.

Duncan side-eyed him. "And I want to share legal guardianship of that most insistent dog."

I laughed, tears ready behind my eyes. I'd hoped this was coming—you don't move halfway across the world to be with a man and not have at least an inkling—but it still stunned me in the moment.

"Wait. I'm missing something." Duncan let me go and held up a finger. "Don't go anywhere."

Standing there in my shorty pajamas, my answer to his proposal at the ready, I wasn't likely to run.

He dashed up the stairs. This time I did hear him clomping around up there. I hadn't moved an inch when he came back down, a little black box in his hand.

"I was going to do this at Arundel Castle this afternoon, but I never could resist you."

He lowered himself to one knee. My heart went absolutely wild: fireworks and pinballs and insane galloping all at once at the sight of my big strong man so vulnerable. He opened the box, revealing a square cut solitaire.

"Molly, my heart. I don't know how I got to be so lucky as to meet you and fall in love with you—and best of all, convince you to love me—but I want nothing more than to be your husband. Will you be my wife?"

I was soaring, flying, drifting up into the heavens. I needed a second to remember how to make words.

"Yes. One hundred percent yes."

His eyes shone as he stood and caught me up. We kissed long and hard, tears mingling on our faces. He slipped the ring on my finger—a perfect fit.

"How did you know?" I stared down at it sparkling in the morning light. From the size to the specific shape I would have chosen, everything about this ring was exactly right.

"Jill. I'm afraid she's known about this for a few weeks. Her silence came at a price, though. I may have promised to tour her around *Outlander* locations when she visits."

"You know you're going to have to read book passages in your thickest brogue, right?"

He looked to the ceiling. "Oh, aye."

"The girls are going to lose their minds that we're getting married."

That soft look that seemed reserved just for Louisa and Sophie came into his eyes. "I love how much they love you."

"I love them, too." We'd got on better than I ever could have hoped. "Can we get married in Scotland?"

He hugged me closer. "I was going to say."

"And have a piper at the wedding?"

He nodded. "Done."

"And have Stewart tartan everywhere?"

"For you? Absolutely." He pushed my loose hair behind one ear, trailing his fingers down my neck. "I heart you."

I laughed at our sweet inside joke, courtesy of the Edinburgh airport.

"I heart you, too."

THE END

Genny Carrick

Get a bonus scene from Molly's 40th birthday when you sign up
for my newsletter!

# also by genny carrick

The Magnolia Ridge series

Say the Words

Have a Heart

Stay this Christmas

Make it Real

# acknowledgments

This book has been a long time coming, and I have a lot of people to thank!

Thank you to my early readers, Kelly & Lindsay! You had a lot to wade through in that first draft so many years ago! Thank you to Claire & Amanda for always giving thoughtful and thorough feedback! Thank you to Allison & Gwen for reading enthusiastically! And thank you to Aimee for making sure my Brits sound like Brits!

Thank you to Laura for seeing the potential in this book and trying to find it a home. Even though it didn't get picked up, I'm grateful for all your efforts.

Thank you so much to my ARC team for reading & loving & hyping up my books!

Thank you to Melody for this phenomenal cover and for creating the illustrated M&D of my dreams!

Thank you to Cindy for your insight & patience fixing my comma mistakes.

As always, I'm grateful to my husband & kids for putting up with all the time I spend writing! You're more than I deserve, and I'll never stop thanking my lucky stars for you.

# about the author

Genny Carrick is a sucker for an HEA, especially if there's a whole lot of laughter along the way. She writes romances and rom-coms about stubborn women and the men who fall for them.

When she's not lost in swoony reads, she's probably up to something crafty or trying to get her dog and two cats to love her.

Genny recently moved to Texas after a lifetime in the Pacific Northwest. She brought her brilliant husband and two hilarious kids with her.

Stay up to date with book news at gennycarrick.com